"Oh, Casey, I'm sorry!" Regan muttered contritely. "If there was only something I could do or say to make up for—"

"To make up for what?" Casey gave a short hollow laugh. "To soothe my having the misfortune to love the wrong person? Tell me, how could you possibly make that up to me?"

She cringed at the bitterness in the hard lines of his face, realizing too late that she had said the wrong thing.

"Just how far would your pity let me go, sweet Regan?" There was a dead quiet to his words that alarmed her. His arms closed around her and one strong hand began stroking the base of her neck with rhythmic sensuous movements that made her tremble. "I felt you shudder when I kissed you. It was difficult, wasn't it? Would your pity be great enough that I could get away with making love to you?"

Dear Reader,

It is our pleasure to bring you a new experience in reading that goes beyond category writing. The settings of **Harlequin American Romance** give a sense of place and culture that is uniquely American, and the characters are warm and believable. The stories are of "today" and have been chosen to give variety within the vast scope of romance fiction.

Elizabeth Glenn has great insight into the psyche of exceptional people. As a cotherapist in a marriage counseling group, she encounters many interesting individuals. Her first novel, *Dark Star of Love*, deals with the capacity of two strong-willed characters to overcome their own prejudices. We are sure that you will find this novel a compelling read.

From the early days of Harlequin, our primary concern has been to bring you novels of the highest quality. **Harlequin American Romance** is no exception. Enjoy!

Vivian Stephens

Vivian Stephens
Editorial Director
Harlequin American Romance
919 Third Avenue,
New York, N.Y. 10022

Dark Star of Love

ELIZABETH GLENN

Harlequin Books

TORONTO • NEW YORK • LONDON
AMSTERDAM • PARIS • SYDNEY • HAMBURG
STOCKHOLM • ATHENS • TOKYO • MILAN

Published July 1983

First printing May 1983

ISBN 0-373-16014-3

Printed in Canada

Chapter One

Looking back on it later, Regan thought it was unfortunate that the whole fiasco occurred. She had come within an inch of not bothering with the yard again this summer, telling herself that the small brown cabin at the lake was nearly hopeless. Standing vacant nine months of the year, it could hardly be expected to put on airs and sparkle just because Regan had arrived home from college. Since her parents had bought it only three years ago, Regan had no idea how old the cabin was, although she suspected it was a relic of World War II at least. Its paint had long since chipped and peeled off, the roof sagged in places and careless weeds had taken over the patio. Last summer she had ignored the problem, but then last summer she had still been in shock over the recent loss of both her parents. The cabin at Bowic's Landing had seemed a haven of refuge, a sanctuary where she could hide from the rest of the world to lick her wounds.

This year, she noticed that the Johnson grass had choked out even her mother's stubborn morning glories on the east side of the cabin and was rapidly threatening the honeysuckle. The low stone wall that edged the dusty patio was more ragged than ever, with chunks of rocks crumbled at its base. The idea of repairing the damage was unappealing. In fact, the only prospect more bleak was that of spending another long summer with the property in its present disreputable state. What would her mother say?—dear Mom, who had spent warm mornings nurturing blossoms and vines and pulling weeds so the evening cookouts overlooking the lake could take place amid beauty and fragrance.

"I guess it would cost me a fortune to fix my place up," she remarked wistfully to Ronald Barnes, the gentle, homely bachelor who owned the one combination service station and garage in Bowie's Landing.

"Oh, I don't know about that." Ronald suspected—correctly—that her income must consist of Social Security and the meager benefits of her parents' small life-insurance policies. The automobile accident that had taken her mother and father had of course been unforeseen; her optimistic, disorganized father hadn't been prepared for death and had left his only child far from well off.

"A friend of mine owns a nursery over at La Grange," Ronald added. "If you were to take my pickup truck over there, now, and get yourself some seeds and such, I think you'd find he'll treat you right."

It would take more than a few seeds to brighten up the exterior of her poor, sad little cabin. Mentally Regan ticked off the items she'd need: bulbs, seeds, bedding plants, mulch, plant food, a little potting soil, pots, and mortar mix for the wall. She recalled her small bank balance and gulped.

"You'll loan me your truck?" she asked, half hoping he wouldn't.

"You betcha," he agreed. "And if I didn't have to keep the station open, I'd come along and help you."

"Thanks," she said faintly, "but I'll manage just fine."

And she did, once she made up her mind to spend the money and not worry about it. Two back-breaking days of weeding and another of kneeling on scratched and grated knees to set out the young plants and tenderly pack warm black dirt around the roots, and Regan was done.

Done in, as well, she might have added, but proud. Rubbing the ache in her back with one grubby hand, she stood and surveyed the patio with pleasure. Gone were the Johnson grass and careless weeds, the brambles and stickers, that had declared her home uninhabited and unloved. The flower beds spilled a rainbow of blue forget-me-nots, creeping phlox with its delicate pink blooms, white-flowered Japanese spurge, and oxalis in pink, yellow and white, onto the old brown flagstones. Violets, periwinkle, and strawberry begonia in red clay pots perched at intervals on the mended wall and accented the one-step rise to the screened patio door. Baskets of wandering Jew hung from the eaves, swaying in the slumbersome Texas heat.

"How does that look, Mom?" she asked aloud, pushing back a persistent wing of dark hair from her forehead with a muddy finger. Somehow Regan knew her gentle, nature-loving mother would have been as pleased to see the cabin today as she would have been distressed at its earlier state, and she sighed with satisfaction, feeling that the awful expense was worth it.

Although the sun was still far too high in the sky, Regan brought the garden hose around the corner and turned on the water to soak the flower beds and potted plants until puddles stood around them on the stones. She hosed down the terrace, splattering her bare brown legs in the process, and when she was finished, wiped her hands on her cutoff Levi's. Mindful of her mother's meticulous gardening habits, she rolled the hose in a neat coil and hung it from the hook around by the kitchen door on the other side of the house.

Regan's head ached. Too much sun, she decided

grumpily. Her legs were stiff from crouching. She was hot and thirsty and in a rather bad mood. The screen door banged behind her as she went through the kitchen and into the bathroom to fumble around in the medicine cabinet for the aspirin bottle. The mirrored reflection of her thin, tanned face, dirt-streaked, damp and flushed, was enough to make her laugh wryly. "If the kids at school could see me now!" she muttered, pushing back at her long hair to get it out of the way. "Regal Regan" she was sometimes called by those who barely knew her because her tall straight carriage made one think of royalty. Her close friends knew better. They had seen her warmth, her vivid spirit, and her well-hidden vulnerability. They had experienced her quick temper and her just-as-quick apologies. Regan, they knew, was a study in contradiction.

In the kitchen, she sat down at the table with a glass of iced tea and popped two aspirin into her mouth, settling back to wait for the headache to go away. It was some time later, as she sat half-asleep with her chin on her fist, that the faint noises outside the patio door registered in her tired brain, and even when she heard them she was too exhausted to care what the sounds were. There was muffled scratching and something that might have been a low whining, and occasionally she could have sworn she heard a pebble skitter across the flagstones. Regan sat in a stupor of exhaustion until the series of crashes began.

And then it was too late.

She flew across the living room to the patio door and found the disaster she had suddenly known she would see: Her lovely, carefully planted patio was in shambles, the new growth dug up and cast about in limp disarray; pink, white, blue, yellow, and violet, all lay under a layer of dark crumbled soil which the dog had flung about with his huge clumsy puppy paws.

That horrid dog! He was bounding back and forth across the patio now, trying to catch a mockingbird that flew, teasing and squawking, just out of reach above him. With every other lunge, the half-grown black-and-tan German shepherd slammed against Regan's new clay pots, sending most of them teetering and crashing in pieces on the terrace.

He was a friendly dog, putting up not a whimper of protest when Regan opened the patio door and stepped outside with deceptive calm. At once his cavorting stopped, and he ambled over to lick the hand she reached out to him.

"There, boy." She spoke in a low voice, stroking his sleek head with fingers that trembled. She bent and examined the gold dog tag on his black leather collar, drawing back when he tried to press his cold wet nose against her face. "Oh, no you don't! You've got more than your fair share of nerve, trying to make up to me."

And so do your owners, she added grimly when she read the name on the dog tag. Charles McKeever, indeed! It couldn't be just any old stray dog who destroyed her flowers. No ordinary mutt, this one. His name, according to the tag, was Ciao, and he belonged to the wealthiest family in Bowie's Landing, Texas.

Ciao's shining coat was matted with mud from the flower bed where he'd rolled in cool delight. He was perfectly still now, the picture of good-natured innocence, panting a little in the heat and watching Regan with big brown eyes as she sat back on her heels and surveyed the damage. "Well!" she exclaimed a time or two, not really knowing what else to say. As she gazed at the ruin, she grew angrier and angrier at the McKeevers, who evidently hadn't much consideration for others if they let their dog run loose to wreak his own particular brand of havoc on the neighborhood.

Standing up decisively, she grabbed Ciao's collar and said, "Come along. I'm taking you home."

She half dragged the reluctant animal down the rocky steep, over boulders and fallen tree trunks, to the sandy white beach below the cabin. And then, not wanting to hurt him, she released his collar and found that he followed her willingly as she stamped along the edge of the water toward the McKeever place. It wasn't far, barely a quarter of a mile of empty beach faced with rugged wooded inland, and then the beginning of the most elegant estates on the lake: the Jonsson place, the Vandevers' summer cottage and the enormous white McKeever house.

Her steps slowed in spite of her anger, and she almost halted completely, so great was her awe of the McKeevers. Every summer Regan had eyed the prominent house with interest, although always from a distance. It was difficult to ignore, a big brick structure, painted white, with huge round pillars and a wide marble veranda in front. There was a look of old wealth in its balconied second-floor windows and its black-trimmed shutters.

The McKeevers themselves were not highly visible among the summer people. In the three summers she had spent at the lake, Regan had glimpsed Charles McKeever, Jr.—"Dr. Charley," as the townies, or year-round residents, called him—only once, at Woodman's Grocery Store on a busy Saturday night. He'd been carrying his own bag of groceries to the car—*just like a regular person,* she had thought in amazement at the time. She had never seen the father, Charles, Sr., a Houstonian known for his Midas touch when it came to oil and land investments; nor his beautiful second wife, Elizabeth; nor the younger son, Dr. Charley's brother, Casey, who was a lawyer. It was probably having never seen them that had blown all out of proportion her respect for the legendary McKeevers, Regan told herself.

She clutched at the evaporating traces of her indignation for courage and started up the perfect green lawn from the boathouse and dock.

The slope was gentle, the grass velvet-smooth underfoot, as Regan's long, slim legs propelled her closer to the looming white house. Ciao remained politely at her side until they reached the flat terrace level with its marble-bordered swimming pool and its brick patio laid in a houndstooth design. Regan saw two figures moving swiftly down the length of the pool, arms cutting the water with clean strokes that made barely a splash in the afternoon silence. Since they didn't appear to notice her, she stood on the terrace edge and studied the surroundings resentfully.

This, she decided, *is how my world would look if I could manage it.* Obviously, the owner hadn't had to count his pennies when it came to landscaping. A virtual forest of tropical plants—tall bamboo, graceful fan-leaved sago palms, assorted ferns, and trailing vines in dense plantings—protected the generous pool and patio area from view on either side. To her right, through an archway in an ivy-covered brick wall, Regan glimpsed a paved parking area and four-stall garage housing a couple of Mercedes-Benz automobiles. Directly in front of her, though still some distance away, long sheer-curtained French windows hid the cool dark expanse of the mansion's interior.

Drawing her attention back to the reason she was here, Regan watched as Ciao deserted her abruptly to circle the pool in an awkward gallop, barking loudly. The two in the water, male and female, reached the far edge, and the girl pulled herself out at once to sit on the side. The man clung to the edge of the pool with one hand and reached up with the other to rub the whimpering dog's head, murmuring in a soothing voice, "Take it easy, old man. Hey, my friend, where have you been? You look as if you've been through a swamp." He grinned at the girl. "You owe me a beer. I told you he'd come home on his own."

The girl smiled back at him. "You lose," she said, nodding in Regan's direction. The man turned his head and looked at Regan silently as she marched around the pool until she could glare down at them.

"Your dog, I presume!" She almost spat the words at him.

The girl's eyes widened and the man looked up in surprise at her anger. Drops of water shone on his dark hair and glistened on his bare sun-bronzed arms and chest. Regan thought she had never seen a man so incredibly handsome, so perfectly even-featured, and the thought only served to increase her anger.

"Yes, he's mine," he admitted readily, fingering the collar and tag around the dog's neck. His voice was low and his pronunciation perfect. The thought occurred to Regan that he must have been educated at exclusive schools. "Technically," he amended, "he'll soon belong to my brother. Thank you for bringing him home. He's not used to the place, so he takes advantage of every opportunity to run away." He turned smoky gray eyes to the raven-haired beauty whose feet still dangled in the water as she watched the interchange with interest. "Would you put him back up, Peg?"

"Certainly." The girl drew her shapely legs up and stood immediately, stretching and shaking, sending tiny droplets of water in all directions. She was older than Regan, curvaceous and extremely fetching in her white bikini. Her blue eyes assessed Regan for a moment with enviable confidence. Turning away, she snapped her fingers smartly and padded toward the archway, leaving damp footprints on the bricks. Ciao followed obediently at her heels as she disappeared through the gate.

"Very well trained," Regan said under her breath, and the man looked at her again.

"Ciao's an obedience school dropout," he offered. "Not the brightest of the litter, but he does have his good points."

"I was referring to your girl friend," Regan snapped. He narrowed his eyes a little, watching her, and she looked back defiantly. There was something familiar about his face, and it dawned on her that he must be the lawyer brother, Cascy McKeever. There was a strong resemblance to Dr. Charley in the regular features, the straight, high-bridged nose and the flat-planed cheeks. His eyes, squinting against the glaring Texas sun, were the same gray shade as his brother's. His brown hair was thick with just the slightest tendency to curl. No one could be that handsome, she decided cynically, without being very much aware of it.

"I hope Ciao didn't annoy you." The man spoke abruptly. "He can be very playful."

"As a matter of fact, he annoyed me a great deal," Regan answered. "He dug up and smashed around forty dollars worth of plants and pottery. He destroyed in less than five minutes what it took me three days to accomplish."

"I'm terribly sorry," he said, and he sounded sorry. "I'll pay for it, of course. Perhaps you can replant—"

"Replant! Take a good look at me! I've been down on my hands and knees for the last three days, digging in the dirt"—she motioned at her grubby clothes to illustrate her point—"getting hot and tired and—and just plain sweaty! If you think I have the energy to put myself through that ordeal again, you're mistaken."

"Maybe there's someone who could help you?" he suggested hopefully.

"I'm afraid not."

"No family around?" he asked, and she resented his probing even though there was more concern than curiosity in his tone. Also, unreasonable as it might be, she resented the fact that he hadn't offered to help her himself.

"No family *anywhere*," she corrected him.

At that, his gray eyes studied her soberly. "You live alone?"

"Yes," she managed to say in a civil voice, although she wanted to tell him it was none of his business.

"How old are you?"

"I can't see that this has anything to do with my ruined flower beds," she muttered, her temper rising.

"Look," he said quickly, "how would it be if I send over the man who does my yard work? He'll have the place looking great in one afternoon—"

"No, thank you." Her response was immediate and emphatic. She had no wish to be on the receiving end of the McKeevers' charity. "What you could do is just use a little common sense and keep the dog fenced in from now on."

His mouth twitching with amusement at the scolding, he nodded. "I had him locked in the garage until half an hour ago. I saw him streak past the pool—"

"And you let him go," she finished for him. "The least you could have done was chase after him. You might have caught him before he chewed up my yard."

"*Me* chase him!" he exclaimed in clear astonishment, as if she had suggested that he sprout wings and fly. His amusement vanishing, he squinted up at her more carefully, and Regan tossed her head under his look, sending dark hair swaying. "Perhaps you don't recognize me," he said finally. "I'm Casey McKeever." As if that explained everything.

"And I'm Regan Allison!" she retorted sarcastically. "Oh, I know who you are, all right. Just because your name is McKeever, that doesn't excuse you from common courtesy. Some people may bow and scrape to you, but I won't."

An odd look came into his gray eyes as she spoke, a

look that Regan didn't understand. Despite her hot words it wasn't anger that she saw, although she had expected to anger him.

"I don't think I'd find you half so attractive if you bowed and scraped to me, Miss Allison," Casey McKeever said wryly after a moment of silence.

Attractive! The word reminded Regan of how awful she must look in cutoffs and T-shirt, with mudstreaked face and legs. Her head still pounded from heat and temper. Flushing in embarrassment she tried to think of a response, but the lawyer spoke again before she got a chance. "You may not believe me, Miss Allison, but I usually manage to keep Ciao under control." He sounded sincere. "I've had him in the garage until my brother can pick him up this weekend and take him to Houston. If Peggy had been here when he escaped—or Katy, my housekeeper—but Katy's at the store and Peggy just arrived a few minutes ago. I assure you it won't happen again. I'll see that Katy is extra careful, now that I know Ciao likes to dig."

His smile mesmerized Regan for a moment. She stared at him with wide green eyes, her generous mouth wanting to return the friendliness, but then she gave some thought to what he had just said.

"You'll see that *Katy* is careful!" she gasped. "Surely you can't be as lazy as that!" She shook her head incredulously. "Or do you consider it beneath your dignity to perform such menial labor as catching your own dog? You'd rather just let your housekeeper or...or your girl friend do it for you! Well, if they're willing to let you lord it over them, that's fine with me. Just keep your dog away from my place, although heaven knows there's nothing left for him to tear up."

Regan thought with precious little satisfaction that she had effectively wiped the smile from the man's suddenly grim mouth. His lean brown hands gripped the edge of the pool so tightly that the knuckles were white, and cold fury put ice in his eyes, but he didn't reply to her accusations. Without another word between them she turned and made a dignified exit around the pool and down to the lake.

Something she had seen in his face puzzled and troubled her. Casey McKeever, she was positive, was a man capable of taking the upper hand in any relationship—a man accustomed all his life to coming out on top. If he had wanted to, he could have cut Regan to shreds; she had no illusions about that. How had she, a mere college senior, brought that look of enraged frustration into the eyes of a successful lawyer?

The question continued to bother Regan. It bothered her too that she had lost her temper and made an enemy of one of Bowie's Landing's most powerful summer residents. The next day when she received in the mail a personal check from Casey for several times her actual loss, she didn't even consider cashing it. Instead she burned it on the hearth.

It was not more than a couple of days later in the post office that she overheard the postmistress, Clara Reeves, remark to someone what a shame it was that Casey McKeever had decided not to stay in Bowie's Landing all summer. "Sort of sudden, him leaving like that, wasn't it?" Clara asked a grandmotherly-looking lady in gray.

The lady nodded, her forehead wrinkled with concern. "That it was. He had been planning to stay through August, but he said something came up in Houston. Said his father needed help on some legal problem." She spread her hands. "Myself, I think it was something he was unhappy about here...maybe a quarrel with his girl friend, the way he acted. But his dad said it was a godsend for him to come to Houston, so maybe I'm wrong."

The gaunt, bespectacled Clara clicked her tongue. "You still try to mother that boy as if he were ten instead of over thirty. Let him grow up. If he had a fight with his girl friend, he can mend his own heart. He don't strike me as wantin' a nursemaid, Katy.''

Katy—the McKeever housekeeper! Before she gathered up her mail and waved good-bye to the post-mistress, Regan stole another glance at Clara's friend, the short plump lady whose brown eyes were bright behind her glasses. "Old habits are hard to break,'' Katy was observing. "I've been mothering Mr. Casey so long now, it's strange to think of him not needing it any more. Anyhow, I miss him something awful, bless his heart!''

The rest of the summer turned out to be strangely flat. Even the young people Regan knew in town didn't help. She found that the young men bored her, and the girls thought her attitude peculiar.

To keep from sitting at home every night, she dated several college students who either lived in the area or were visiting nearby, but all too often she found herself comparing them unfavorably with her memory of Casey McKeever. It was a puzzling tendency, she thought, since her contact with him had been brief and not at all satisfactory. What was there about the man that she couldn't seem to rid herself of his image? And why did it seem, when she looked back on it now, that the expression in his eyes that she hadn't been able to identify that day was sadness? Why should their con-versation have made him sad?

And, for heaven's sake, why did she keep looking for him every time she went to the post office or Woodman's? Why did she drive by his house at every opportunity, craning her neck for a glimpse of someone on the front veranda or the driveway?

At any rate, she never saw him, and despite the dates she really didn't enjoy, she felt alone and lonely. Worse, she felt as if she deserved to be lonely. By now she ought to be used to it, she thought with self-pity, but it was a new, raw loneliness, and she was glad when September came and it was time for her to close up the cabin and return to Austin for her final year of college.

"Oh, wow, I hope I get this job!"

The girl in sundress and sandals didn't seem to be talking to anyone in particular—there were three of them waiting to be interviewed for the position—so Regan turned to look at her fully and said, "I'm hoping for it, too," in an agreeable voice.

"Oh, sure," the other girl laughed, and shrugged. She had waist-length straight blond hair, and Regan saw to her complete surprise that she was chewing vigorously on a lump of gum. The girl had a remarkably young look about her in spite of her low-cut spaghetti-strapped dress. Regan wondered briefly if perhaps they were applying for two different jobs. The blonde hardly seemed old enough to vote, much less teach.

On the other hand, the girl sitting next to the door with her nose stuck in a book appeared much more qualified. Undoubtedly her hair in its tidy brown bun and the rather thick eyeglasses she wore added to the impression that she would make a splendid special-education teacher. Certainly she didn't seem much older than Regan's own twenty-two years.

Regan amused herself for a while by imagining that the plain young lady in her stern-looking brown suit—was it really wool in May?—was actually a French novelist in disguise, come to Bowie's Landing to write about the lives of the real people who inhabited the small lakeside town year round and not just during the summer season.

"My boyfriend has his own business in Springer. He services swimming pools—makes a bundle at it too." The blonde interrupted Regan's thought with her announcement. Springer was a town a few miles downriver from Bowie's Landing, slightly larger and having about the same attraction as a weekend home for wealthy city dwellers. Springer's main advantage was that it had been selected some eighty years earlier as the seat of county government. "I'll just *die* if I don't get a job nearby," the girl declared, looking at Regan earnestly, as if Regan simply must understand the terrible urgency of her plight.

"I can imagine," Regan murmured dryly. Just to make conversation, she asked, "Where did you get your degree?"

The blonde looked complacent. "What degree? I've heard the Bowie's Landing school board is so desperate to fill this job, they've dropped that requirement."

At that statement, the girl with the bun looked up from her book and snorted in disbelief.

"I have two years of college," Miss Spaghetti Straps continued. "Well, nearly two." She leaned closer to Regan and whispered, "I also have connections."

Before Regan could ask what sort of connections she meant, the boardroom door opened and the thin young man who had been called in previously came out. A lady with little half glasses perched on her nose and a stenographer's notebook in her hand followed him out and shut the door. "We'll be in touch, Mr. Denton," the lady said briskly, steering him to the exit before turning to the blonde. "Miss Fontaine?" She looked down her nose in disapproval. "This way, please."

Regan drifted back into her daydream about the French novelist, although she admitted this time that few researchers would waste much time on the Bowie's Landing townies. No, they'd write about the aristocrats, the summer people, most likely the macho McKeevers. She imagined the novelist whipping off her glasses and loosening an abundance of long thick hair from her bun, throwing herself into Casey McKeever's strong arms and confessing to being "madly, desperately" in love with him. Regan was so far into her

daydream that she could scarcely believe it when the
boardroom door swung open again and the blonde
rushed out, looking pink and huffy.

"Evidently her connections weren't as good as she
hoped," the girl with the bun remarked dryly to Regan.
Regan couldn't help feeling a touch of sympathy for
the childish blonde, for whom a waitress job might
have been a more realistic goal.

"You're next, Miss Allison."

The words snapped Regan to attention and she came
out of her chair eagerly, pushing back a wing of dark
hair from her temple and tugging at the short jacket of
her smart cranberry pantsuit, which looked as if it had
been made just for her—long and slim and stylish,
vivid with a hint of reserve. Regan followed the board
secretary confidently, walking with the long-limbed
grace of a ballerina. She knew she looked good, she
knew she was right for the job, and she had reason to
believe she could convince the men in the adjoining
room to hire her.

These school-board members were not big business-
men like those in Dallas or Houston, she knew. They
were leaders of the community, it was true, but most of
them were friends of Regan, men she had come to
know well in her past summers here.

Following the older woman into the room, Regan
smiled at the group assembled around the table and
nodded at those she knew. She had to choke back a
laugh at the wink Fred Woodman, the gray-haired
grocer, gave her. Ronald Barnes grinned broadly at her,
and the nice young farmer, Bob Cox, whose kids she
sometimes baby-sat for, returned her smile with a little
wave. She had never met the school-board chairman,
Roy Coffman, and one or two others, but—

Regan's attention froze when it reached the man
seated next to the chairman, and her thoughts scrambled in horrified confusion. It couldn't be—not Casey

McKeever! What in the world would he be doing on the school board at Bowie's Landing? He was a summer person! She blinked and shook her head slightly as if her vision might be defective, but when she looked again, the outrageously handsome man in the three-piece gray pinstriped suit was still there, staring back at her with recognition and surprise in his charcoal-colored eyes.

Chapter Two

It was May now, nearly a year since Regan's unhappy encounter with Casey, and she wasn't pleased to find her heart beating rapidly with the memory of that day last June. She was a fool, she had told herself innumerable times, to have made such a big deal over the antics of a puppy. She should have been calm and reasonable about the damage and gracefully accepted Casey's generous reimbursement. He had been awfully nice about it at first. Had she imagined the rage on his face when she stalked away from the pool that day? Never mind—she wasn't imagining the cool speculation that came into his eyes as he faced her now. Regan's heartbeat became a roar in her ears.

"Miss Allison?" Mr. Coffman spoke loudly. "I asked if you would have a seat please?"

"Yes, thank you." Regan tried to pull herself together. She took the seat offered her, at the opposite end of the table from the board chairman and Casey McKeever. For encouragement, she glanced at Fred Woodman, who smiled at her in a fatherly way.

Mr. Coffman's first questions were routine and her answers unremarkable. Yes, she would graduate from the University of Texas at Austin within the month, her degree would be in education, and she would be certified to teach special education at either elementary or secondary school level. She would complete her student-teaching requirements this spring at a rehabilitation-center school in Austin where she was presently working with both mentally and physically handicapped children. Yes, she felt capable of serving as special-education or resource-room teacher for the fifteen or so elementary-school children in Bowie's Landing who had been identified as having some sort of disability requiring special help.

Regan responded in a clear calm voice to the board chairman's questions. By avoiding looking directly at Casey McKeever, she even managed to regain some measure of the self-confidence she had lost so suddenly upon finding him in the room. And then, during one of Mr. Coffman's pauses when he consulted her application form and college transcript, the unsmiling attorney broke crisply into the silence: "If you don't mind, Miss Allison, I'd like to ask you a question or two." He waited for her nod of assent, which she gave with sinking heart. "First of all," he said, "I'm curious. Just what made you think you want to be a special-education teacher?"

She took a deep breath. "I think," she said slowly, "I've wanted to teach kids with special problems for as long as I've wanted to teach, which has been a long time. Most of my life, in fact."

"A long time, indeed," he murmured, and the other board members tittered.

"It has seemed a long time to me," Regan said with dignity, flushing at the laughter. "When I was in first grade, a deaf girl who was my age lived across the street from us, and I always resented the fact that she had to go away to school, that she couldn't be taught in public schools in the community where we lived. It occurred to me that one day perhaps I could teach children like her."

"I see." He leaned back in his chair, pulling at one earlobe as he studied Regan. "You think you have something special to offer? Some insight into the problems of the handicapped?''

She moved her shoulders uncomfortably. "I don't know that I would put it exactly like that, although some of my professors at the university think I have a gift for working with handicapped children." She nodded at her application papers in Mr. Coffman's hands. "I think if you read my letters of recommendation, you will find that the children in my class accept me and seem to enjoy learning under my instruction."

Without even glancing at the letters he asked smoothly, "Would you tell us please what you think about Public Law 94-142?"

Regan adjusted her thoughts dizzily to his abrupt change of subject. Public Law 94-142 was a piece of federal legislation that said that all children are entitled to a free public education, regardless of physical or mental limitations, and that handicapped children should be taught whenever feasible in public schools and in the most normal, or the least restrictive, educational setting possible. Regan believed strongly in the justice of the law.

"I approve of it," she said cautiously, "but I'd be a fool to say otherwise, wouldn't I, since it's the law?"

Casey shrugged. "A great many educators are resisting PL 94-142. Its financial implications have the potential to ruin some school districts, and ours could be one of those ruined. Resource teachers, interpreters for the deaf, special classroom aides—all of these cost a great deal of money, Miss Allison. Tell me, why do you favor bringing handicapped children into the classroom rather than teaching them at home?"

"Because they've been hidden away at home long enough!" Her face and voice were warm with feeling. "Many of them have been denied an education because of architectural barriers—steps which they can't

manage on crutches or doorways too narrow for wheelchairs. And home-bound teaching isn't always as good
as classroom teaching. It certainly isn't *equal*. It doesn't
expose the handicapped child to normal learning stimu-
lants, to other children—"

"Now there's another problem," Casey interrupted
her. "In fact, you've just mentioned two very good reasons for keeping the handicapped child out of public
schools. What do you propose that we do about the
steps here at the elementary school?" His cool voice
challenged her. "Did you happen to notice any steps
when you came in?"

"Of course I noticed the steps! Teaching handicapped children makes one aware of the presence of
architectural barriers. You may not know it, Mr. Mc-
Keever, but the world is full of barriers for the handicapped."

"Is it really?" He raised an eyebrow, rather sardoni-
cally she thought.

"Yes, it is. And you will have to build ramps to get
students in wheelchairs into the buildings. And widen
the doorways, and make the bathrooms and water
fountains accessible. The law says so!"

"And where are we to get the money for these
changes?"

Regan smiled sweetly at him. "The same place you get
money for educational services that benefit normal children. The same place you get money for the athletic programs, and band, and teachers' salaries, for that matter.
From the general budget of the school district. The federal government will contribute some, of course, but the
rest is your responsibility."

A murmur passed among the school-board mem-
bers, but Regan couldn't tell if it signified agreement or
disapproval. Casey inclined his head and scrutinized a
paper on the table in front of him, rolling a slim gold

pencil between his palms. Without looking at her, he asked, "Don't you think it might be somewhat depressing for the able-bodied kids to have"—he paused slightly—"cripples in the public schools?"

There was a taut silence as the other board members waited for Regan's response. Her anger flared at his use of that word. "That's an archaic idea," she said through clenched teeth. "It's as outdated as racial segregation! No, I do *not* think it would depress normal kids to be around handicapped kids, Mr. McKeever. That you should even suggest it seems to me to be an indication of your own prejudice against the handicapped."

A shocked gasp went through the room. Regan regretted her sharp answer immediately, but she would not change her words. The only one who didn't look positively scandalized by her rudeness was Casey McKeever. He watched her with a half smile that made Regan suspect she had played right into his hands.

"Harrumph!" Mr. Coffman cleared his throat noisily. "Miss Allison, surely you must be aware that Mr. McKeever is a strong supporter of the rights of the disabled!" His voice was gently reproachful. "As a concerned school-board member, he was merely playing the role of the devil's advocate in order to determine your stand on the issues involved here."

Regan wanted to protest, to tell him that Casey McKeever had a much more devious reason for baiting her. Using his considerable skill with words, he had given her enough rope to hang herself. The board would never hire her now—not after she had insulted him in front of all of them. She looked helplessly at her friends, but they wouldn't meet her eyes.

As if to confirm her fears, Mr. Coffman added uncomfortably, "We do, er, appreciate your coming from Austin tonight for this interview. I realize you have classes tomorrow and hope it didn't inconvenience you too much. The board will be, er, reaching a decision soon and will let you know what we have decided."

Regan blinked back the tears that stung her eyes and rose numbly to leave the room. She must have stumbled a little on her way out, because Ronald Barnes was suddenly gripping her by the arm and escorting her past the prim, frowning secretary into the waiting room, where the girl with the bun looked at them with interest.

"Regan, honey," Ronald mumbled in her ear, sounding troubled, "how well do you know Casey McKeever?"

"I met him once before. I insulted him that time too. You don't have to tell me what a fool I am, Ronald." She straightened her shoulders. "Go on back and do your job, and for heaven's sake don't worry about me! There are other special-education teaching jobs in Texas."

Freeing herself from his grip, she grabbed up her purse from the chair where she had left it and almost ran outside to her car.

Driving back to Austin through the warm spring night, Regan wondered distractedly what to tell her professors, who would certainly be curious to know why a prospective graduate with her qualifications had failed to get the job. After all, Regan's grades were outstanding and her references excellent. Her friendship with several of the school-board members, plus the fact that she was a Bowie's Landing property owner and summer resident, should have given her a definite advantage in competing for the teaching position.

"Don't tell them anything, yet," her roommate Andrea advised her the next morning. "They probably won't ask you how the interview went for a few days. In the meantime, you can think of some way to convince them you didn't want that old job!"

"But I *do* want it!" Regan sighed. Standing before the

mirror in the dormitory room the girls shared, she stared into her own wide-set green eyes which clearly reflected her misery. As usual, her face was scrubbed clean of makeup. Regan's healthy, long-legged, golden-tanned kind of good looks couldn't be described as ordinary prettiness. This morning dark smudges under her eyes told of her sleep loss. "Oh, Andy, you can't imagine how much I hoped for that job!"

"Yes, I can," Andy contradicted her, enveloping Regan in a hug. And because they had been roommates for nearly four years, and had shared their deepest confidences with each other, Regan knew Andy spoke the truth.

"Me and my big mouth! How many times have I said that? How many times have you told me my temper would get me in trouble?"

The smaller, towheaded girl grinned at Regan's lament. "Evidently not often enough. It really did mess you up this time. Looks like you'll have to come to New York with me after graduation. You can join my repertory theatre group and we'll starve together...."

Regan was laughing at the idea as she went to class.

As Andrea had predicted, Regan's professors didn't mention the disastrous job interview that day, which was Friday. It was on Saturday morning that she received a registered letter from the Bowie's Landing school board. The letter must have been written at Thursday evening's meeting.

"Oh, my! They certainly believe in giving prompt notice that you bombed out!" Andy joked as Regan ripped open and scanned the single sheet.

Her heart thudding noisily, Regan looked up at her friend. "They want to see me again. They want me to attend this Thursday's meeting," she whispered with dread. "No explanation. Just 'Please try to come.' Oh, Andy, couldn't they just let me go in peace? I never want to see Casey McKeever again as long as I live!"

"Really?" Andy asked skeptically, clearly not believing her.

As it turned out, Casey McKeever was not present at the next meeting. After all her sleepless nights, the source of Regan's anxiety wasn't even there! None of the other job applicants were there, either, she noticed.

"Thank you for coming back, Miss Allison," Mr. Coffman addressed her with a smile. "I assure you it will be the last trip you have to make on our account until you begin teaching school in September. That is, if you accept our offer—"

Regan wasn't sure she had heard him correctly. "Your offer?" she repeated in a weak voice.

Mr. Coffman nodded. Ronald Barnes and Fred Woodman beamed at her, and Bob Cox and the other men looked very pleased.

"That's right. There was no question but that you were the best qualified of our many applicants, my dear," the board chairman assured her. "All of us are in agreement that Bowie's Landing needs more teachers with your sort of training and your caring nature."

Stunned, Regan stared about at the men, duly impressed that they had dared to hire her against Casey McKeever's wishes. For she had no doubt that the board had not been in complete agreement about choosing her, at least not when Casey was there to cast his vote.

"I thought—" she began and stopped to take a deep breath.

"Yes?"

"I thought last week when I left that—" She stopped once more. "That is, I didn't think you'd want to see me again. I was afraid I didn't make a very good impression, losing my temper with Mr. McKeever the way I did. I do hope it didn't cause any bad feelings."

"Not at all, not at all!" Mr. Coffman insisted. "As I told you then, Mr. McKeever was merely playing the devil's advocate. By the way, he would have been here tonight except for a sudden business conference he had to attend in New York. His secretary called from Houston to say he had gone up there yesterday and couldn't make it back in time for our meeting." The chairman put on his glasses and pulled a set of papers from his briefcase. "Now, if we can get down to basics like salary...."

When Regan walked out the door an hour later to drive back to Austin, she had signed a contract for a job that would have brought forth hearty approval from her teacher-parents, had they been around to witness the signing. Along with her job, she acquired a genuine hometown and made a secret vow that she would stay in Bowie's Landing for a long, long time. No more moving every couple of years as her parents had done, from one challenging teaching job to another, usually attaining a promotion but never quite finding what they were looking for.

Regan's long legs were cramped from being folded under the steering wheel of her white Volkswagen bug. She pulled into Ronald Barnes's service station and switched off the engine. Climbing out of the car, she threw her arms around the startled Ronald. "I'm home!"

"Well, now, you sure are." He blushed around his smile of welcome. Not accustomed to being hugged in public, the tall gangling man squirmed until Regan took pity on his embarrassment and released him. "Got yourself all graduated, huh?" he asked with relief.

"Uh-huh. Yesterday. Mortarboards, 'Pomp and Circumstance,' and the works. Oh, fill it up, please, Ronald." Because her stomach was sending out reminders that it was lunch time, Regan surveyed the cheese crackers and soft drinks in the vending machines for a moment, then turned away. Instead of snacking, she would stop at Woodman's Grocery Store and get enough supplies to last. "Do you suppose Billie Riddle-hoover got around to opening up my place?" she asked Ronald, referring to the handyman at the lake marina who hired out to do odd jobs for summer people.

Ronald nodded at her from his post by her gas tank. "He was over there this morning. Always puts a thing off till the last minute, but he does it up right when he gets around to it. He said your chimney is all cleaned out and safe to use—not that you'll be needing your fireplace, hot as it's been here lately." Ronald paused and a worried frown creased his high forehead. "Billie said it looked to him like someone'd tampered with your kitchen door and a window or two. He had to re-place a pane of glass. You'd better be careful, Regan. Folks around here would be mighty upset if anything happened to the new teacher in town."

The news didn't greatly disturb Regan. It had been nine months that the cabin had stood empty, a long time for curious kids to keep away. She did some shop-ping at Woodman's, collected her winter's supply of junk mail from her post office box, and drove on to her cabin, secure in the knowledge that—thanks to Ronald Barnes, Fred Woodman and Clara Reeves—everyone in Bowie's Landing would know by nightfall that Regan Allison had come home.

When Regan was halfway through the extensive housecleaning always necessary on opening up the cabin each year, a car from the county sheriff's depart-ment pulled off the pavement and stopped behind her little VW in the driveway. Regan watched curiously through the window as a tall, powerfully built man in a deputy sheriff's uniform approached the kitchen door and knocked. The sun glinted off the badge on the man's broad chest as he stepped back from the door and half turned to look around the unkempt yard.

Regan padded in barefooted silence to the screen door, but he turned back abruptly to face her as if he had heard her coming. She found herself gazing into a pair of startling blue eyes, set in a hawk-nosed, dark-complexioned face. Except for the blue eyes, he resembled a native American—with an Afro hairstyle, Regan amended as she took in his unruly curly black hair. He held his big cream-colored cowboy hat in one hand and flashed her a white-toothed smile. "Hello, Regan Allison!" he said enthusiastically. "You're even prettier than I've heard."

She gaped at him in surprise.

"Hey, I didn't mean to embarrass you," he added quickly. "It's just that in a town this size you often hear about people before you meet them, and sometimes they don't live up to their descriptions."

"You've heard about me?"

He nodded. "All good, too." His look settled approvingly on her hair.

Raising a hand to touch it self-consciously, she saw that her arm was smudged with dirt from her cleaning tasks. She glanced down at her dust-streaked jeans and cotton shirt and grinned ruefully. "Some first impression I make! I've been getting rid of nearly a year's accumulation of dust and cobwebs. Cleaning *me* up when I finish will be another major undertaking, I'm afraid."

He nodded again, face solemn. "You look like my sister when she helps Mom with spring cleaning. Like a chimney sweep out of *Mary Poppins*."

Regan burst out laughing. "A chimney sweep!" she sputtered. "Listen, Officer, those would be fighting words if I weren't too exhausted to fight right now."

"Did I forget to introduce myself?" the handsome young giant asked. "I'm Deputy Sheriff Dunivan of the county sheriff's department. Call me David. I'm here on business, by the way." He looked suddenly serious. "I came by to check your place out—see how safe it is. I understand there have been some uninvited visitors to the cabin within the last few months."

Regan opened the screen door and let him into her cosy, patchwork-decorated little cabin. She was amused to find that word had already gotten out about her broken window. "Is this part of the usual treatment provided by the sheriff's office?" she wondered aloud.

"Ordinarily we wouldn't come unless you asked us to," he said, placing his well-shaped Stetson on a chair with evident pride. "I'm here because a friend suggested it might be a good idea."

"What friend?"

David, who had already started inspecting the kitchen window with its new pane of glass, spoke over his shoulder. "Casey McKeever."

"Casey McKeever!" she repeated in such astonishment that David turned to look curiously at her.

"That's right," he assured her. "Does that surprise you? I just came from his place, and he asked me to look in on you. He wants to know whether it's safe for you to stay here alone."

Regan followed him through the cabin, silently digesting the fact that not only was Casey back in town but that he had taken it upon himself to send a deputy sheriff to snoop around her cabin and report back to him. It was certainly food for thought.

"This is crazy, David," she said when he had nearly completed his tour. "Why on earth did Casey send you, anyway?"

"Why?" David looked puzzled. "Does he need a reason besides his concern for your safety?"

"Casey McKeever doesn't care two hoots for my safety! He doesn't even like me. Not that I blame him. We've never hit it off very well. So why should he care whether or not I'm safe?"

David snapped the lock on the final window and

turned to face Regan again. "This place is a disaster area," he said bluntly, ignoring her remarks about Casey. "The windows are bad enough, but the locks on both doors are next to worthless. An inept ten-year-old could break in. I notice you don't have air conditioning, which means in this hot weather you'll keep the windows open all the time, won't you?" At her nod, he shook his head. "And you don't have a telephone. Bad news."

"I'll get around to having the phone installed one of these days. I'm not afraid."

"Well, you ought to be!" David ran a hand through his curly hair. "Bowie's Landing is getting to be more like a city every year. New people move here, old-timers leave. The place loses more of its friendly small-town spirit all the time. I've been away four years, so I can see the changes, Regan. That's what Casey's thinking of, I'm sure. You're too trusting if you assume it's okay to go to bed at night with your windows and doors wide open. And you're wrong if you think Casey doesn't care for your safety. As hard as he's worked to hire a special-education teacher for Bowie's Landing, there's no way he'll let anything happen to you."

"He didn't hire me!" Regan protested indignantly.

"Yes, he did," David said firmly. "Casey's been the moving spirit behind getting that position filled, after it had been vacant for several years. Oh, the school board wanted to hire a special-ed teacher. They just didn't have Casey's determination. Last fall he ran for a place on the school board and was elected by a landslide, thank God! And he's keeping his promises. He made sure the salary was competitive. It was Casey who suggested that the school district send out notices about the job vacancy to the directors of every special-education teacher-training program in the Southwest. Believe me, Regan, if Casey hadn't felt you were right for the job, you wouldn't have gotten the contract, even if he had been wild about you personally. Casey, you see, inherited a large share of the famous Mc-Keever integrity."

"You sound like a commercial! What is he, a special friend of yours or something?" Regan asked suspiciously.

"Oh, sure," David admitted. "My older sister Peggy and I grew up with Casey and Charley. The McKeevers have been coming here every summer since I can remember. Mr. McKeever used to send his chauffeur over in the Rolls to pick up Peggy and me and bring us back to the big house to play with the boys."

"Ah, wealth!" she muttered. "So it's his father who is to blame for Casey's being so spoiled. I guess that's only to be expected."

David had an incredulous look on his face. "Spoiled! Are you joking, Regan? Casey may have some faults, but being spoiled isn't one of them. Although the Lord knows he's had plenty of opportunity to turn out that way."

She faced David Dunivan squarely in the middle of her small living room, her chin up. "I won't argue with you about it. Perhaps I simply misinterpret everything Casey does. One thing's for sure: *You* certainly seem convinced of his sainthood." She smiled suddenly, a wistful smile. "I hope someday I have a friend as loyal to me as you are to Casey McKeever."

"I'll work on it," he teased. "But I'll have to get to know you a lot better—after all, I've known Casey all my life." His face took on a hopeful look. "Why don't we begin getting acquainted Saturday evening? I could take you to dinner for a start."

Regan accepted his invitation, glad to have something to look forward to.

"This place"—David gestured around, shaking his head, all business again—"Casey's not going to be happy to hear about the condition of the locks. I'll send the telephone company around tomorrow to install a phone. And don't you forget to lock up when you go to bed tonight. Even if the locks aren't much protection, they're better than nothing."

But at bedtime, Regan went to sleep with her windows raised high to catch the night breeze from off the lake, murmuring defiantly into her pillow, "I don't take orders from you, Casey McKeever! David Dunivan may, but I don't!"

Chapter Three

Traditionally Saturday evening was the only night of
the week to dress formally to attend the Bowie's Landing Country Club. The current trend to go casual had
further modified dressing habits in Bowie's Landing,
but Regan compromised with tradition by wearing a
floor-length cotton sundress in white with tiny blue
daisies sprinkled across it. Since David Dunivan was a
few minutes late, she used the time to add a light touch
of eyeshadow that matched the cornflower earrings she
had put on at the last minute. The dress emphasized
the long slender lines of her figure. Excitement and
hours in the sun had given her bare arms and shoulders
and cheeks a peach-colored glow and her wide green
eyes a vibrant shine.

"You look like an advertisement for fresh air and
vitamins," David commented when she opened the
door to him. "I like whatever you did to your hair."
She had pulled it into a rather loose knot on top of her
head and twisted a blue satin ribbon through the dark
strands. David gave her a quick friendly kiss before
they left her cabin.

He looked very nice himself in a dinner jacket with his
curly dark hair somewhat subdued and his blue eyes
smiling. "What rotten luck that I've missed out on
knowing you these past few summers," he said, shaking
his head as he drove. "Believe me, if I'd known who

bought the Robertsons' cabin, I'd have come back to Bowie's Landing a lot sooner. I'd have gone A.W.O.L. or something."

"Where have you been?"

"Washington, D.C., mostly," he answered, "although I saw quite a bit of Europe, too. With the army, of course. I got out last September and spent a month doing absolutely nothing before I made up my mind to fulfill one of my childhood fantasies."

"What was that?"

"Become a policeman—or Bowie's Landing's equivalent to a policeman." He grinned like a little boy, then sobered up. "Actually, I take my job seriously. It's just that I'm not sure this is what I want to do with the rest of my life. Maybe in a year or so I'll know for certain."

His small car followed the winding route of Old Orchard Road as it climbed to the highest point overlooking the lake, where the club sprawled with its tennis courts and golf course. As David parked the car Regan asked with interest, "What are your alternatives, or do you know yet?"

"Well..." He drew the word out, taking his time answering her. "Casey McKeever is trying to talk me into studying law." Regan got out of the car and joined him on the sidewalk before he could come around to open her door for her. "I have to admit," David drawled, "he can be very persuasive."

I'll just bet he can, she thought.

The country club was a low, rambling, Spanish-style structure with white stucco walls, a red-tiled roof and arched windows and doorways. Courtyards laced the inner floor plan of dining room and lounge areas. Palm trees and yucca plants both inside and out helped simulate an atmosphere of Old Mexico, and strolling mariachi bands sent Spanish music echoing into every corner of the club.

"I love this place," Regan confessed as they stepped

from the foyer into the main dining room, where the mirrored walls, the dark beams supporting the ceiling, and the heavy wrought-iron chandeliers with their hundreds of tiny flickering bulbs set the mood for an evening Regan was determined to enjoy.

"Mmm-hmm," David agreed.

As the maitre d' led them in the direction of a table near the windows, Regan was too busy scanning the crowded room to single out anyone she knew; however, David paused in mid-stride and exclaimed, "Peggy! I thought you were going to see a play in Austin—"

Regan smothered her gasp of surprise when she focused on the foursome who had a moment before been engrossed in their menus. Her initial shock came with the recognition that the girl David addressed—his older sister Peggy—was none other than the blue-eyed, black-haired beauty who had been swimming with Casey McKeever the day the pup tore up Regan's patio. That in itself was disturbing, but Regan couldn't stifle the sinking feeling that gripped her when she realized Peggy Dunivan was seated at a table with Casey and his brother, Charles, and a lovely girl with short sandy hair.

Charles McKeever, Jr., rose immediately and pounded David's back in hearty greeting. Casey merely leaned back in his chair and nodded politely to them, his eyes opaque but his mouth betraying annoyance at the interruption. David apparently didn't notice Casey's unenthusiastic welcome. He was too busy listening to Peggy explain that she hadn't known when the McKeevers picked her up that their plans for the evening would change because Charles might get called back to the hospital in Houston at any time.

"Of course you'll join us for dinner," Casey's brother said graciously. Without waiting for an answer, he told the head waiter, who stood by patiently, "We'll need two more places here, please, Carlos."

David looked to Regan for confirmation. With Casey's disapproving frown still uppermost in her mind, she wanted to say with dignity, "I'd rather die than join them for dinner." But she'd look like an idiot and embarrass David unforgivably if she were honest, so she nodded her agreement.

Casey didn't lift a finger to help rearrange the chairs. Instead, he sat silent and aloof, watching the others shuffle the chairs around him. Regan's face burned at this outright insult, which no one else seemed to notice.

David introduced her to his sister and to the other girl, whose name was Geneva Jonsson, and to Charles, who was "Charley" to everyone present. "And of course you know Casey," David concluded.

"Yes. Hello, Casey." Deliberately she gave him her brightest smile, as if she were really glad to find him here in evening clothes, looking even handsomer than she had seen him before, if that were possible.

Although Regan didn't know Casey very well, her previous encounters with him had led her to believe he was scrupulously well-mannered. But now he made no attempt to return her smile. He said, "Hello, Regan," with obvious reluctance.

So much for the social amenities, she thought bitterly as she sat down beside David in the chair Charley held for her.

Peggy gave no hint that she had seen Regan before. As if sensing Regan's discomfort, she made a special effort to bring the newcomer into the conversation. "I hope David has told you how pleased we all are—especially those of us who live in Bowie's Landing all year—to know you've been hired to teach," she said after Carlos had taken their order. "And I must tell you, you're lucky to have an advocate in Casey. Most school-board members are out of their element when it comes to special education—"

"If you don't mind, I'd rather not hear shop talk tonight," Casey cut in rudely, to everyone's surprise.

After a moment of shocked silence, David said, "Casey's right. If we talk about school business, you'll also have to let me tell you about the high point of my week, which was the false alarm Reverend Tillman turned in—by accident, of course—and I'll have to ask Charley to describe the tonsillectomies he's performed lately."

The others laughed rather nervously, and seeing Regan's blank look, Peggy explained, "Charley doesn't remove tonsils. He's an orthopedic surgeon."

Studying Charley obliquely during dinner Regan decided he must be a great success as a doctor if his bedside manner were anything like his easygoing friendliness tonight. Blonder and larger than Casey, otherwise he looked remarkably like his brown-haired younger brother, but their personalities were miles apart. Charley smiled frequently and listened sympathetically, and Regan liked him, even as she soon discovered she liked Peggy, instinctively. They both made everyone else feel comfortable.

Geneva Jonsson didn't have Peggy's vivacious personality. She sat back and observed the rest of them and occasionally smiled rather shyly at one or the other. In the end, Regan had to admit she liked Geneva too, although she would much rather have disliked the sweet-voiced young lady who was Casey's date.

By the time coffee was served, it was apparent that everyone was finding Casey exceptionally moody. From comments the others made Regan gathered he was usually a nonsmoker. Yet tonight he smoked one cigarette after another, watching the glowing ash with more attention than he had given anyone all evening. Regan thought Geneva was being patient about being ignored. To be fair, though, Casey appeared not so rude as simply preoccupied.

When the band started playing, Charley and Peggy got up to dance. David and Casey launched a discussion of the Houston Astros baseball team, which Regan found easy to tune out. She returned Geneva's smile a little awkwardly, noticing the way the girl's fingers were tapping the table in time to the music. Didn't Casey care that Geneva wanted to dance? Evidently not, from the indolent way he sat now and talked to David. Several numbers later, when Peggy and Charley returned to the table, David asked Regan if she would like to dance, to her great relief. It was a slow song, and he held her off a little so he could look down into her face. "Foxy lady," he commented. "I should have known you'd be good at this."

"Thank you for the flattering words." Forcing a smile, she wished she could shed the depression that had settled over her in Casey's presence.

"You'll get no flattery from me, Regan. Just honest praise. You know, I'm almost sorry we came here tonight."

Me too, she thought fervently, but she only asked, "Why is that?"

"Because I'd rather have kept you all to myself so I could find out more about you. For instance, do you always shake men up like this?"

"Like what?"

"Like Casey. I don't think I've ever seen him lose his cool before."

So David had noticed! Regan flushed. "I told you the other day he doesn't like me, but you didn't believe me. We just seem to irritate each other."

"Funny—he doesn't look at you with dislike."

That was a peculiar thing to say. "David, he hasn't looked at me all evening!"

"Well," David mused, "he has been sort of furtive about it. Do you always affect men that way?" he repeated.

"I'd have to be pretty egotistical to think I'm responsible for Casey McKeever's bad mood," she said. "Unless he's a snob."

David laughed outright. "No, Casey's not a snob. Where'd you get such a notion?"

"Well, he doesn't seem exactly overjoyed to see me tonight. I'm certainly not in his income-tax bracket, so I thought—"

"Regan!" David protested, his voice gentle. "Casey's not like that at all. Good Lord, you don't think Peggy and I are in a class with the McKeevers, do you? My dad was a farmer until his retirement. I mean a *small* farmer. Casey's not class-conscious."

"Mmm," she mumbled thoughtfully. "Okay, maybe he had a fight with his girl friend, then." When David made no comment, she pressed on. "Are they engaged, or what?"

"No, although I think Neva would go for that idea. She's a sweet one." He shook his head and grinned. "How many times have I heard Casey swear off women!"

"But he always comes back for more?"

"Sure, but I have to wonder how serious he is. There are usually at least two or three girls waiting on Casey hand and foot; all the while he's telling me privately that he's a confirmed bachelor."

Remembering the first day she met Casey, she wondered how to ask the next question tactfully. Finally she settled on the direct approach. "Is Peggy one of those who hang around spoiling Casey?"

They were dancing nearer their table and the song was about to end. David agreed hastily. "She's his number-one fan, all right, but her heart belongs to another McKeever. She and Charley are engaged, you know."

Regan hadn't known. It was coincidental that when they got back to the table they found Peggy alone and deep in earnest conversation with Casey. They had been talking a little heatedly, Regan thought, but she couldn't be positive because Casey clammed up at their approach and Peggy said brightly, "David, dear, while Charley's dancing with Neva, I'm going to teach you the latest dance step."

David looked as mystified as Regan felt, but he seated her, cast a quizzical glance across the table at Casey, and took his sister off to the dance floor. Acutely aware that she and David had interrupted something private, Regan searched about for small talk, for anything to ease the tension between Casey and her. She was even prepared to apologize, but he beat her to it.

"Peggy tells me I've been making everyone uncomfortable tonight," he said in a tight voice. "If that's true, let me assure you it wasn't intentional."

"It's perfectly all right," she answered. "Perhaps the evening would have been more enjoyable for you if David and I hadn't been here."

Rather than soothe Casey's temper, as it was meant to do, her statement seemed to annoy him. "Don't be ridiculous! Why does everyone keep insisting my bad mood has something to do with you?" He glared at her. "Peggy just accused me of being unnaturally preoccupied with you. I told her there would be nothing strange about that if it were true." There was a dangerous glimmer in his eyes. "You expect men to find you irresistible, don't you? One dance and you've made a conquest—isn't that how your charm usually works?"

The scorn in his voice was biting. His harsh words were a shock to Regan, who was expecting another encounter with the cool smooth lawyer she had met before. Her tension peaked after a trying evening, and she reacted with amazing venom of her own. "You'll never get a chance to find out if that's the way my charm

works, Casey McKeever, because I'd never dance with
you in a million years!''

He gave her a slow acid smile. ''Believe me, Regan
darling, it would never occur to me to ask you to dance.
Not even in a million years.''

Regan sat in speechless hurt and anger, her flaming
cheeks turned away so Casey couldn't see the tears in
her downcast eyes. Gritting her teeth and gripping her
hands together in her lap, she wished miserably that
David would return so they could leave.

As if he had read her mind, Casey broke into her
thoughts. ''It's too early for David to take you home.
You may as well stay and add Charley to your collection
of male scalps—I imagine he'll want to dance with you
before the night's over. Just try to remember that he's
spoken for.'' His gray eyes raked mockingly over her,
stripping her soul bare, and then looked away with disgust. ''As a matter of fact, *I'm* going home....''

The other four, converging on the table when the
dance ended, overheard Casey's last words and raised
an immediate protest. ''Why are you leaving?'' Charley confronted him bluntly.

''I'm tired,'' Casey said. ''It's been a long week.'' He
was perfectly calm now, finishing off his drink and
pocketing his cigarettes with a nonchalance that suggested he and Regan had just been exchanging pleas-
antries. He looked up. ''Do you mind leaving, Neva?''

It occurred to Regan that this was the most concern
he had shown for his date all evening, but the girl
shook her head, reaching out to touch his thick brown
hair in an eager caress. ''Whatever you want to do,
Casey.''

''Well, if you insist, go ahead,'' Charley finally
agreed. ''We'll be along later. We'll get a taxi or hitch a
ride.''

''Charley and Peg can ride home with us,'' David
assured Casey.

Regan wished he would just hurry up and go so everyone would stop hovering around him. She found it hard to keep the anger out of her eyes as Casey pushed back from the table and stood up, taking his own sweet time, she thought. An instant later, however, she forgot her resentment in sheer astonishment when Charley retrieved a pair of aluminum crutches from somewhere and handed them to his brother. Casey fitted the metal cuffs onto his forearms casually, as if he'd been using them for years, leaned on them for a moment while he and Geneva said good night to the others, and turned to walk slowly across the room without even a glance at Regan.

Chapter Four

"Are you all right?"

David's concerned voice sounded unnaturally loud in Regan's ear. All of a sudden the atmosphere in the dining room was suffocating her, and she thought she would faint if she didn't escape. Jumping up, she dropped her handbag, its contents spilling under the table, but she didn't notice. "Excuse me," she whispered, pressing a hand to her temple. "Please excuse me." With only a vague impression of the glances David and Charley McKeever were exchanging, she stumbled past the other diners and skirted the edge of the dance floor to duck into the powder room in its little alcove.

"Regan!" Peggy was right on her heels. "Sit down here." With firm hands, the older girl pressed Regan down onto the chaise. After digging around for a minute in a cupboard, she came up with a clean white linen towel which she wet under the cold water tap and used to sponge off Regan's hot face.

"Thanks," Regan murmured gratefully. "That helps."

Peggy sat down beside her. "I thought for a minute you might pass out."

"I thought so, too."

"Not too much to drink?"

Regan tried to smile but it resembled more of a grimace. "No. Sort of a similar feeling, though."

"You're awfully pale. Is your stomach upset?"

"It feels a little better now. I think I'll be okay if I can just sit here for a minute."

"Would you like me to leave, or shall I stay with you?"

Regan touched Peggy's arm quickly. "Oh, don't go, please! I want to ask you something." She swallowed, a difficult job considering the huge lump in her throat.

"Yes?" Peggy prompted her when she remained silent.

"I didn't know—that is, I hadn't heard Casey had hurt his leg." She finally managed to get the words out.

Peggy looked blank. "What are you talking about? Casey hasn't hurt his leg as far as I know."

"If he hasn't, then what are the crutches for?" Regan asked as casually as she could.

Wide blue eyes stared into green ones. "Regan!" Peggy gasped. "You're not trying to tell me you didn't know about Casey's handicap? I thought you *knew* Casey!"

"I've met him a couple of times before tonight, but if he had crutches, I didn't notice them." That sounded ridiculous. How could she have missed a thing like that? "At the school-board meeting, he was sitting at the table with the other board members when I came in. The first time I met him—you were there, remember?—I thought he was the most attractive man I'd ever seen." Regan's voice was faintly accusing. "He was swimming in the pool that day, and he looked downright athletic!"

"He's an excellent swimmer," Peggy explained. "There's nothing wrong with his arms and shoulders. If anything, they're unusually strong. Crutch walking does that for a person, you know, and he's been using crutches since he was—let's see—fifteen, I think."

"That long?" Regan's voice trembled and threatened to break. Shutting her eyes and bowing her head, she felt a trickle of warm tears on her cheek. She licked the salty taste off her lips and looked up to ask hoarsely, "His handicap is permanent, then?"

Peggy tossed her head impatiently and stood up to walk across the room. She turned and studied Regan's white fearful face. "Think about that," she ordered Regan sternly. "After all this time, his handicap isn't likely to disappear all of a sudden, is it?"

"I guess not." Regan sounded small and lost. "What happened to him?"

"When he was fourteen, he had polio."

Suddenly everything clicked into place with dreadful precision: Casey's astonishment that Regan should expect him to catch his own dog, Mr. Coffman's insistence that Casey was an advocate of rights of the disabled, and Casey's apparent refusal to help make room at the table for Regan and to dance with Geneva Jonsson.

Regan slumped in utter dejection. "No wonder he hates me. I hate myself! I acted awful to him, Peggy, just awful! I thought he was a self-indulgent, spoiled rich kid, and I called him lazy to his face. Lazy! Can you imagine? I tried to shame him for letting his poor old housekeeper do something I thought any red-blooded American male ought to do himself." Covering her mouth with her hand, she muffled a groan. "Do you know I actually accused him of being prejudiced against the handicapped? After hearing that, it's a miracle the school board hired me."

Peggy had a suspiciously amused gleam in her eyes. "Now that I think about it, David did say you had some peculiar notions about our friend Casey."

"This isn't funny!" Regan protested. "It was bad enough just knowing I'd made an enemy of Casey McKeever, but knowing why is much worse! I feel like a fool." Dabbing at her eyes with the tissue Peggy handed her, she asked anxiously, "How in the world can I make it up to him? Do you think he'll forgive me? I'll go over there first thing in the morning and explain to him—"

"Hold it a minute, Regan," Peggy said in alarm. "What will you say? 'I'm sorry but I didn't know you were crippled. If I had known, I'd have been much nicer to you!'" she mimicked in a gushy voice. "How will that sound to him? It sounds awful to me."

But Regan would not be dissuaded. "I'll think of something. I have to!"

When they rejoined David and Charley, she looked almost back to normal. To David's query, she replied truthfully enough that she had been swimming in the lake at noon and might possibly have gotten too much sun. She didn't think Charley believed her excuse from the odd way he looked at her. David opened his mouth to speak, but Peggy quickly hushed him.

"For heaven's sake, can't you see Regan's had a day of it!" she exclaimed, for which Regan silently thanked her. "Let's take her home so I can tuck the poor kid in bed. Maybe she'll feel better tomorrow."

The men sat for a while in Regan's living room, lounging on the bright patchwork slipcovers on the chair and sofa, admiring her hand-embroidered mural of a lake scene that hung over the fireplace, while Peggy heated milk for hot chocolate in the kitchen portion of the L-shaped room. When Regan asked, Charley gave her a progress report on Ciao, his German shepherd, who he said had the run of the family estate in Houston.

"How do you happen to know about Ciao?" Charley asked curiously, but Regan was saved from having to answer the question when Peggy brought in the tray with heavy mugs of chocolate for each of them.

"This should relax you and help you fall asleep," she

told Regan, and Charley nodded his mock-sober professional approval. "Don't think about anything tonight—just forget it all and rest," Peggy advised her in an undertone.

"I'll try," Regan promised.

David and Charley checked all the windows to make sure they were locked before they left, and David whispered in her ear, "I'll call you."

With the windows closed, the air in the cabin quickly grew stuffy. Regan lay in bed with the covers flung off, hoping for sleep, for anything to shut out the unforgettable image of Casey McKeever that kept limping through her mind. "Poor Casey," she groaned into the hot darkness. Tears of remorse dampened her pillow before she finally fell asleep.

She dreamed dreams, hazy and sad, in which she confused Casey with all the children she had taught, the lonely ones whose minds and hearts were hurt as badly as their bodies. She couldn't reach him. She tried all the methods she had learned in college, but nothing seemed to work because he was embittered and hostile. Each time he looked at her, it was with accusation and hatred, and she couldn't figure out what he was accusing her of.

The dreams were mere flashes, and it seemed as if she hadn't been sleeping very long when the sound of breaking glass woke her. For a moment, Regan thought the noise had been part of her bad dreams, but the next instant her skin prickled and her pulse raced. From the kitchen she heard the distinct sound of glass shattering and dropping with almost melodious tinkles to the floor. Frozen with fear, she lay still, wondering what to do.

Regan didn't own a gun, nor did she even now regret it. She had heard too often of people being overpowered and killed with their own weapons. Even so, she had no intention of waiting to be murdered in her own bed without putting up a struggle. If only she could muster her courage—

The scraping sound of a window being raised mobilized her into action. The thought occurred to her that her chances for survival were better if the intruder never made it inside the cabin. Telling herself she had no choice but to frighten the intruder away, she jumped out of bed and stomped on the floor with the intention of making as much noise as possible. She rattled a dresser drawer open and shut, kicked the cabin wall and grabbed her tennis racket from the corner where it stood, groping about vainly in the dark for a pair of shoes. Frustrated, she clumped barefoot but with resounding footsteps down the short hall to the kitchen, trembling in spite of the racket clutched over her head for protection. *Dear God,* she begged silently, *let this be a nightmare!*

She could see nothing in the blacked-out cabin, and she tried not to be frightened of the silence. Moving blindly forward, her right foot came down heavily on a jagged piece of the broken window pane and Regan let out an outraged howl. In a reflex action of fear, she swung the would-be club with all her strength and heard the wood crack as the racket struck sharply against the hard enamel of the sink. There was a searing pain climbing from her foot to her knee.

Silence again, and she felt a rush of cool air on her cheeks from the opened window above the sink. Regan stood on one leg and bent over to touch the bottom of her right foot. Her fingertips felt something warm and wet and sticky.

Nothing broke the silence. Regan stood like a crane for what seemed to be hours, tensed, waiting, dreading, barely noticing the pain. After an interminable time, she finally dared to move again and hopped to the telephone in the living room to call the sheriff. It wasn't until she heard the comforting assurance that a car would be dispatched immediately that she began to move mechanically through the cabin, turning on lights and grabbing a pink robe to cover her long, filmy nightgown. With jerky movements, she sat down on the edge of her bed to take a good look at her foot. Staring at the deep straight gash that no longer hurt, she realized that she must be in shock. She wrapped a clean towel around it to stop the steady flow of blood and glanced up at the wall clock. Two A.M.

Nerves on end she felt a ridiculous compulsion to be doing something. She was standing on her good left foot, sweeping up the broken glass, when a car screeched to a stop outside. Seconds later, David Dunivan yelled through the kitchen door. "Open up, Regan! Are you okay?"

Regan hopped over to let him in, clinging to the door for support as a strange light-headedness struck her. "I'm fine, David," she told him. "I must have scared away whoever it was. How'd you get here so fast?"

"The dispatcher called me at Casey's place." David put both hands on her shoulders and squeezed as if to reassure himself she was in one piece. She told him briefly what had happened, omitting the part where she cut her foot, and when she finished, David kissed her soundly on the forehead. "Thank God you're not hurt!" he breathed. "I'm going outside to look around." The door banged shut behind him, and Regan stood with her face pressed against the screen, straining to follow him with her eyes.

It was no more than a couple of minutes later that two more cars slammed to a halt in quick succession on the pavement beyond Regan's driveway. One was the sheriff's car, its red lights flashing boldly in the dark. From the shouts she guessed that several men had joined David with spotlights and guns drawn to scour the wooded area surrounding the cabin. It was too dark to see the other car, but in another minute there was a

sound on the porch and Casey McKeever stepped into
the patch of yellow light that slanted over Regan's
shoulder.

Startled, she pushed open the door silently and
hopped back to let him in. Casey still had on the black
trousers and white silk shirt he had worn at dinner. She
supposed he hadn't gone to bed yet, although his coat
and tie were gone and the top several buttons of his
shirt were undone, revealing his strong bronzed throat
and chest. His usually immaculate brown hair was tou-
sled a little on his forehead, but even as Regan stared at
him, he released one crutch and reached up a hand to
smooth the hair back. Coming a step farther into the
room he glanced around swiftly at the broken window
over the sink, the tidy little stack of shattered glass that
Regan had swept together, and the pool of blood in the
middle of the floor. In an instant his gray eyes had
taken it all in and focused back on Regan's crudely
bandaged foot and her death grip on the doorknob.

"Go sit down," he told her in a no-nonsense voice,
jerking his head toward the couch.

Casey worked quickly and for the most part silently
to make her comfortable so that when Charley Mc-
Keever came inside with David a few minutes later,
they found Regan settled on the couch, her injured
foot propped up on a small stool. She was drinking a
glass of tomato juice Casey had brought her rather
awkwardly from the refrigerator.

"You should have told me your foot was hurt!"
David chided her, his face contrite as he watched
Charley unwrap the wound.

"You're the public protector around here, David.
You should have noticed!" Casey's voice was sharp,
and Regan winced at his tone. Casey turned his back on
them and stood looking out Regan's patio door at the
few lights that could be seen twinkling on the lake. She
eyed his crutches covertly, thinking how incongruous

they looked with his tanned, attractively lean form. He wasn't bent and deformed. He didn't *look* crippled, her mind raged. It wasn't fair!

"Did you find any sign of the intruder?" Casey asked after a moment. There was a tautness about his posture, in the way he held his head and the set of his shoulders, that made Regan wonder how he felt about not being able to help in the hunt. Her stomach churned with compassion for him.

"No," David answered. "Nothing other than a few footprints in the mud beneath the window. We'll dust for fingerprints as soon as the man gets here from La Grange with the equipment."

Charley bound a fresh towel around Regan's foot. "In the meantime, you'll have to come with me so I can clean this and stitch it up," he said, smiling his reassurance at her. "Unlike the Girl Scouts, I'm not always prepared. Casey was in such a hurry to get over here that I went off and left my black bag in my own car."

She glanced down at her negligee. "I'm not exactly dressed to go out. Do you suppose you could wait until I get my clothes on?"

"You can go just as you are," Casey informed her coolly. He had turned to face them again, his handsome features set. "You're certainly not coming back here to stay by yourself tonight. David can pack a bag for you and bring it over to my house later."

Regan sat straight up in alarm. Although she didn't relish the idea of staying by herself, she couldn't have Casey feeling obligated to shelter her, not considering the way he felt about her. "Thank you for offering to take me in for the night, but I can't let you bother."

His voice was hard. "I'm not inviting you. I'm telling you." She stared at him, shocked. She was not used to being ordered about. Strong-willed as she had always been, her parents had known better than to put ultima-

turns to her; rather, they had given her alternatives. A sharp retort rose to her lips, but she bit back the words when her eyes slid down to his crutches. His eyes narrowed angrily at the pity reflected in her face, and his lips thinned to a grim line. In spite of his crutches he moved quickly across the room to the kitchen door. He pushed open the screen with one crutch and paused on his way outside. "Charley," he snapped, "or David," he added as an afterthought, "one of you carry her to the car."

Charley shrugged agreeably and bent to scoop Regan up in his arms. He followed his brother, while David went ahead to open the car door for them.

"Tall as you are, I'm glad you're on the thin side," Charley teased her as he deposited her in the plush back seat of a big silver Mercedes-Benz. Casey, behind the steering wheel, started the engine impatiently and watched in the rearview mirror as Charley straightened her leg and made sure her foot was in a comfortable position.

"I'll probably bleed all over your car!" Regan protested, eyeing the soft gray leather upholstery with doubt.

"No, you won't." Charley grinned at her. "It's Casey's car, so you wouldn't dare. Besides, the blood seems to have clotted and the towel is good and thick." He climbed in front beside Casey, waved to David, and the car took off smoothly.

Using hand controls Casey drove the car with skill and considerable speed, and the elegant Mercedes took the dips and bumps so gently that Regan felt no jarring pain in her foot. In the course of a couple of minutes they had wound around Old Orchard Road and turned into the oak-lined drive that led to the Mc-Keevers' big white house. Only when she saw the lights blazing a greeting from the windows of the white-pillared southern-colonial-style mansion did it occur to Regan that she would really be sleeping here tonight, in a house she had admired from afar for three years.

Despite Charley's extreme kindness as he sewed up the cut on her instep; despite the warm interest of Peggy Dunivan, who had waited there for the men to return; despite the concern of the grandmotherly housekeeper, Katy Danetz, Regan didn't feel welcome when Charley carried her up to bed an hour later. She sighed as she looked around at the feminine room with its soft yellow walls and dotted Swiss bedspread and the yellow velvet easy chair in the corner. It was a lovely room with a private bath and dressing room and a little balcony that no doubt afforded a breathtaking view of the lake in daylight. A thick fluffy white carpet covered the floor and a basket of Boston fern hung before the sheer white curtains on the French windows. Regan rubbed a finger over the polished oak of the heavy four-poster bed and sighed again.

It was the finest room she had ever stayed in. She had no complaint about her quarters. What bothered her was Casey's attitude. After insisting that she come here he had completely ignored her, sitting across the solarium from her and talking in a low voice to Peggy while Charley put the stitches in Regan's foot.

"He's not hurting you, is he?" Peggy asked once, gesturing toward Charley's deft fingers.

The orthopedic surgeon had deadened her foot with a local anesthetic, so Regan shook her head and smiled at the three of them. Casey's response was to look through her as if she weren't there, his eyes remote. Regan felt her heart lurch as she thought how justified his contempt was. *If only I could apologize to him,* she thought wretchedly, her green eyes filling with tears.

"Can you feel the needle, Regan?" Charley asked, his concern obvious. He was looking down at the tears on her dark lashes.

"No." She shook her head again and furtively brushed the side of her hand across her eyes.

Charley had finished soon after that and given her a sleeping pill from his black medical bag before carrying her up the stairs. The pill, or perhaps it was sheer exhaustion, overcame her and she fell asleep with the lamp on, still wondering what she could do to obtain Casey's forgiveness.

Chapter Five

Shortly after noon on Sunday a distant throbbing pain in her foot woke Regan. She lay between crisp, fresh-smelling sheets, surveying with drowsy curiosity the airy yellow-and-white dream room streaked with sunshine, taking in the highly polished oak chest of drawers and dresser, and the Wedgwood vase filled with fragrant yellow roses on the table beside the bed. A large oil painting hung on one wall, a scene of two small boys playing beneath a willow tree, done in shades of yellow and peach and chartreuse. When her eyes slid to the white louvered dressing-room doors and she saw her familiar blue overnight case on the floor nearby, she remembered where she was and how she had come to be there.

She sat up hastily and threw off the cover, drawing up her gown to expose her foot. "Not bad, Charley," she said as she lifted a corner of the bandage to admire the neat black stitches. "Not a bad job at all."

"Thank you, ma'am." The door had opened without a sound, and Regan turned in surprise to find the doctor leaning against the frame, smiling at her. Decked out in tennis whites he tapped the head of a racket against a sun-bronzed knee. He came into the room and laid the racket on the foot of her bed. "How's it feeling today?" His touch was gentle as he bent to re-dress the wound.

"It hurts," she admitted.

Charley straightened up and nodded. "Looks good, though. No sign of bleeding." Reaching into the pocket of his shorts he pulled out a small amber plastic bottle and handed it to her. "I picked you up some pain medication on the way home from church. It's not too strong—can't have you getting addicted to anything, you know—but it should get you over these first couple of days."

"Thanks. I guess I can use a little help."

He brought a glass of water from the bathroom for Regan to take one of the capsules and then sat down on the bed beside her. "How are you feeling about last night? A little nervous?" he asked.

Regan hesitated. Charley couldn't know she was oddly more concerned about her belated discovery of Casey's handicap than she was about the cabin break-in. "Well, naturally I hope they catch whoever it was," she said at last. "I'll feel a lot safer at night when they do."

"Naturally," he agreed.

"They haven't, have they?"

"Caught him? No. David was out most of the night and probably will put in a lot of overtime until they apprehend the guy. Bowie's Landing is a peaceful little place. Everyone I saw at church this morning was upset that something tragic nearly happened to you." Charley studied the laces on his tennis shoes for a moment while Regan in turn studied him. *He has something on his mind,* she thought with interest, but after a moment Charley merely looked up and said, "Katy will bring a tray up to you soon. You can get dressed if you like. Peggy went through and picked out some of your clothes to bring over here. For some reason she thought you'd like her selection better than David's." His cheeks creased in a boyish smile. "Katy put them away for you. By the way, Katy's ecstatic about having you here to look after. The McKeever men, I'm afraid, are not very appreciative of her maternal instincts.''

"Not even Casey?"

"Especially not Casey!" Charley said emphatically. "As I said, you can get dressed if you like, but I'd rather you didn't move around much by yourself today. I don't want you to take any unnecessary chances with your foot. It could start bleeding again. Peggy and I are going to play a couple of sets of tennis at the club, but when I get back I'll take you downstairs. Can you be patient?"

Nodding, she lowered her lashes. "Will I be here by myself?"

"No, of course not." Charley stood up and took himself and his tennis racket over to the door. "Katy will be here if you need anything." He started out. "Oh, yes. Casey is swimming right now, so he'll be around the house, although I doubt if you'll see him. He doesn't come upstairs often, as you might have guessed."

As soon as Charley had shut the door behind him, Regan put her left foot to the floor and hopped over to the dressing room with its big walk-in closet. She pushed back the doors and gaped at the row of dresses, pantsuits and assorted shorts and tops which Peggy had evidently instructed David to bring from Regan's cabin. Most of her clothes hung in front of her taking up relatively little space in the large closet. Her shoes had been placed in orderly rows on the shoe rack. Regan hopped back over to the dresser, opened a drawer, and discovered her underwear in tidy stacks inside.

She sank down on the edge of the bed in confusion. Just how many changes of clothes was she expected to need today? Hadn't Casey said she was coming to spend the night? It looked as if she could stay a month.

Before Regan could sort out her thoughts, Katy arrived with a heavily laden breakfast tray. Instead of Regan's usual toast and coffee there was a cheese omelet, bacon, homemade biscuits dripping in butter, a dish of homemade strawberry jam, and a tall glass of milk. "That's beautiful," Regan sighed. "Will you get mad if I don't eat it all?"

"I won't, Miss Allison, but Mr. Casey might. He said for me to fatten you up some," Katy answered with candor, indicating by her tone that whatever Mr. Casey said was regarded as law.

"Oh, he did?" Regan was stung. "I happen to like being thin! Besides," she reasoned, "I won't be here long enough for you to fatten me. I'm going home today."

"I don't know anything about your leaving." Katy obviously didn't believe a word of it. "Mr. Casey said you'd be staying with us for a while. That cabin of yours isn't a safe place for a young girl like you, especially with your foot hurt the way it is." She had arranged the food on a bed tray and stood back now to inspect it with satisfaction. "Now then, sit down and eat before everything gets cold," she said, shooing Regan over to the yellow velvet chair in the corner.

Regan obediently hopped to the chair and plopped down so Katy could place the tray over her lap. "I don't know where Casey got the idea I should stay here," she said calmly, taking a bite of her bacon. "It's not his responsibility to take care of me."

"That may be so," the housekeeper conceded. "Mr. Casey lives by his own code of behavior, though. He feels bad that he didn't do something earlier about your cabin being unsafe, since he's known about it most all week. It's a good thing there are still a few men like him around, if you ask me. When he feels responsible for someone, he acts responsible. He doesn't wait for other people to make him do a thing just because it's the law."

"Very admirable of him, I'm sure. But I don't want

to stay here. I want to go home," Regan insisted obstinately. It was somehow absurd to be denouncing the McKeevers' hospitality even as she sat in their luxurious home and ate their delicious food.

Katy's kind face showed her amazement at a young lady so foolish as to prefer a simple cabin to the comfort of the McKeever mansion. "Well, Miss Allison, that's between you and Mr. Casey, I suppose." She shook her head as she went out and shut the door.

When she finished eating, Regan set the tray aside and went over to the French windows. Pushing aside the curtain she looked out at the slope of velvet lawn that ran into white sand on the beach. The early afternoon sun made the lake seem white, bleached out the greens of grass and trees, and sparkled on the azure swimming pool almost directly below the window as if it were a precious gem. Charley had said his brother was swimming, but Regan could see no sign of Casey outside.

Shrugging off the knowledge that Charley had more or less restricted her to her room, she swore suddenly to find Casey and talk to him. She jerked a raspberry-colored blouse and white culotte set off hangers in the closet and dressed, pulled her thick dark hair back into a low ponytail and tied a white scarf around it. Critically she looked down at her long brown legs and bare feet. She shrugged again. Bare feet it would have to be.

It was easier than she had expected to search the house undetected. Hopping stealthily down the curving staircase into the entry hall below, she discovered that the thick soft cream carpet on the stairs effectively muffled her thudding foot. She bounced as silently across the polished hardwood floor in the foyer to peek into the cool blue living room, which stood vast and empty. The solarium, a green-and-white oasis of sun and tropical plants and summery wicker furniture, where Charley had sewn up her foot last night, was likewise unoccupied. Regan could hear Katy's faint humming voice through the closed door to the kitchen, so she turned the other way and faced the big, cool oak-paneled hallway.

She stopped when she saw all the closed doors ahead of her. *Dare I open one?* she wondered, shuddering at the thought of risking Casey's wrath again. She was tempted to give up and return to her room when the floor beneath her foot creaked in the silence.

"Katy?"

She knew the deep voice that came from behind the third door on her right. Afraid of losing her nerve, she knocked quickly and waited.

"Come on in, Katy!" Casey McKeever called out rather impatiently.

Regan hesitated only a second before she turned the fine brass doorknob and pushed open the heavy door to enter. Casey sat behind a large desk in the impressively book-lined room thumbing through a folder of papers. When he raised his head, she saw that his freshly combed hair was still damp from swimming and that the bridge of his nose was a little red, as if he had gotten too much sun. As she watched, his smoky eyes darkened to charcoal and he scowled at her. "What are *you* doing down here?"

"I wanted to see you."

"I'm busy!" he snapped.

She took a deep breath. "I promise not to take up much of your time."

He looked back down at the papers. "I can't give you even five minutes right now. Maybe tomorrow."

"You mean you *won't* give me five minutes. I notice you had plenty of time to swim."

His voice was even. "That's right, and I still don't have five minutes for you." He shuffled through the documents for a while, blatantly ignoring Regan, who stood before him and fumed in silence. All that kept her from exploding was the memory that she deserved whatever he said to her. After several minutes, he looked up again. "Would you go away please?"

She shook her head stubbornly.

"Didn't Charley tell you to stay off your foot?" he demanded.

"I *am* off it. I hopped down here."

He looked exasperated. "Then hop back upstairs, for Pete's sake, and leave me alone. I have work to do."

Infuriated by his rudeness, Regan burst out, "You want to be left alone? Terrific! I'll leave you alone!" She hopped closer to the desk and snatched up the telephone. "If I may use this, I'll just call Ronald Barnes to come get me and take me home right now. I certainly don't want to interrupt your work—"

His strong brown hand came down on Regan's and took the receiver away from her. Shoving the folder aside, he leaned back in his chair and looked at her. "Okay, talk. Only sit down, please, or you'll have Charley jumping all over both of us!"

Regan sat in the brown leather armchair across from the desk, caught off guard by his abrupt acquiescence. She fastened her gaze on Casey's lean, finely shaped fingers, and then on the front of his green-striped shirt, and finally on his chin. She tried to meet his eyes but found that she couldn't.

"Regan," he said with exaggerated patience, "I'm waiting."

She nodded and swallowed, still watching the lower half of his face. "There are a couple of things I want to talk to you about. First of all I'd like to clear the air between us."

"Clear the air?" he repeated. "As in 'apologize'? Oh, Lord," he groaned, "I hope this isn't where you tell me how sorry you are for calling me lazy!"

Her head shot up and she pushed a wing of hair off

her forehead, staring at him with indignant green eyes.
"Did Peggy tell you—"

"Peggy told me nothing," he cut in shortly. "It's just
that you're not all that original, Regan. There have
been other spitfires before you who told me off for not
playing Sir Galahad to the hilt, for not leaping out of
my car to rescue their strategically dropped handker-
chiefs or carry their packages."

"There have been?" She was mortified to hear her
own behavior described in such scathing tones. "And
did they apologize to you?"

Casey took a cigarette from the carved teak box on the
desk and lit it. "Only the ones unfortunate enough to
run into me later and discover their faux pas." He took a
long drag on the cigarette, then slowly expelled the
smoke toward the ceiling. "You know, I never thought
that would happen here. Bowie's Landing is so small, I
thought *everyone* knew about the crippled McKeever."
His mouth twisted. "Trust the one person who didn't
know to be a hotheaded kid with a big mouth who likes to
spout off before she knows what she's talking about."

He was right, of course. Regan knew he was right,
but he didn't have to be so—so superior about it!

"It's not my fault you don't look as if there's anything wrong with you! Did it ever occur to you," she
asked through gritted teeth, "that if you didn't hide
your crutches, you wouldn't run into that problem?
Where are they, by the way?" Her eyes swept the
room, then glared back at him. "Are you ashamed of
them? Trying to pretend you don't need them?"

It was an incredibly awful thing to say to him. Regan
wanted to bite out her tongue when she saw his face
pale and a nerve begin to jerk in his cheek. "I gave up
pretending that a long time ago," he said, and his voice
was flat. Horrified, she watched as he leaned over to
pick up his crutches from the floor one at a time and
prop them against the desk. "There. Satisfied? Or

would your sadistic streak like me to wear a sign that says 'cripple,' just to be sure everyone gets the message?"

"Of course not!" She shook her head in distress. "Listen, Casey, for some reason you bring out the worst in me! I say the most horrible things when you're around, and frankly you're not always so pleasant, either."

He drew once more on the cigarette, then crushed it in the ashtray. "Really?" He looked bored.

She stood up and put her hands on the edge of the desk, leaning toward him earnestly. "Yes, really. I think I'd better just go now. It would be easier if David hadn't brought so many of my clothes over here. I can't imagine what he was thinking of. As it is, it may take another trip in my car, after my foot gets better, to haul it all home. If you can't spare the time to drive me now, I'll wait until Charley gets here, I guess. I'd walk down the beach if it weren't for this darned foot...."

Casey watched her without expression, letting her run out of steam before he straightened up and put his elbows on the desk. "Finished?" he asked. "Now I'll tell you why you're not going back to your cabin. A smart girl like you with a straight-A average in school should be able to figure it out for herself." He ticked off the reasons on his fingers. "Number one, somebody broke into your cabin last night—someone who is still running around free today. Number two, your cabin wasn't safe even before last night. You should never have been staying alone in a place with inadequate locks on the doors and windows. Number three, your foot has ten stitches in it and you won't be able to walk properly on it for at least a week, so you couldn't even outrun me. Number four, if you're too foolish to recognize the danger, I'm not, and I won't allow you to go back to that cabin. Do you want to hear numbers five and six?"

"What do you mean, you won't allow me?" Regan raged. "I don't believe I need your permission to return to my own home!"

Casey's voice was deadly quiet. "It's not stretching the point very far to say I'm your employer. I hired you and I can get you fired, so I would suggest you rethink that last statement."

Regan drew herself up straight and tall. "Go right ahead. Fire me! That should show David Dunivan just how much of the so-called McKeever integrity you really inherited! I suppose next you'll tell me that you'll see to it I never get another teaching job as long as I live."

"How did you guess?" he asked calmly. "I have connections in every state, and I wouldn't hesitate to pull a few strings if you leave us high and dry without a special-education teacher this year."

"*Me* leave *you* high and dry!" she gasped with fury. "Aren't you getting things backward? You're the one who's threatening to fire me, remember?"

He shrugged. "The choice is yours. I'm not going to stand by and let a teacher with your potential get herself murdered or raped just because she doesn't happen to feel comfortable around me." A devilish smile flickered across his handsome face. "Strange as it may seem, some people actually enjoy my company. But since you don't, I'm sure we can manage to avoid each other, don't you think?"

From what she knew of Casey Regan suspected he was making no idle threat. She didn't really think she had any choice but to agree to stay at the McKeever house. Not if she wanted to keep her job, which she did. *I'll leave the minute they catch the prowler,* she told herself firmly.

Chapter Six

Casey upheld his part of the pact to avoid Regan. At dinner Sunday evening when Charley told her his brother had gone out for the night, she acknowledged mentally that she felt thoroughly relieved. Her apology to Casey had been a dismal flop. Their relationship, if it could be called that, was moving downhill at a steady pace, and she was certain to come out on bottom.

Peggy and David Dunivan joined Regan and Charley for dinner beside the pool, and afterward Peggy and Charley wandered off toward the lake hand in hand, oblivious of the other two.

David looked at Regan and smiled. "Alone at last."

She lay back against the cushions on the redwood chaise longue, thinking that there was something scandalous about being waited on hand and foot like this, carried about solicitously by Charley or David and not having to worry about cleaning up after herself or preparing her meals. "Isn't this heavenly? I think this must be the loveliest spot in the civilized world."

In the early dusk the silver lake was darkening to black, and myriad stars were popping out overhead. Regan could see clear white lights blink on in windows of houses across the lake. The air was heavy with the scent of magnolia blossoms.

"I agree," David said. "It's the perfect time of day, and this is the perfect spot for a little foolin' around."

He pulled up a chair next to hers. "I'd take you for a walk, but I don't think your doctor would approve."

Regan laughed. "I don't think my *foot* would exactly be thrilled, but Charley wouldn't know the difference at the moment. He's got other things on his mind." She let David pick up her hand and hold it, thinking about the absent couple. "I didn't realize until Charley mentioned it at dinner that Peggy's a physical therapist. How'd she come to study that?"

"She was influenced by the McKeevers," her brother explained. "She always had this thing about wanting to share Charley's work."

"I'll bet Casey bullied her into it," Regan muttered under her breath, but David heard her and grinned.

"He's coming across to you as a tyrant," he guessed, and she nodded vigorously. "He impresses some people that way, but what else would you expect? Casey is chief legal counsel for his father's conglomerate, and that means he's responsible for a lot of money. Not just McKeever money but the investments of the stockholders as well. If you had invested in the company, you'd hardly want someone in that position who was weak. On the other hand, Casey's not heartless. He serves on the board of trustees of half a dozen charitable organizations and as such donates not just money but time to run hospitals and children's homes."

"You're sounding like an advertisement again," Regan grumbled.

"Sorry. As I started to say, Casey didn't try to bully Peggy into becoming a therapist. Unless I'm mistaken, when she made that decision, Casey was too busy going through his own personal crisis to hassle anyone else. From what I gather, college was a sort of hell for Casey."

"Why?" Regan asked, immediately curious, but David squirmed and changed the subject. Peering at her hand in the rapidly descending darkness, he pretended to read her palm. Soon he had her smiling with his silly predictions about her falling in love with a tall dark stranger wearing a badge and gun.

Lying in bed later in the yellow-and-white room, Regan decided that David's uncomplicated friendliness was like a breath of fresh air after Casey's overbearing criticism.

When Charley left to go back to Houston early the next morning, Regan felt bereft. With David working long hours she didn't get to see much of him that week. Although Casey had secluded himself in the library to work, she learned that he took time out to swim for exercise for at least an hour every day before noon. On Monday she sat on the little balcony just off her bedroom, hugging her legs, chin on her knees, observing his laps with grudging admiration for his tireless perseverance. Peggy came by on Tuesday to swim with him, and Neva joined him in the pool on Wednesday.

There was little for Regan to do. Charley had warned her that she couldn't swim or even wear a shoe on her right foot for at least a week. The wound stopped hurting after a few days, but she still favored her injured foot and used the antiseptic solution which Charley had given her for the cut. Her enforced inactivity bored her nearly to tears. There was probably some excellent reading material in the well-stocked library, but with Casey working there behind a forbiddingly closed door, she didn't have the nerve to ask if she could come in to select a book. David brought over her VW and parked it in the four-car garage, but Casey somehow had managed to pocket the key to it. Besides, she admitted, she couldn't drive with her foot injured the way it was.

"Mercy, child, I believe you're losing weight!" Katy exclaimed on Wednesday when Regan limped into the delightfully old-fashioned-looking kitchen with its dark ceiling beams and its rack of copper pots hanging over the chopping-block island. "After all my efforts to fatten you up, I seem to be failing. What have you been doing with my cooking—throwing it out on the lawn to feed the birds?"

Regan looked down at her long limbs in the snug tan jeans and sleeveless black sweater she wore. "I should have told you, I just don't gain weight, no matter what I eat."

As she continued peeling potatoes for dinner, Katy kept an eye on Regan. "I think you might if you weren't so lonesome. Your mother and daddy haven't been gone very long, have they?"

"A couple of years now."

"And you're still missing 'em. Well, that's only natural."

Regan scraped at an imaginary spot on the counter with her thumbnail. She swallowed. "I guess I do miss them a little."

Katy clicked her tongue. "And here you are with no one but an old gray-haired woman to talk to. Seems as if Mr. Casey could at least eat lunch with you, if he insists on working all day and half the night."

"It's all right," Regan hastened to assure her. "Honestly, Katy, I enjoy eating with you. I know how Casey..." She paused and rephrased her words mentally. "I know how Casey wants to complete this business he's working on."

The potatoes were plopped alongside carrots and onions simmering with the juicy pot roast on the stove top. Katy clamped the heavy lid back on the cast-iron pot and wiped her hands on her apron. "Well, he'll be finishing up with that soon, and then he can start spending some time with you," she declared with satisfaction.

"But I'm doing fine, really!" Regan cried, horrified by the idea that Katy would try to persuade Casey to entertain his houseguest.

It was useless to argue with Katy. The housekeeper

had blinded herself to the possibility that Regan and Casey didn't like each other. Casey was Katy's adored employer who could do no wrong, and she made no secret of the growing fondness she felt for Regan.

Regan hoped frantically that the prowler would be captured soon so she could go back home before Katy started trying to play cupid to an unwilling Casey.

Halfway down the curving staircase on her way to join Katy for dinner as usual in the kitchen that evening, she realized Casey was in the middle of a conversation on the white telephone in the entry hall. He stood with his back to her, and she had no trouble hearing his words.

"In another day or so, I'll have the papers ready for Dad's signature. I'll see you when I come to Houston to close the deal. Holly, my girl, I've missed having you around." He laughed. "I know. I don't appreciate you half enough when I'm there."

Regan halted in consternation. Could he be talking to a girl friend? Who in the world was Holly? In a moment curiosity overcame her good intentions, and she proceeded downstairs at a snail's pace, continuing to eavesdrop.

"I'll probably drive down Friday," he was saying. "Uh-uh. Just for the weekend." A pause. "Well, I've gotten myself into a rather awkward baby-sitting job and I can only be gone while Charley's here to take my place.... Yes, me, really. It's hard to explain over long-distance."

Baby-sitting job indeed! Regan's cheeks burned. They were still flaming when she reached the bottom step just as Casey concluded his conversation and hung up the receiver. Her green eyes were shooting sparks at the back of his head when he turned abruptly and faced her. "Well, well, Miss Allison, so you're still around. I was beginning to wonder. Still angry, too, I see." He grinned wickedly.

"Angry? Me?" She started to sweep past him with as much dignity as her funny hopping limp would allow her. Casey, however, raised his right crutch, pressed the tip of it against the banister and effectively blocked her path toward the kitchen.

At five feet ten Casey was only a few inches taller than Regan, yet he had the self-assurance of a giant. His handicap might not have existed at that moment, she thought with a bewildering mixture of resentment and admiration.

"You *are* angry!" he observed. "What have I done now?" He looked nonchalant and unconcerned, his thick hair smooth, his ivory-colored linen slacks and sandy-beige oxford-cloth shirt flawless, his brown loafers polished to a high gloss.

Reacting once again to his goading she glared into his gray eyes. "You do *not* have to stay in Bowie's Landing and baby-sit me!" she said vehemently. "I didn't want to stay here with you in the first place, in case you've forgotten, and as far as I'm concerned you can go to Houston and never come back!"

Unperturbed he asked, "Do you have a habit of eavesdropping? Perhaps I should make my telephone calls in my bedroom from now on."

"Perhaps you should!" She shook her long hair back and gestured around the foyer. "Since I am forced to stay with you, it's hardly fair of you to claim this as your private domain. I couldn't help overhearing. And I don't appreciate your ridiculing me to your friends and blaming me for your not being able to stay in Houston."

At least he had the grace to look mildly ashamed of himself. "I didn't mean to ridicule you, but I couldn't tell her I was staying here with a beautiful young woman, could I? Do you think she would understand?"

Regan didn't really think Casey cared what people

thought about him. "There you go again!" she
stormed. "You keep saying you're staying with me!
Who are you kidding? This is the first time I've seen
you since our little talk on Sunday. If you're under the
impression you're doing me a big favor, y-you can
think again!" Her voice quivered annoyingly and sudden tears blurred her vision. She bit her lip, angry with
herself for the childish display of self-pity. "I think
you're rude and—and awful! Just leave me alone!"

He offered no resistance when she pushed his crutch
out of the way and escaped past him. A minute later
she heard the firm closing of the front door, and after
that, the sound of the Mercedes leaving. Regan told
herself wearily that she hadn't done anything to improve the situation.

It cheered her considerably when David Dunivan
came in just as they were finishing up Katy's pot roast.
"I hope you came to tell me you've caught the man
who broke into my cabin!" Regan exclaimed with feeling.

"Not yet," David answered. "I just got an hour off
and thought you might enjoy a ride around the lake.
You probably haven't been out much this week—"

"Oh, David, I'd love it!" She threw her arms around
his neck and kissed him, a move which delighted him,
as it amused Katy.

"Better watch yourselves, children," she teased.
"You could get carried away being that grateful, Miss
Regan, and find yourself in hot water."

Regan laughed and hugged Katy too. "Don't you
worry about me."

The sun was low in the sky when they left the
McKeever house in David's small car. The air blew
through the open windows, cooling her face as they
sped along Old Orchard Road, curving up and down
among the hills. She gazed out, admiring the cotton-
wood trees and willows that grew almost down into the

lake on the summer estates with their graceful homes, and the live oak and pecan trees that grew farther back from the water.

"Looks like Casey's got a date tonight," David commented, nodding at the familiar silver Mercedes parked on the Jonsson drive as they passed. "By the way, are you two getting along any better?"

"Just peachy," Regan said facetiously. "As long as I don't see him, we get along fine."

Well, well, she was thinking in surprise. *So the sterling Casey McKeever's got a hot thing going with Holly Whatever-her-name-is in Houston and Geneva Jonsson in Bowie's Landing at the same time.* Not bad for someone she had been pitying for his unfortunate handicap. She thought with a tiny smile how nice it was to be aware of Casey's penchant for playing around. It was just as well too, that she didn't have to waste her time feeling sorry for him anymore. She suspected from her own experience that Casey, with his good looks and his crutches, had a way of tugging at the heartstrings of the women who knew him. Feeling sulky, but not knowing why, she told herself that he was taking unfair advantage, whether he meant to or not.

David parked the car on a scenic overlook near the top of a ridge and turned to her with a devilish grin. "Now, beautiful lady," he murmured, his voice heavy with a fake German accent that still sounded comically tinged with the Deep South. "Come to me and I will teach you all about love."

His blue eyes dancing with humor he took both her hands and slid her across the seat toward him. Regan looked at David and saw instead a pair of opaque gray eyes in a lean handsome face with a firm mouth that didn't smile nearly often enough for...for what? For his own good, or for hers?

Alarmed by the unwanted image of Casey, and the unbidden thoughts that had stolen into her mind, she closed her eyes and let David pull her into his arms. When he kissed her thoroughly and soundly, she kissed him back, and if she suspected herself of using David, he didn't need to find out. That would be her own secret shame.

The next morning she was in the kitchen and up to her elbows in flour, rolling out pie crusts for Katy, when Casey walked in. Though he smiled when he saw Regan's activity, she detected no malice in his amusement. "Where's Katy?" he asked.

"Doing the laundry in the utility room." Regan, busy with the dough, could spare him only a nod in the right direction. Determined to be decent to him if it killed her, she added helpfully, "You can go back if you like."

Instead he moved over to the counter where she worked. "Actually I was looking for you."

Regan came very near to gasping, but Casey ignored her poorly concealed surprise. After watching her work for a moment with interest he propped his right crutch against the cabinet. He reached out to brush her cheek with a warm finger and his touch sent a shock through her. This time, however, she managed to show no reaction. He held up his finger for her inspection, and there was a smudge of flour on it.

"You have a little white dab on your nose too," he informed her, grinning. "You look very domestic. It becomes you."

"It—it does?" Regan stammered, thrown off guard. *Just another of the many moods of Casey McKeever,* she thought.

He nodded. "Can you really cook, or is that apron just for show?"

Regan touched the frilled smock that, having been made to accommodate Katy's bulk, swallowed her own slender figure. "I'm only helping Katy," she admitted with characteristic honesty. "At home I live on peanut butter and hot dogs."

"I see." His look had turned solemn. "Too bad. If you'd like to learn, I'm sure Katy would be happy to teach you."

As a matter of fact Katy had given Regan her first official cooking lesson earlier that morning. Regan didn't tell Casey that, however, because she guessed that he was merely making conversation and would get to the real point of his visit soon enough.

Regan thought she had better be wary of Casey in this particular mood. His charm could be devastating when he turned it on. In fact, she found him more dangerous when he was being nice than when he was arrogant.

"By the way," he said casually, as if to prove what she had been thinking, "I have a couple of tickets to a concert in Springer tonight." He mentioned a nationally popular writer-performer of progressive country music whose name was well known to Regan. "If you think your foot is up to it, perhaps you'd like to go?"

Regan's first impulse was to accept his invitation eagerly. She owned quite a few of the artist's albums and she knew that the concert had been sold out for weeks. Momentarily, though, she wondered about Casey's motive for asking her. If he had purchased the tickets weeks ago, as he must have, whom had he planned to take? And why was he now, at the last minute, offering to take Regan? Had someone rejected him, or what?

Pounding the dough with flattened palm, she eyed him with suspicion. "I suppose Katy made you invite me," she murmured in a matter-of-fact way.

"Katy?" He looked genuinely puzzled. "Why in the world would you think that?"

"Didn't she?" Regan demanded.

"Darling Regan," he said patiently, "Katy doesn't tell me what to do. She may want to, but she's not my nursemaid anymore. What made you think she might have?''

"Because she thinks I'm about five years old and terribly lonely. She feels sorry for me." Regan rolled the dough vigorously. "I don't want that from her—or you, either!"

Casey threw back his head and laughed, as Regan stared uncertainly at him. "That's beautiful!" he finally managed. "You realize, of course, that you stole my line! I'm the one who's supposed to tell you I don't want your pity."

Regan flushed. "It's not necessary to tell me that. I don't pity you." Thinking of Neva and Holly she realized it was true. Casey didn't need her pity or anyone else's. He could take very good care of himself.

"I'm glad to hear it." His gray eyes contemplated her with sudden thoughtfulness. After a moment, still looking pensive, he slipped his sun-bronzed forearm into the cuff of his crutch and turned to leave.

"Casey?" Regan spoke up shyly. He swung around to face her again. "What time should I be ready tonight?"

His eyes narrowed a fraction, appraising her anew. "We'll leave at seven," he said, so curtly that she thought he regretted having asked her.

Chapter Seven

Casey looked across the front seat of the Mercedes at Regan. "I should have warned you to wear something long-sleeved. The coliseum is usually ten degrees too cool for comfort."

That, she thought, explained the cream-colored suede jacket he wore with his pale yellow shirt and beige slacks. He also wore expensive-looking square-toed suede boots, but then of course everything he owned had an exclusive, Neiman-Marcus look to it. Katy had mentioned once that the McKeevers did all their shopping at Neiman's.

Regan herself had spent the afternoon worrying over what to wear. Her fingers itched to grab the pearl-white silk evening dress from the closet in an attempt to impress Casey with her elegance, but she remembered in time that her right foot would be bare and that she could not safely hop around on a single high-heeled shoe. Besides, she reminded herself, they were going to a country-music concert, not the opera.

She sighed. Nice as it looked, her white-and-green linen dress would afford her little protection in an air-conditioned coliseum. Her tanned, smooth legs would have been more comfortable in a pair of warm jeans.

The drive to Springer took fifteen minutes. When they arrived at the coliseum, easily the largest building in the county, Regan saw that the parking lot was jammed even though better than half an hour remained until show time. Thinking that they might have a long walk from the car, she glanced at Casey worriedly, but he didn't seem concerned. The fat, balding guard at the gate spoke respectfully to him. "Good evening, Mr. McKeever. Your usual space is waiting for you. I hope you enjoy the concert, sir."

"You have your own parking place?" Regan asked, impressed.

He shrugged. "It comes with the name." He said nothing else by way of explanation before he pulled the gleaming silver car into a space at the very foot of one of the entrance ramps to the building, tucked in at the base of the looming glass-and-steel structure. A small bronze sign declared the parking space RESERVED FOR MCKEEVERS ONLY, with the warning that OTHER VEHICLES WILL BE TOWED AWAY AT OWNER'S EXPENSE.

More than slightly awed Regan limped in silence beside Casey up the long concrete ramp. Quite a few concert-goers passed the two of them, many of whom spoke to Casey, calling him by name. When they reached the top, he smiled at Regan easily, as if climbing the incline had been no effort at all for him.

In the throng in the lobby Casey could hardly take a step without being slapped on the back and welcomed by everyone from the mayor of Springer on down to the less affluent year-round residents, who obviously thought a great deal of the handsome lawyer. "Sorry," he growled in Regan's ear when their progress into the auditorium was halted for the umpteenth time for a handshake.

"Have you thought of running for political office?" she whispered back, just beginning to recognize his enormous popularity.

"Certainly!" he retorted, grinning. "I'm on the school board, remember?"

They had excellent aisle seats near the front and

center. Regan sat for a moment, scarcely daring to believe the view she would have of the famous singer, before she turned her attention to the concert programs she had been given on entering. Handing one to Casey she looked at her own, and the lines directly beneath the performer's name seemed to leap out at her: "In concert at the Sam Houston McKeever Coliseum, Springer, Texas."

The Sam Houston McKeever Coliseum? Regan looked around at the packed auditorium with its red plush seats, its balconies and huge stage and red-carpeted aisles. She turned to Casey, feeling bewildered, thinking that this was much bigger than just having a reserved parking space and everyone knowing your name.

Seeing her confusion Casey leaned toward her until she could smell his masculine fragrance. "What's the matter?" he asked.

For a moment his unexpected nearness shocked her into silence as she experienced the warmth of his hard-muscled shoulder against hers, the clean sexy smell of him. She swallowed, not even attempting to answer his question, almost mesmerized by the slow pulse she could see beating along his brown throat.

"Regan?"

She raised her eyes to meet his and saw quizzical amusement in the arching of his eyebrow. Blinking, she struggled to recall just what it was that had caught her attention a moment earlier.

"Oh, er, I was just wondering...who in the world is Sam Houston McKeever?"

He pretended shock. "You mean to say you don't know Houston McKeever!" he teased her. "He was my grandfather—a proud, irascible old gentleman." When she still looked puzzled, he asked, "Are you asking why the coliseum is named for him? He was active in county politics most of his life. He grew up in

Bowie's Landing—no, I mean *really* grew up here, not just summers.''

To her relief he leaned back in his seat then and she found that she could breathe almost normally again, although she knew a flicker of alarmed amazement at his effect on her.

"Granddad was a certified native," Casey continued, evidently unaware of her physical reaction to him. "He held just about every office you can think of in county government and was a long-time member of the Texas Senate. About the time his cronies were being put out to pasture, he went on to serve five terms as a United States Senator. Granddad would roll over in his grave to hear you say you've never heard of him." There was a gleam in his eyes that made Regan think he was somehow pleased at her ignorance. "He donated the land the coliseum is situated on and helped procure the funds to build it, which I'm sure had a little something to do with its being named for him."

The lights dimmed and the program began just then. Regan's thoughts were torn between her still-chaotic heartbeat and the questions she wanted to ask Casey about his grandfather, but he was watching the stage. After a while, forcing herself to concentrate on the entertainer, she forgot everything except the gentle-flowing music that merged soft rock and country and folk sounds, guitar and bass and piano, and the singer's husky baritone. It wasn't until the concert ended an hour and a half later and the lights went up that she realized Casey had slipped his coat around her sometime during the show. She hugged it to her for warmth, and a funny little shiver of emotion went through her as her arm brushed Casey's. She blamed the shiver on the fact that her mind still swam in the bittersweet music, but did that explain the sudden pounding of her heart? *Calm down,* she cautioned herself in desperation.

As if by unspoken agreement they waited until the crowd had thinned out before Casey bent over to pick up his crutches and they both stood up. Moving up the center aisle at Regan's limping pace, sharing a comfortable silence, she felt a peculiar closeness to Casey and, at the same time, a new shyness of him. Was he responsible for all those strange feelings she'd just had? The sudden suspicion nagged her that she had a lot to learn about Casey McKeever.

"Are you hungry?" he asked when they reached his car. "I am. I'm starved in fact. How would you feel about seafood?" She nodded, wanting to prolong whatever it was that had created this rare tranquility between them.

They drove down the river to Christy's. The restaurant was crowded with after-concert patrons, but the waiter, hailing Casey as a valued acquaintance, miraculously found them a table without delay. Casey ordered fried catfish and gumbo for both of them. The night was cooler than usual for June and breezy, and they sat companionably by windows overlooking the fishing craft tied up to the docks just outside. Lit by floodlights, the boats rocked jerkily on the wind-whipped river.

"Were you close to your grandfather?" Regan asked Casey as they waited for their food.

From his expression when he turned his head to look at her, she thought he hadn't been expecting the question. "Very close," he said and was silent for a moment before adding, "He was a paradox to me. In a lot of respects, he was a typical doting grandfather, but he was frequently a tyrant...a colorful sort of character who set standards that were next to impossible to live up to. He was reminiscent of the white-suited Southern colonel, straight out of an antebellum novel. For a long time he was my hero, even to the exclusion of my own father."

"Where did your grandfather live?"

"In my house." He leaned back in his chair while the waiter placed his bowl of gumbo before him. "Naturally, it was Granddad's place then. He built it in the thirties."

Regan stirred her thick gumbo, watching the steam rise. "Doesn't it really belong to your father?"

Casey shook his head. "Dad lived there off and on as a boy, when the legislature wasn't in session in Austin. But he's a Houstonian by choice. Besides, Granddad willed the house to me, although naturally Dad would be welcome if he ever slowed down long enough to settle in Bowie's Landing."

"Not much chance of that, though?"

He smiled. "Obviously you haven't met my father or you wouldn't even ask."

When they had finished eating, she sat with her chin on her fist, watching him with interested green eyes. "When did he die?"

He glanced over at her and lifted one of those finely etched eyebrows. "I presume you mean Houston McKeever? He died ten years ago." The waiter brought their coffee, and Casey sipped it, his face suddenly tight and introspective. Regan wondered if she had been kind to remind him of the painful loss, but after a few minutes he seemed to relax. "His death came very suddenly, following a heart attack, just a month after the coliseum had been dedicated. Granddad was a great one for pomp, and he really loved the dedication celebration. He made us—Dad and Charley and me—walk in with him and stand beside him the whole time he was being honored. Damn, it seemed like a long ceremony!" Casey looked out the window at the night-blackened river, talking mostly to himself. "You know"—he sounded a little surprised—"I believe he was actually prouder of the fact that the coliseum had no steps than he was that it was named for him. A journalist once called him an activist for the disabled, but Granddad put it in simpler terms: 'I intend to see that my grandson can go any damn place he wants to go!' There were no laws to help him when he set about getting rid of the barriers that kept me out of some of the county's more prominent buildings. What he accomplished, he did through his own influence in the community. And then he informed me in no uncertain terms that I had better get out and start using those buildings. He wouldn't let me sit at home feeling sorry for myself.''

Regan felt a warm glow of appreciation for the old man's wisdom. ''What buildings were affected?''

''Hmmm? Oh, the county courthouse and jail. The post offices in Springer and Bowie's Landing. And the church in Bowie's Landing. As a matter of fact that's the first building that he ever saw to it was barrier-free. When I was sixteen, he decided that if I was ever to attend church again—which was very important to him, by the way—he'd have to make sure Bowie's Landing got a new sanctuary. At that time, you see, he still harbored the hope that I'd become a minister.'' Casey grinned again, boyishly.

Regan wanted to keep him talking. ''So he built you a church?''

He nodded. ''As chairman of the board he got the rest of the board's approval—by hook or by crook I imagine—and they had the old church torn down. It had been built around 1900 and was solid as the Rock of Gibraltar, but there were something like thirty steps leading up to the front door. They put up a huge tent and folding chairs down by the lake and held old-fashioned campground meetings all summer, until the new church was completed. You know what it looks like?''

Regan knew it well. It was a beautiful arched building with an aged look to it, made of native stone, with exquisite stained-glass windows along the sides and over the altar. Most remarkable, its front door was level with the ground. It had never occurred to Regan just how unusual that feature was in such an old-looking church.

"I imagine there are a lot of elderly people in Bowie's Landing who can attend church now, but who never would have made it up those thirty steps," Regan mused.

"So Clara Reeves's father tells me every time he sees me. He's ninety-four years old and teaches Sunday School. He considers me responsible for the fine state of his soul," Casey laughed.

"But you didn't become a minister," she prodded him.

"No, but I go to church whenever possible. Houston McKeever would haunt me for sure if I stopped going."

"I wish I could have known him." She thought Houston McKeever must have been a fascinating, vital man, a lot like his younger grandson.

"Everyone should experience at least one grandparent like mine. What were yours like, Regan?"

"I don't know. My grandparents had died by the time I was big enough to know them," she said.

"I see." He paused. "Tell me about your parents, then."

She did, with difficulty at first, and then warming to the task, describing her tall dark father and slender mother and their passion for academic life that led them to continually chase rainbows in the form of one research or teaching job after another. She described the dedication to learning and the succession of rented houses in one college town after another. Somehow the inevitable loneliness and lack of roots found their way into her voice without her knowing it, until she realized she had said too much and shut off the flow of words abruptly. "I'm sorry," she mumbled in contrite embarrassment.

"What for?" He gave her a level, unreadable look.

"For boring you. You should have told me to cool it."

Smiling wryly, he gave his head a single shake, but he didn't contradict her.

As they drove back home Regan curled up in her corner of the comfortable front seat, Casey's jacket blanketing her now from the night chill. To keep the soothing motion from putting her to sleep Regan studied his profile through half-closed eyes. His mouth looked hard, but it could have been a trick of the dim light from the dashboard. Casey could be very hard and unyielding at times, she knew from painful experience. Had he overcompensated for his handicap by purging himself of gentleness, kindness, the tender emotions? Was he afraid of being thought weak? Or was there a soft side to Casey too?

It was nearly midnight when they pulled into the driveway. Casey stopped the Mercedes in the circle before the big white house and they went inside together. Standing in the light of the lamp Katy had left burning in the foyer, Regan fingered the soft suede jacket she had folded over her arm. "Would you like me to hang this in your closet?"

He motioned to the antique ladder-back chair beside the telephone. "You can put it there," he said and watched as Regan did so.

She turned back to him, reluctant to say good night and end the evening. As she hesitated, his eyes, charcoal-colored in the soft lamplight, met hers and held them so she couldn't look away. Indeed, she suddenly wanted to go on looking into his dark eyes forever. She had the feeling of being caught in a strange dream and hoping she wouldn't wake up.

As if in slow motion, he came a step nearer. Releasing one crutch, he reached out and touched her cheek with his hand, and the hand felt warm and strong. With a gently caressing motion his thumb stroked her lower lip, tracing back and forth over the soft fullness, sending agreeable little tremors of electricity racing through her.

Regan almost stopped breathing, her pleasure was so great. Her widening eyes clung to his, begging him to ... *what?* Hold her? Kiss her? She didn't know; she couldn't think.

In that curiously bewitched condition she surprised herself by reaching for Casey with both arms. She hadn't imagined she would ever do a thing like that to a man who inspired such anger in her at times, but when he pulled her to him, her arms stole around his waist and she held on to him for dear life. Pressing her face against his neck she let herself be overwhelmed with a flood tide of sensations that were too confusing yet too incredibly enjoyable to resist.

She felt good all over. Her head was light, her stomach alive with feather-winged butterflies that danced for joy. Her heart whispered shyly, *Casey? Can it really be you that I'm wrapping myself around?*

As they held tightly to each other Regan's focus gradually shifted from her own body to Casey's. She sighed, settling even more snugly against him, delighting in the hard warmth of his embrace and the masculine reminder of his aftershave lotion. It was as if she had found a home in his arms, a secure shelter from a world that hadn't been easy of late. *Nice,* she thought dreamily. *This is so nice, I could stay here forever.*

She didn't know how long they stood that way, but it was Casey who pulled away first. He rubbed his hard cheek against hers and brushed his lips across the wing of dark hair at her temple, straightening up to smile as he withdrew his arms from around her. "Good night, Regan," he murmured, his voice low.

She sighed to herself again. "'Night, Casey," she said meekly.

For a brief moment she tried to read the look in his eyes, but couldn't, so she turned to limp upstairs. When she reached the top, Casey still stood in the middle of the entry hall below, watching her with a trace of a smile.

Chapter Eight

Regan came downstairs early the next morning, hoping she could join Casey for breakfast. She first peeked in the door to the sunny dining room, but found it empty. Perhaps he was sleeping late. She hurried on to the kitchen and surprised Katy, who was reading the newspaper over a cup of coffee.

"Aren't you an early bird today! And you're not hopping, either!" the housekeeper greeted Regan, laying aside the paper with pleasure.

"What?" Regan said distractedly. "Oh, no—my foot's much better this morning." She had discovered quite by accident that her foot could bear her weight without pain, as long as she walked cautiously. "Is Casey already at work in the library, or did he sleep in?"

"Mr. Casey sleep in!" Katy sounded as if that were a truly novel idea. "Mercy, I can't remember the last time he slept this late! No, he's gone to Houston. He left nearly an hour ago."

"To Houston!"

Katy nodded. "I thought you knew he was going."

Regan dropped down into a chair across the table from the older woman. "I did know, but—" She bit her lip to keep from finishing the sentence: "But I thought he'd at least tell me goodbye." Instead, she mumbled, "I didn't realize he would leave quite so early. I wanted to talk to him."

"Oh, dear, I *am* sorry, Miss Regan. I hope it can wait until he gets back Sunday. Otherwise you can call him at his father's."

"No, of course not." Her voice was flat with disappointment. "It's not important."

Admit it, she urged herself as she moped away the endless afternoon on the beach, soaking up sun in shorts and halter. *Your feelings are hurt. You thought last night was special, because Casey opened up to you about his grandfather.* Something in his voice had given her the idea he was telling her things about the old man that he'd never told anyone else.

And the good-night embrace! That had been special too. Regan's face burned with shame when she recalled the eagerness of her response to Casey. If he hadn't stopped first, she might have clung to him indefinitely. It had felt good. Too darned good! *Which just proves how practiced Casey is at that game,* she concluded bitterly. It had obviously meant nothing to him.

Regan strolled aimlessly back up to the house, shoulders slumped, just as Charley slid his low-slung red Porsche to a stop before Casey's empty garage stall. "Hello, sweet young thing," he called to her, climbing out of the car and coming around to give her a brotherly squeeze. "You're walking better than I expected. Come on inside so I can take a look at that foot." He herded her through the archway, down the long terrace and in the kitchen door, stopping to tell Katy his week had been routinely hectic, and then guiding Regan into the sunny solarium. Easing her down onto a white wicker chair to examine her foot, he probed with deft fingers as he asked, "Does this hurt? This?"

Regan shook her head.

"It's really coming along beautifully." Charley looked satisfied. "Deep as the cut was, I'll leave the stitches in until next weekend, just to be safe. Meanwhile, you can swim, wear a shoe, do whatever you want to do that doesn't hurt. I wouldn't advise you to climb mountains or dance on it yet, but everything else is okay.''

"Who would I dance with, anyway?" Regan retorted a little petulantly, and Charley sat back on his heels to study her downcast eyes.

"Do I detect a little self-pity, Miss Allison?"

Her lower lip stuck out. It had been a miserable day. "What if I do feel sorry for myself?"

"Then I'd say you were only normal," he responded without hesitation. "After the boring week you've just had, I'd say you'd have to be pretty unusual not to be feeling some self-pity right about now. I don't suppose my brother helped much?"

"Casey? What do you mean?"

"Did he do anything to occupy your time?"

Regan looked down at her hands, folded in her lap, and answered, careful to show neither the pleasure she had experienced on the date nor the rejection she was feeling the day after. "He took me to a concert last night."

Charley's face broke into a grin. "Well, good for him!" He seemed relieved. "Anything else?"

"Well, he's been awfully busy all week, working on the Hughes contract, you know. I didn't expect him to sit around holding my hand."

"Mmm...." Charley looked thoughtful and just a shade disappointed. "I know how wrapped up Casey gets in his work. He'd forget to eat if Katy didn't remind him once in a while."

Dinner that evening was a candlelit affair in the intimate dining room that resembled a greenhouse with its polished brick floor and banks of areca palms, lush ferns, and climbing vines on the windows. Peggy was tied up with some recreational function at the nursing home in Springer, Charley said with what sounded like resignation in his voice. Regan knew he was somewhat down in the dumps himself over Peggy's absence, and figured that it must have been his suggestion to Katy that prompted the housekeeper to break out the best china and silver and a bottle of vintage wine from Casey's well-stocked cellar. Drastic measures to cheer them both up, she suspected. Trying to get into the spirit of things, she dressed up for the first time in a week, in a long emerald green caftan and thin-strapped sandals. Her hair fell soft and dark about her shoulders, and Charley looked at her with unconcealed admiration as she came down the stairs to meet him just before eight.

"My God, Casey's a fool," he muttered to himself.

Startled, Regan halted and stared at Charley. "I beg your pardon?"

Shaking his blond head he took her arm and walked with her into the dining room. "My younger brother amazes me. He ought to have his head examined," he said ironically. "You're a foxy lady. Casey knows that, though. He's certainly not blind. How he can stay in the same house with you and not fall under your spell, I don't know."

"Maybe I'm not his type."

She said it in an off-hand way, as if it didn't matter that Casey didn't pay much attention to her. Charley eyed her quizzically as he seated her and sat down across from her at the round natural-pine finished table. "I don't think it's a question of types at all. Casey has had his mind made up about women since he was eighteen years old."

Regan perked up with interest at that odd statement, but Charley evidently regretted his words immediately. He promptly changed the subject and talked about trivia throughout dinner.

"Why did you become an orthopedic surgeon?" she asked him later, in the library. She sat on the couch with her long legs and bare feet tucked beneath her, sipping a glass of the wine they hadn't finished off at dinner. Charley relaxed in a deep leather chair nearby, his long legs stretched out, his head back.

"Why did you become a teacher?" he countered lazily. "Lifelong dream? That's how it was with me."

"You were a born doctor, you mean?" It sounded almost too corny to be true.

Charley's eyes were shut. "Something like that. I was doing heart transplants on frogs years before anyone heard of Christiaan Barnard. It was just a matter of shifting my interest after Casey had polio. I started transplanting muscles. I thought I'd find a cure for him."

"Really?" The idea intrigued her. Brother healing brother.

He opened his eyes and grinned at her. "Well... not exactly. But I did become interested in orthopedics while he was in the hospital. His doctor encouraged my interest—he made arrangements for me to observe during one of Casey's operations. Every summer for several years Peggy and I worked out a physical therapy program for Casey and put him through a daily routine of exercises in the pool. We probably saved Dad a fortune in therapy fees, and Peggy went on to become a super physical therapist."

"Did Casey appreciate what you did?"

"The exercises? He hated them! We spent hours in the water, stretching and bending his legs. At the time he was nearly always recuperating from one muscle graft or another, and the therapy must have hurt like hell. But he never gave in to the pain. And since he never eased up on himself, we couldn't very well go easy, could we?"

Regan took a tiny sip from her goblet and looked over at Casey's desk. She was glad he wasn't there, listening to them talk about him. It was somehow frightening to hear Charley speak so calmly of Casey's ordeal. "Why weren't the operations successful?" she asked.

"Who said they weren't successful?" Charley's voice was sharp, and he sat up abruptly. Elbows on his knees, hands clasped together, he leaned forward, his handsome face intent. "Damn it, people expect miracles from doctors! We're only human, after all. I'm not a miracle worker, and neither was Casey's surgeon. Casey underwent some relatively minor procedures—at least, they were much less complicated than the complete knee and hip replacements I perform on severe arthritics today, for instance. They accomplished what they were intended to do. Casey has more use of his legs than he would have had without the muscle transplants. Matter of fact, he walks better now than he did ten years ago."

Regan had had no idea Charley could get so worked up about anything. She got up to pour herself some more wine and gulped down a long swallow of the burgundy liquid. She offered Charley some but he declined. "In what way does he walk better now?" she asked.

As she watched, an alert wariness stole over Charley's features, as if he felt he had said too much already, and she realized he didn't want to discuss this. He was silent a moment, and when he spoke he chose his words with care. "You may not be aware that Casey wore braces on his legs for a long time. Through persistence and hard work, he trained himself to use the muscles that remain functional, so the braces are no longer necessary. He can't walk without crutches, but he can stand unsupported for a short time."

Having worked as a student teacher with children who needed braces to walk, Regan could well imagine the magnitude of Casey's accomplishment. "That's remarkable," she breathed in admiration.

"Yes, it is," Charley agreed. "Walking requires a great deal of concentration and effort from Casey."

"He makes it look so easy!"

"He'd like people to believe it is easy."

Regan sipped her wine again, her spirited green eyes for once soft and pensive. Charley was still watching her rather suspiciously, looking a lot like a fair-haired version of Casey, and like his brother he seemed capable of exploring the very depths of her soul. She fidgeted and pushed the hair back from her forehead. Raising the slender-stemmed crystal to her lips, she took another quick drink for courage and blurted out the question that had been haunting her since last week at the country club.

"Isn't there some chance that further therapy or ... or surgery will improve his condition even more?"

When Charley's eyes clouded, she realized he had been dreading that very question. "Not a chance in a million!"

Although his brusque voice didn't encourage Regan, she had to pursue the idea. "But if he's improved as much as you say, Charley, isn't there reason to believe that will power—exercise—*something* can help him?"

"Do you realize how long it's taken him to get where he is today?" Charley demanded roughly. "Nineteen years! Nineteen years of spending more energy than you can imagine, trying to be what other people hoped he could be again: normal, able-bodied, uncrippled. And there's simply no more potential for improvement." Rising from the chair, he paced the room, an angry scowl looking out of place on his usually easygoing countenance. "Too many of the muscles are gone. Dead." His grim words hit her with the force of physical blows, almost taking her breath away. "It's cruel of you to expect Casey to keep striving for a physical perfection he can never reach."

She huddled in misery on the couch and stared

through welling tears at the gold-and-onyx pen set on the desk. "I'm sure you're right." She should have known better, and she was angry at herself, but still, his words hurt.

Charley stopped pacing to study her. The scowl smoothed itself out. "I'm sorry," he said contritely. "You didn't deserve that." Moving swiftly he crossed the thick carpet and sat down next to Regan. "I lose all patience when it comes to this particular subject. Why dwell on the things people can't do? It makes more sense to focus on a person's assets. Instead of feeling sorry for Casey, why not think about the fact that he earned his pilot's license when he was twenty, and that he is a part-time member of the faculty of a law school in Houston? You see, Regan, you're not doing him any favors to fantasize about a complete recovery for him. He doesn't need a miracle. What he needs is to be accepted as he is. Like him or hate him, but don't just see him as a cripple."

She sat in silence, blinking away the tears as she clenched her hands at her sides. She sniffled once, and Charley looked at her, concerned about the torment on her face.

She was wondering with considerable shame if she really could have been thinking of Casey only in terms of his handicap. It was a startling possibility. An hour earlier she would have sworn she had learned long ago to recognize human values unrelated to physical or mental perfection or limitations. But now—

She swallowed unshed tears and tried to defend herself. "I only thought how marvelous it would be for Casey if he could walk without crutches."

Charley picked up her hand and clasped it between both of his. "There are worse things than having to use crutches, Regan," he reminded her gently.

She raised her eyes to meet his, tears glistening on her dark lashes. "I know," she said, and she suddenly realized he was right. There were plenty of things worse than Casey's affliction. In spite of it he was quite a man: intelligent, successful, sophisticated, and dangerously attractive. Look at the way she had fallen for him last night at the concert. He had been so nice, so much the Casey McKeever who was universally liked and respected. "You know what I think, Charley?" she asked, her heart lightening. "I think Casey is remarkable, crutches or no crutches."

Casey's brother smothered a grin. "I think you're right," he agreed. "But it's just as well we confined this discussion to the two of us. Let me warn you, curiosity about his physical condition is one thing he doesn't handle very well. He resents the hell out of questions. I do my best to avoid the subject, to keep from ruffling his feathers."

"I'll keep that in mind."

She smiled at Charley with gratitude, feeling that he had helped her come a little closer to understanding his complex, coolly fascinating brother and to sorting out her own perplexing thoughts about him.

With her head tilted to one side, long hair parted in the middle and falling over her cheek, the slim length of her looked exotic and enticing in the caftan. Charley placed his arm around her shoulder and hugged her, a decidedly fond look in his eyes.

Warmed and encouraged by his hug she asked, "What did you mean earlier? Why did you say Casey had made up his mind about women a long time ago?"

He chewed his lip as he debated whether to finish what he had unwisely started, but the sharp jangle of the telephone on the desk interrupted. Looking relieved he leaped up and grabbed the receiver.

"Dr. McKeever," he murmured into the phone and then grinned. "Hi, there!... Yes, I got in around six.... Tired. How about you?" A sudden glance at Regan. "Yes, she is.... Uh-huh...." He turned slightly and put his back to Regan, who slid her feet to the floor and watched him alertly. "Uh-huh . . . uh-huh. . . . I see. Yes, you may be right. . . . No-o-o-o, I guess not, if that's what he said." There was a longer pause. "Mmm-hmm, that sounds good to me. Let me ask her." Charley turned to Regan and held his hand over the mouthpiece. "David wants to know if you would like to join him tomorrow morning at the marina for the Bowie's Landing Aqua Festival. In the past it's been a tradition for the Dunivans and McKeevers to go out in our boat and make a day of it. I had forgotten all about the festival until David reminded me just now. How about it?"

"You mean David actually gets the day off?" Regan asked in surprise. As of yesterday he was still putting in extra long hours, as were all the deputies, because the prowler was still at large.

"Evidently so," Charley shrugged, looking impatient for her answer.

"It sounds like fun to me," Regan said.

Charley stayed on the phone a while longer, finalizing details about the next day's outing and then responding to David in terse phrases that left Regan confused as to exactly what they were discussing. When he hung up, he hustled her off to bed with a brotherly concern that was partly an urgency to get rid of her, she thought. Probably he was afraid she would begin asking questions about Casey again, questions that he didn't want to answer, so Regan went to bed without a fuss.

Chapter Nine

At four o'clock on Sunday afternoon Regan stood gazing at the rows and rows of books in the library. Plato and Socrates and Homer held places of honor on shelves next to leather-bound periodicals from the American Bar Association. Casey's taste in reading was varied, anyway. There was everything from a collection of Hemingway and a selection of medieval literature to the complete works of Kahlil Gibran. She found a volume of Carl Sandburg's poetry that interested her and had just settled down with it on the brown leather sofa when the housekeeper tapped on the door and looked in on her.

"It's threatening to rain, Miss Regan, so I'm going to run on to Woodman's and buy some bread and milk. We're nearly out. I meant to ask Dr. Charley to pick some up when you all came home from church this morning, but it plain slipped my mind." She tied a dark scarf over her curly gray hair. "I'll only be a few minutes. If Mr. Casey gets in, tell him I'll whip him up something to eat soon as I get back."

Regan listened to the kitchen door slam and one of the McKeever automobiles start up in the garage. She sat for a while with the book on her lap, too tired to begin reading. Spending yesterday in the Texas sun on the lake had exhausted her, burned her golden skin darker and made her feel almost feverish. She had rid-

den in the boat all day, Charley having told her sternly
that her foot wasn't healed well enough for her to take
part in the aquatics. He showed her how to operate the
controls of the powerful speedboat and let her drive
while the other three skied in the boat's wake.

There had been boat races, skiing competition, and
water ballet for spectators massed along the shore near
the marina. For the less energetic participants, there
were prizes for most and largest fish caught. Luncheon
was served for the whole community on the picnic
grounds, and the festivities closed with a late supper at
the country club. Regan could do little more than
struggle to keep awake through the last award presenta-
tion.

She stared trancelike at the closed volume of poetry
on her lap, remembering how persistently Casey's
image had intruded itself on her yesterday, as if he refused to be ignored. Probably it had been the thought-
provoking conversation with Charley on Friday night
that triggered it. When David made a passing comment
that the Aqua Festival had never been one of Casey's
favorite events, she began evaluating it from his view-
point and decided that perhaps all it did for Casey was
remind him that he was different.

All day long, watching the graceful athletes on skis
performing for an appreciative audience, Regan felt a
curious urgency to see Casey, to judge for herself if he
were well-adjusted or if he found it hard to bear his
affliction. It was all very well and good to tell herself
that being dependent on crutches was no big deal, but
how did Casey feel about it?

Thunder shattered her reverie. She started, dropping
the book to the floor and drawing in a sharp breath, just
as the telephone shrilled on the desk. It sounded unnaturally loud in the heavy air and she scrambled to cut
short its summons. "McKeever residence," she said.

The connection was poor, but a confident feminine

voice carried over the static. "Katy? Is that you? You sound a little funny. This is Holly Bridges."

"I'm sorry but Katy isn't in right now," Regan answered politely. "Did you want to speak to her?"

"Oh..." There was a brief pause. "Oh, no. I just assumed that you were Katy. I'm really calling Casey. May I speak to him, please?" There was a clear businesslike tone to the voice, which sounded as if its owner were in her mid-twenties and very, very sure of herself. This must be Casey's Houston friend, Holly!

Rain started to patter against the window, gently blurring the view of the lake through the trees. Regan's hand tightened on the telephone receiver. "Casey isn't here, either, I'm afraid. He hasn't returned yet from Houston. Would you like to leave a message?"

"He isn't there yet? I certainly hope he didn't have car trouble. Well, he should be arriving any time now." The voice sounded as if there could be no doubt about it. "He left here at two o'clock, so he's had more than enough time to make it." Regan silently digested the fact that Casey had been with Holly Bridges before leaving Houston today. "Would you please ask him to call me as soon as he gets there? He knows my number," Holly said.

When Katy returned from the store, Regan joined her in the kitchen with the news of Casey's departure time from Houston. "There's nothing to worry about," Katy assured her. "Mr. Casey's the most capable driver around. Most likely he's just taking his time in this rain. It moved up this way from the coast, the radio said, so he's probably been driving in it most of the way."

But as the minutes ticked by into hours and he still hadn't come home, they both became jittery. Regan thought to herself several times that she wished Charley hadn't left already to go back to Houston. He would have known whether or not to be worried.

Outside, rain hammered down persistently out of a dark sky.

When the sunny yellow kitchen wall phone rang at six thirty, Katy and Regan fairly jumped out of their skins. The housekeeper answered it before the first ring faded. "Oh, yes, Miss Bridges!" There was mingled relief and disappointment in Katy's voice. "Yes, I know you called earlier.... No, ma'am, Mr. Casey hasn't come in so we haven't passed on the message to him yet." She bit her lip. "I'm sure he's all right.... Yes, ma'am. Good-bye."

Katy sat back down at the table heavily and picked up a spoon to stir her coffee. "Heaven knows, he's been late before," she said momentarily, as if talking to herself. She drank the coffee slowly. After a while she put the cup down with a decisive clink. "Before he left Houston, he must have made another stop that Miss Bridges didn't know about. I'll bet he went by his dad's place again and lost track of the time. He often comes back late on a Sunday night, anyway. He doesn't mind driving after dark." Katy's brown eyes dared Regan to challenge her logic, but Regan merely nodded.

At Katy's urging Regan finally went back to reading Sandburg in the library, or attempting to read, and the housekeeper retired to her room to work a crossword puzzle. When the rain stopped at dusk, heavy gray clouds opened to reveal the sun sliding down behind the hilltops. Regan dropped all pretense of reading and went to stand framed in the long window, awed by the fading pink of the evening sky over the lake.

When she turned back around some minutes later, she found Casey standing in the door, watching her. Regan's eyes widened in surprise. "I didn't hear you come in."

He didn't speak.

"Have you seen Katy?"

He shook his head.

"Then I'd better tell her you're here." Regan hurried around Casey's desk and came up against him in the doorway. "She's worried about you." He narrowed his eyes and looked at her without moving. "We've both been worried!" she went on. "We had no idea where you were."

"Now why should you worry about me?" he wondered quietly, leaning forward a little on his crutches to block her path. "Didn't Katy tell you I frequently get back from Houston late?"

Regan's nod was curt. "And Miss Bridges told us you left her place at two o'clock." She consulted her watch. "That was nearly seven hours ago."

"Holly called?" Casey straightened his shoulders, frowning.

"Twice!" Regan was wickedly pleased to see Casey's discomfort. "She's probably worried, too. Did it really take you seven hours to get back—a drive that ordinarily takes two hours?"

"Of course not!" He sounded impatient. "I stopped by the Jonssons' and got caught in the rain. It just now let up enough for me to get in my car without getting soaked."

For some reason her heart plunged. She met his eyes fiercely. "I guess if it had rained all night, you'd have just spent the night there? Never mind calling to let Katy know what had become of you."

She wondered as she snapped at him what was making her so angry. Uncomfortably she suspected it was the knowledge that he had already spent considerable time today first with Holly and then with Neva, and all the while she had been unable to get him out of her mind. She had an idea that another part of her outrage had to do with the deliberate way he had charmed her the night of the concert—charmed her and then gone off to Houston without even telling her good-bye.

"It didn't occur to me that Holly would have called

to alarm you. Does she want me to call her back?'' At Regan's haughty nod Casey moved toward the desk, leaving the door clear for her. She watched as he sat down in his swivel chair behind the desk. He glanced up at her, his hand poised to drop his forearm crutches to the floor. Instead he propped the crutches against the corner of the desk.

Regan flushed at the deliberate dig. Apparently Casey had no intention of letting her forget her past blunders. Mouth trembling, eyes burning, she turned to escape, but his voice caught her in the doorway.

"Regan!"

She halted.

"Come here, please."

She kept her back to him and shook her head jerkily.

"Please."

Her head gestured again: No!

He was silent a moment before he proposed in a quiet voice, "Would you go and tell Katy I'm here, please? I hate for her to think I still haven't made it home."

For Katy. Only for Katy. "All right," she agreed, still not looking at him. "She'll want to know if you've had dinner," Regan pointed out reluctantly.

"Yes, I have." When she started to leave, his voice stopped her again. "Regan, will you come back here after you've seen Katy? I need to talk with you."

"About what?"

"I'd rather not get into that until you come back. And, Regan—it *is* important so don't conveniently forget, all right?"

Regan gave him no answer but swept out the door, down the hall, and through the kitchen to find Katy. The older women was pacing the floor in her small bedroom, no longer able to pretend she wasn't worried. Relief lightened her face and her eyes misted at Regan's message. "I knew he was all right, of course, but I couldn't help being a little afraid..." she admitted.

Stalling for time Regan drank a glass of milk in the kitchen and searched the refrigerator for something to appease her hunger. It occurred to her belatedly that she hadn't eaten, and she felt sure Katy had forgotten, too. She stood for a minute with her hand on the lid of the cookie jar, trying to think. Had she been that preoccupied with Casey? Heaven help her if she had, because his mind was definitely elsewhere. In Houston with Holly Bridges? Or down the road with Geneva Jonsson? It was becoming increasingly hard to say just to whom Casey McKeever was most attached, though one could safely assume he was not attached to Regan Allison. Strange that what she was feeling seemed so very similar to jealousy. Why should Casey's indifference bother her so much?

She finally chose to ignore her rumbling stomach and get the ordeal over with. Casey was just replacing the telephone receiver in its cradle when Regan appeared in the doorway of the library. The look he gave her was sober but not unfriendly. "Have a seat," he said. As if he was aware of his commanding tone, he added, "Please."

She sat in the brown chair opposite the desk, smoothing the wheat-colored skirt over her knees self-consciously. Raising one hand she pushed back a lock of hair from her face. Casey was watching her, she saw, and he almost seemed to be assessing her, calculating. *Thinking of adding me to your collection?* she wondered silently and resentment flashed across her face.

Still eyeing Regan he patted the shirt pockets under his gray blazer absently, then reached over to take a cigarette from the teak box on the desk and light up.

"You shouldn't smoke, you know."

Regan didn't know what on earth made her say that.

Casey was thirty-two years old, a college graduate with a law degree on top of that. Surely he was intelligent enough to know smoking was bad for him. He raised an eyebrow at her, looked down at the smoke curling up from his cigarette and hesitated only a second before crushing it out in the ashtray.

"You're right, of course," he acknowledged.

"You put it out!" Regan declared in surprise.

"As I said, you're right. I don't smoke often. Just when I'm having a hard time sitting still." He shifted his shoulders uncomfortably. "Something has happened that you ought to know about. The police in Austin have arrested the man who broke into your cabin." He stopped to let her consider that a moment, and then continued. "He's a vagrant, a drifter from out of state who has a long record of convictions for petty theft and burglary." His voice was purposely calm. "He's no one you know—that much police are convinced of. He was just hunting an easy target, looking for something he could fence easily."

She swallowed. "He was arrested in Austin?"

Casey nodded. "His prints match those taken from a window at your cabin, and he has confessed to your break-in as well as a number of others between here and Austin. As I said, he had a record and was wanted in Oklahoma, so law-enforcement agencies all over Texas have been on the alert for him."

"When was he arrested? When did you find out?"

Casey reached for a cigarette again but suddenly realized what he was doing and let his hand drop. From his gesture, Regan suspected that he didn't really want to answer her questions. To his credit, he forced himself to. "He was arrested trying to burglarize a home in Austin— sometime early Friday morning, I believe. David Dunivan called me in Houston that night to tell me."

She recalled Charley's telephone call from David Friday evening and the feeling she'd had that there was more to their conversation than what Charley shared with her.

"Do you mind telling me," she said icily, "why I wasn't informed of the arrest on Friday evening? You told David to keep it from me, didn't you?"

He leaned back in the chair and observed her with speculation. "That's right," he admitted finally. "And you may as well know that David, on my instruction, told Charley not to tell you about the arrest, either. I thought it best for you not to get the news until I returned."

"Oh, really?" she muttered. "Why? Because you're my self-appointed guardian?"

"Because I didn't want you to do anything foolish."

"Foolish!" She was incredulous. "Like what?"

"Like move back to your cabin." His voice turned as cool as hers. He crossed his arms over his chest and Regan recognized the look of determination she had seen on his face before. "Would you have moved back?"

"Probably!"

"Then it seems I was correct in not letting the others inform you of the arrest."

Regan stood up and glared at him, her arms rigid at her sides. "You forget, Casey McKeever, that it's my life and my cabin! Oh, I know, I know your arguments very well. You said I had to stay because I couldn't walk properly. Well, I'm walking just fine now—"

"So I see." His eyes flicked to her foot and back to her face.

"I told you I'd stay until the prowler was captured. I didn't agree to stay a minute longer."

He tilted his chair back and eyed her curiously. "Is it really so awful in my house that you can't wait to get away?"

She tossed her head, sending a swirl of dark hair over her shoulder. "That's beside the point—"

"The point is, Regan, that your cabin is no more suitable for you now than it was a week ago." He brought the chair back down with a thud and leaned forward, his elbows on the desk. His gray eyes were direct and his words brutally frank. "I went over with a carpenter and inspected your cabin thoroughly. The place wasn't meant to be a year-round residence. It has single-thickness walls, so there's no way to insulate it against the cold and heat without major construction work. You'd have to install a heating system and possibly air conditioning, as well. The windows and doors would have to be replaced. The present ones are too flimsy and poorly built to provide adequate protection against the weather and human intruders. Frankly, the place isn't worth what these repairs and alterations would cost."

Regan heard the unvarnished truth in what Casey said. Her father had pointed out most of those facts about the cabin in the past, but he had never considered using it as a year-round home. She sank back in the chair with a sigh and studied the desk between them. "I'll find an apartment, then, or a room to rent somewhere," she said hoarsely. Her throat felt as if there were an enormous lump caught in it that would neither go up nor down.

To keep from losing complete control she concentrated on the silver cuff links on Casey's crisp white cuffs, which extended from under the sleeves of his blazer. One of his finely manicured hands picked up a gold pen and wrote something on a note pad. "Regan," he was saying patiently, as if he were speaking to a child, "there isn't a room to rent in Bowie's Landing. This isn't that sort of town. People here don't cater to strangers. All the summer people own their homes, and outsiders aren't especially welcome. You ought to know that!"

She listened with a growing feeling of alarm. She

knew he was right, but what was he trying to tell her? Raising her head she faced him squarely and gave it one last try. "Surely someone will rent to me! They know me. I'll ask Sara Thompson, the librarian, or—or Clara Reeves—"

He shook his head. "I can't believe you'd impose on those kind ladies. They both live with elderly relatives and have all the problems they can say grace over. Certainly they'd be glad to help the new teacher in town, but would you really be so selfish as to ask?"

Biting her lip Regan swallowed the sob that was building within her. Casey must be able to hear her heart thudding heavily in her chest. Why was he hurting her like this? Her green eyes looked wide and miserable in her thin face. She seemed to stare through Casey for a moment before she gave her head a brief shake and focused on his eyes. "What do you suggest that I do?" she asked, her voice husky.

Casey didn't answer immediately. Although his hands twirled the gold pen idly, his mouth looked anything but casual. Gray eyes studied the notes in front of him with a concentration that was almost fierce in its intensity. After a moment's silence he cleared his throat, and when he spoke, his voice was carefully controlled. "I have a proposal to make that would help both of us, I think. You see, every fall since Granddad left it to me, I've closed up this house and returned to Houston, taking Katy with me. With everything put under cover or out of reach, it really hasn't been practical for me to come up for a weekend now and then, as I would have liked. Then, too, Katy's a native and she dislikes being away from Bowie's Landing all winter. She'd be much happier, I believe, if she could stay here and keep the house open for the family to use as needed. But as you may have noticed, Katy's the maternal type. She thinks she has to have someone here to take care of, to justify her salary."

Casey gave Regan a half smile, and she felt a flutter of hope at the quiet assurance in his voice. "What I'd like," he went on, "what I'm asking is that you live here—keep the same room you have now, if it's the one you want—and let Katy keep house and cook for you. Consider it your own home, where you can come and go as you please. If it works out, I'll be able to get away more frequently when the traffic and pollution of Houston get to me. Charley can come up, or Dad and Elizabeth, and we'll know the place is being looked after."

She stared at him when he finished, not quite believing his proposition. "That's incredible!" she gasped. "I couldn't afford to rent even a closet in a place like this!" Glancing around the library with its appearance of quality and wealth, she sighed. "It's absurd even to think of it."

"I didn't say you'd be renting from me." Casey spoke carefully, obviously weighing his words. "Actually you'd be doing me a favor to stay. I've wished for several years that I could spend more time here in the winter. This would be the perfect solution to my problem."

"It seems more likely that you'd be doing *me* a favor," Regan argued. "I told you once before, I don't want you feeling sorry for me. I mean it just as much now as I did then."

He nodded. "I know exactly how you feel. Believe me"—his voice was dry—"I don't feel sorry for you. I don't want pity and I don't give it. This is strictly a business deal, even though no money will change hands. If it ceases to serve my purposes, I will close the house and ask you to leave. And if you find it unbearable to live here," he said, his face solemn, as if he didn't realize how slim was the chance that Regan would find all this luxury unbearable, "then you may move out. I do ask that you give it a fair try—say at least six months—and give me adequate notice if you decide to leave so I can make other arrangements for Katy.''

She shouldn't consent to an idea that would throw her into such constant contact with Casey. Her feelings about him were too overpowering. Something told Regan she was getting herself involved in a situation that she couldn't handle.

Suddenly, however, she knew she was going to ignore the warning signals. She wanted to stay here. Besides, where else could she go?

''Do you have a contract drawn up with rules to play by?'' she asked, trying to make light of the matter. ''Shouldn't we sign something?''

''Do you agree with my idea, then?''

She nodded once, emphatically, anxious to commit herself and thereby get the decision over with.

Casey's face relaxed. ''I always keep my word whether or not it's in writing, and I trust that you do, too.'' He held out his hand to her across the desk, and Regan a little shyly rose and gave him hers. She felt the strength in his lean brown fingers when he squeezed.

''Mi casa es su casa,'' he said, and smiled an oddly un-Casey-like smile. If she didn't know better, she would swear she saw something like tenderness in his gray eyes.

Chapter Ten

Mi casa es su casa. My house is your house.

What a beautiful thing to have said! Regan hugged it to her secretly as she tried to analyze Casey's gesture. Was he merely feeling responsible for the special-ed teacher, or did he really hope to solve some of his own problems by sharing his home with her? She didn't imagine for even one minute that he cared about her personally. Somehow knowing that Casey's friendship with Holly and Geneva ruled out that last possibility, she spent long hours pondering his reasons for inviting her to live there.

Casey himself was no help in answering her questions. After a couple of long-distance phone calls he drove back to Houston Monday and flew from there to New York with his father for what he expected to be a week of urgent business conferences.

"Mr. Casey told me you've agreed to stay here and be in charge this winter," Katy told Regan after he had gone.

That was a kind way for Casey to have put it. "Yes, I have," Regan answered, wondering how Katy really felt about the idea. "I hope you won't mind not going to Houston—"

"Mind!" Katy stopped dusting the furniture in the elegant blue living room. "Why, Miss Regan, I'll keep house wherever he wants me to, without complaining.

He's that good to me! But I'd just about given up hope of him keeping this place open all winter, after he said no so plain to Miss Bridges last year.''

Regan sat up with interest. ''What did Miss Bridges have to do with keeping this house open?''

''Oh, she came up with the same notion of me staying here all winter so Mr. Casey could spend more time here. He really works too hard, you know. Everyone tells him he needs to relax more, but he takes after his father in that respect. Every McKeever I've ever known has been like that. Anyhow, Miss Bridges volunteered to stay here and work with him. She said she was willing to sacrifice the social advantages of living in Houston if it would help him.''

That was big of her, Regan thought with a twist of dry humor. *No doubt she made the offer without a thought for advancing her own relationship with Casey.* ''And he said no?''

Katy nodded, her eyes twinkling. ''Before she'd hardly got the words out of her mouth. I was right here when it happened. Very polite, he was. He thanked her for her devotion and loyalty and her self-sacrificing gesture, but he said it was best for him to close the house up.''

Regan giggled a little at what must have been a hasty comeuppance for Holly Bridges, but then she sobered up and frowned. ''He must have had quite a change of heart since then!''

The housekeeper reached up to dust around a small porcelain bluebird on the carved white mantel. She took it down and wiped it carefully with a corner of her apron. ''If you want to know what I think, I don't believe he had a change of heart at all. I think he wanted then exactly what he wants now. He told me later that he just couldn't bear to have Miss Bridges around all the time.'' Katy looked mildly penitent for talking about a lady friend of her beloved employer. ''She's a

nice young woman, but she is a little—well, pushy, I
guess you might say. She's been his private secretary
for so long now, she's gotten awfully possessive of Mr.
Casey.''

So Holly worked for Casey! Regan could well imagine the close relationship that might develop between a
man and his secretary. ''That's a perfectly good reason
for him not to want Holly Bridges to live here,'' Regan
agreed, trying not to sound critical of the absent Holly.

''Oh, it wasn't just her,'' Katy insisted. ''Mr. Casey
hasn't wanted *any* young lady around all the time.
That's why I was so surprised and—well, *hopeful* when
he told me you'd be living here. I thought maybe,
maybe the two of you—''

''Oh, no!'' Regan protested aloud, horrified by what
Casey must have thought if Katy had mentioned her
hopes to him. ''It's nothing like that—''

''I know, I know. Mr. Casey set me straight about
that, all right. But still I'm convinced there's hope yet
that he'll get over what that Tiffany St. James, that—
young witch did to him!''

''Tiffany St. James?''

Katy Danetz's face was suddenly shaded with guilt
and something like sorrow. ''I spoke out of turn, Miss
Regan. Forget what I said.''

''All right, Katy, but who *is* Tiffany St. James and
what did she do to Casey?''

Shaking her head Katy begged her, ''Please just forget that! It would hurt him something awful if he knew
I mentioned her. He thinks everyone's forgotten.''

To pacify Katy, Regan dropped the subject of Tiffany
St. James, but she stored the name away for future reference, wondering just what it was that Casey hoped
people had forgotten.

Now that her foot was well enough for her to drive,
the days passed more quickly for Regan. Casey had returned her car keys before he left, and she buzzed

around town in her VW, running errands for Katy and stopping to visit her neighbors at Woodman's or at the post office or drug store. Bob Cox and his wife had been expecting their third child. When the baby was born that week, Regan spent two days at their farm just outside town, keeping the two little boys, who were thrilled with the idea of a new baby sitter. And David, since his hours were back to normal, dropped by to see her often and made a date to take her to church and then out to dinner on Sunday.

On Friday Regan drove to the post office to mail a package for Katy. As she was paying Clara Reeves she noticed a pretty girl of sixteen or so staring at her with fascination. Being eyed with such obvious interest temporarily disconcerted Regan, who fumbled and dropped the small change Clara handed her.

"Oops, watch it, Regan," Clara warned her too late.

Regan knelt to gather up the coins that were rolling in every direction over the ancient wooden floor.

"Here you go."

Regan glanced over at the girl who held out a couple of pennies. She had sun-whitened hair and a sprinkling of freckles across her nose. Although she sounded shy, her blue eyes smiled. Regan smiled in return and murmured her thanks. They walked out the door together.

"You're Regan Allison, aren't you?" the girl asked on the sidewalk outside. At Regan's nod, she hurried on. "Ronald Barnes pointed you out to me one day. I'm Tammy Cypert. We live out on the Springer Highway."

"I'm glad to meet you, Tammy," Regan said, wondering what this was all about.

"I thought—do you have time to walk down the street a little ways, just to Woodman's Grocery Store? There's someone I want you to meet."

The teenage girl seemed so hopeful, Regan couldn't turn her down. Together they walked down the sidewalk, talking about inconsequential things, and when they reached the parking lot at Woodman's, the girl led Regan to a dusty green station wagon and stopped by the front passenger door. There was a small hot boy seated inside, his hair as white as the girl's and his large eyes as blue.

"Miss Allison, I'd like you to meet my brother Michael. Mike, didn't I tell you I'd introduce you to your new teacher?"

Delighted, Regan bent her head and smiled through the open window at Michael Cypert. "Are you going to be in my class, Michael?"

He was a solemn child. He didn't smile. In the back of the station wagon, Regan could see a folded wheelchair, child-sized. Michael stared at Regan, his small hands clenching and unclenching on his lap.

"Can't you answer Miss Allison, Michael?" his sister demanded. "She's going to teach your class in September."

"No!" he burst out suddenly, and his anger surprised Regan. "I don't go to school!"

"Michael!" Tammy admonished him in a stern voice. "You know I've told you that from now on you *will* go to school." She gave Regan an apologetic look. "In the past, a homebound teacher has come to the house twice a week to supervise Michael's lessons. This year will be the first he's been around other kids much." She bent down again. "You'll go to public school in September, Mike, like I do. You'll like it."

"No," he said again. "No, I won't go."

"Why not?" Regan asked gently. "Why don't you want to be in my class, Mike? We're going to have fun, I promise."

The little boy considered that briefly and then rejected her promise with a jerky shake of his head. His chin determined he turned his head away and refused to look at her again.

There were tears in Tammy's eyes. She moved out of earshot of her brother and whispered, "Why won't he believe me? When he was little, he used to beg us to let him go to school. Now that he's really going, he's terrified!" She blinked and turned to go. "I'm sorry for dragging you down here, Miss Allison. I wasted your time." Regan could do nothing but stare after the car, perplexed, as Tammy drove it off down the street.

That evening Charley drove up from Houston for the weekend, arriving late with the smoothly spoken excuse that he had come to take out the stitches from Regan's good-as-new foot.

"You don't have to tell me why you came," Regan laughed as he snipped and pulled on the tiny black threads.

He continued to work rather moodily, his mouth unusually straight and unsmiling.

"You *are* going over to Peggy's tonight, aren't you?" she probed, curious to know what was responsible for his sober mien.

"Oh, sure," he replied, adding almost under his breath, "and if I'm lucky, she might even come home before midnight to see me." It must have suddenly dawned on him that he had spoken his thoughts aloud, because he looked up at Regan with a small sheepish grin. "Sorry. My green-eyed monster's showing."

Charley...*jealous?* But Peggy was absolutely crazy about him! No one could doubt her fidelity.

"Charley," Regan managed in a choked voice, "you don't think Peggy—I mean, er, she isn't—"

He saw her difficulty and shook his head at once. "No, I don't think *that,* Regan. Peg and I are engaged to be married, and she has my complete trust. But sometimes"—his eyes darkened with feeling—"sometimes I just want her all to myself, and I have to share her with her work. And she does such a damned good job of it too."

Regan had heard enough from others about Peggy's skill as a therapist, not to mention her capacity for compassion, to know Charley spoke the truth.

"Lately," he sighed, "it seems as if every time I can manage to get away from Houston, she's got something going on at the nursing home or the hospital in Springer or the pediatric-PT clinic she runs." He shot a mildly guilt-ridden glance Regan's way. "Sounds like I begrudge them her time, doesn't it?"

Regan knew he wouldn't really want to change Peggy's dedication to her work; not Charley, who could have written a book about his obligations as a physician. "It must be difficult for both of you, having two such demanding careers," she said.

"That it is! I'd like to simplify things—marry her tomorrow and take her home to Houston with me."

"What's stopping you?" she inquired.

His expression turned wry. "Tell me something, Regan. If you were Peg, would you give up a place of honor in Bowie's Landing to become just another physical therapist in Houston? There's a lot to be said for small-town life, you know, and I'm not sure I can compete for her. The people around here never let her forget how much they love and appreciate her. Hell, Regan, in another year they'll be treating you the same way! One day"—he smiled at her with ironic affection—"the guy you love is going to have the very devil of a time trying to pry you away from here, because you like it in Bowie's Landing, don't you?" She nodded. "Well," he muttered, sounding moody again, "maybe you'd better plan to fall in love with a native, then. That way he won't have to worry about uprooting you."

She wondered privately if she would ever be in a position to face that particular dilemma.

In the meantime Charley put away his black bag and pronounced her cured.

"Don't forget to send me your bill, Doctor," Regan reminded him only half in jest.

"Are you kidding? You ought to know I don't charge members of my own family." He shoved his hands in his pockets. "You might as well be family. I understand you're going to be living here."

She lowered her lashes demurely. "Word certainly has a way of getting around, doesn't it?"

Charley laughed, his good humor well on the way to being restored. "Were you planning to keep it a secret? I hope you're not worried about gossip, because you've got an unimpeachable chaperone in Katy."

Regan managed to remain cool despite the blush his words inspired. "No, gossip doesn't really bother me. I guess maybe I'm just still not sure whether I should be staying here, for reasons of my own. And maybe I'm a little scared that Casey will change his mind about wanting me to stay."

"Why would he do that?" Charley gave her a hug. "Katy thinks you're good for Casey, did you know that?"

To her chagrin Regan felt her blush deepening. *For heaven's sake,* she thought, *Charley doesn't mean anything by his teasing.* "Good for him?" She tried to sound nonchalant. "Why?"

He touched a finger to the tip of her nose and smiled into her eyes. "Because, my sweet, you're young and the right sex and awfully nice to look at. Because our maternal, romantic Katy thinks Casey has been too serious for too long when it comes to work and not serious enough when it comes to young ladies." Still smiling, he shrugged, pulled a ring of car keys out of his pocket and dangled them from his finger as he started out the door. "Who knows? Katy may be right. And there's a thought, by the way. Around here, Casey's the next best thing to a native. Maybe you ought to marry him. *That* would certainly stop any gossip that might arise over your living arrangements.''

The upshot of Charley's teasing was that Regan began thinking about Casey at the most inconvenient times. The increasing frequency that his handsome brown-haired image intruded into her daydreams was a source of great irritation and puzzlement to her. Even sitting beside David in church on Sunday she was reminded of Sam Houston McKeever and thus of his grandson Casey. In her mind the simple beauty of the little stone sanctuary had come to symbolize the old man's love for the boy. She bit her lip and frowned at the association, knowing that church would ever hereafter bring Casey McKeever to mind.

"You okay?" whispered David, who was out of uniform and ruggedly attractive in his western suit and boots.

Regan nodded, her face averted in her embarrassment. *Damn you, Casey, get out of my mind,* she thought with a very unholy passion that brought tears of shame to her eyes.

If Peggy or Charley, sitting on Regan's right, noticed her tears they were tactful enough not to mention it a few minutes later as the four of them exited among the usual Sunday morning crowd.

"Charley."

Regan recognized the soft voice and turned to see Neva Jonsson take the doctor's arm and tug gently to get his attention. "Casey called me yesterday," the girl with short-cropped fair hair was saying. "He said it looked as if he wouldn't make it back in time for our date on Wednesday, and he asked me to tell you, in case he doesn't get a chance to call you himself. Casey thinks the meetings may stretch out another week."

Regan was shocked at the unmistakable jealousy that washed over her at Geneva's announcement, like the huge wave in the Gulf of Mexico that had once knocked her flat when she swam there as a child. Her face froze in a mask of whatever expression she had been wearing, but the others kept talking as if nothing whatsoever were wrong. Meanwhile one thought played over over and over in Regan's throbbing head: *Why did Casey call Neva and not me?*

It was an absurd question. Casey'd had a good excuse to call Neva, whereas there was no reason for him to call Regan. *No reason at all,* she thought with painful clarity, *except that I desperately want to hear his voice, and to know that he cares enough to call me.*

There was the problem. Kind as he was to the special-education teacher, Casey didn't care a thing about her personally, and Regan cared so much that her chest hurt with the weight of her longing.

That was why she had agreed to stay in his house; even more important that was why she *wanted* to stay so badly! Not for the security it gave her, not for the once-in-a-lifetime chance to live in luxury, but for love! For love of Casey McKeever!

It was a shattering revelation. Regan was appalled to discover that she had allowed herself to fall in love with a man who didn't return the feeling. Whatever his other qualities, and she recognized that he had many fine ones, Casey had no intention of getting serious about Regan Allison. He was much too content dividing his time among his harem—weekends with Holly, a regular Wednesday date with Neva, and the bittersweet memory of a mysterious girl named Tiffany St. James, who must have hurt him badly once.

Still numb from the trauma of her discovery Regan went along quietly with David and Charley and Peggy for Sunday lunch, only half listening to the conversation around her. They ate at a popular restaurant in La Grange, where she couldn't do justice to her rib-eye steak, baked potato, and salad.

"You sure you're not feeling sick?" David's concern was obvious in his gruff but soft inquiry.

She reached deep inside herself and came up with a shaky smile. "I'm fine. Really!" she insisted when he raised an eyebrow at her. *Come on, girl, prove it,* she thought. She fluttered her long eyelashes at him. "It's just so terribly hot today. I can't wait to get back to the house and change out of this dress. You'll go for a swim with me, won't you, David? I really want you to—"

She broke off, aware that all three of them were staring at her—David with both eyebrows raised now—and that there must be something unconvincing in the urgency of her tone. Inwardly she groaned at her lack of acting prowess.

"I really want you to swim with me, David," she repeated, her voice calm now. Looking down at her plate, she hoped they believed her. *Please,* she begged them silently, *don't guess that I've been so idiotic as to fall in love with Casey!*

David spent the afternoon with her on the beach below the house, and she put forth considerable effort to make up for her earlier blue mood by being as cheerful yet serene a companion as he could wish for. She congratulated herself on a job well done when as he was leaving David put both large hands on her shoulders and gazed down into her eyes. "I like you very much, Regan Allison," he said and bent his head to kiss her.

Regan willed herself to respond, reminding herself that David was a wonderful young man . . . good-looking, outgoing, and one of the nicest persons she'd ever dated. All of that was true, yet the spark just wasn't there. His lips were persuasive, his hands firm and strong as he held her, but her only conscious thought was that she would rather be kissing Casey.

After a moment David drew back and assessed her, his blue eyes grave. Was that disappointment in their depths? "Anyway, I like you," he murmured and patted her cheek awkwardly before he left. She felt wretched and guilty for not being the right girl for David.

Regan didn't fare very well during the second week of Casey's absence. A restless kind of energy, almost a caged feeling, drove her to go for walks along the lake every day, spending hours sitting on a fallen tree trunk with her toes dug into the sand, staring across the gray water. She avoided the spots where the summer residents usually swam, preferring the solitude of the stretch of beach between the McKeever house and her own now-deserted cabin.

Part of her was terrified of the time when she would have to face Casey again, certain that he would guess immediately that she loved him; but the rest of her felt as if she were caught in a state of suspended animation that would hold her immobile and miserable until Casey returned and broke the spell.

Just in case he tried to call, Regan stayed close to the telephone every evening. Afraid of missing the hoped-for call, she refused to go out with David twice when he came by. The second time she turned him down, David got that look in his eyes again and mentioned, apparently out of the blue, that Casey's business in New York might drag on yet a third week.

"How do you know?" Regan asked more sharply that she intended. "Has he called Neva Jonsson again?"

"I don't know if he's called Neva, but he called me," David replied. "Matter of fact he's called several times."

"He has? Why?"

"Casey likes to keep informed about things." David was watching her closely. "He always asks about you."

When David left, Regan scrubbed the tears from her eyes furiously. "He always asks about you," David had said. How very kind!

She made a solemn vow to herself that she would

never again sit home waiting to hear from Casey
McKeever. She thought bitterly that she didn't care if
she never heard from him again. He could call Neva
and David—heaven only knew how many others in
Bowie's Landing he called! But he wouldn't call Regan.
As if she had seen the future in a crystal ball, Regan
knew he would never call her.

Chapter Eleven

Casey arrived home from New York with a touch of summer flu, and Katy put him to bed despite his protests. Regan wished somewhat deviously that she had been there to see Katy humble the arrogant Casey; however, she'd been baby-sitting for the three Cox children while Bob took Mary out alone. It wasn't until she got home at midnight and saw the silver Mercedes in the garage that Regan realized Casey was back.

At breakfast the next day Katy told her Casey was sick. "It's like I've said, he's working too hard," Katy fretted. "His resistance is down. He hasn't got any business trying to do the work of three men, bless his heart, but you can't convince him of that."

At her first stirring of sympathy Regan hardened her heart. "He's not an invalid," she responded tartly. "The fact that he had polio doesn't lessen his endurance. Casey seems to me to be an exceptionally strong person, even with his handicap."

"Well, I suppose you're probably right. But"— Katy clung tenaciously to her protective attitude—"he shouldn't work such long hours. He ought to take better care of himself." Her face brightened. "Better yet, he ought to get himself a wife to take care of him."

When Regan went down to supper that evening, she found Katy stirring a pot of chicken soup, her forehead creased with a worried frown. "What's wrong?" Regan demanded.

"I don't know what to do, Miss Regan," the housekeeper sighed. "I got a call a little while ago from my niece in Austin, wondering if I could come stay with her children while she goes into the hospital for a couple of days."

"Oh, dear! Is she very sick?"

"Not exactly. She needs some tests, I believe she said."

"That sounds urgent. What's there to decide? You'll have to go help her, of course."

"I know I should," Katy began, "but with Mr. Casey sick too—"

"Oh, I forgot." Regan glanced involuntarily in the direction of Casey's bedroom. His illness did present a problem. *Someone* had to keep him supplied with aspirin and chicken soup. She drew a deep breath. "I'll make sure Casey gets everything he needs."

"You'll take care of him?"

Katy sounded so hopeful, it was impossible to be annoyed at the secret pleased look in her kind brown eyes.

When she had seen Katy off in the station wagon, Regan prepared a tray of soup and crackers and stood for a moment at Casey's door, dreading the ordeal to come. Balancing the tray on one arm she tapped and then opened the door without waiting for permission to enter. One thing she would not do was let Casey intimidate her.

The room was dim, late afternoon sunlight filtering in through louvered French windows that opened onto the terrace. With difficulty Regan made out a bed near the windows and a still, dark form half buried in covers and pillows. Impatiently she groped for the wall switch, and suddenly Casey's room was bathed in light.

She gasped in surprise at the restfully attractive decor. There was a Polynesian theme in the blue-green-gold tropic flora design of the wall covering and the soft green carpeting. Several arched wicker bookcases stood side by side on one wall, holding shelves of asparagus fern and philodendron, as well as books and a stereo system. One corner was filled with a heavy copper pot of areca palm whose fronds reached almost to the ceiling.

The figure on the bed stirred and blinked sleepily at the brilliance. Smoky eyes focused after a moment on Regan and her tray, seeming rather dazedly to be trying to make sense of what he saw.

"Hello, Casey," Regan murmured. She set the tray on the bedside table.

"Regan." Casey whispered her name and shut his eyes. Regan gazed down at him, wondering at the half smile on his lips. For once he seemed young and vulnerable, lying in a tangle of sheets with one arm flung out across the bed. Shirtless, he wore only the bottoms to a pair of deep blue pajamas. Her pulse suddenly racing Regan had to tear her eyes away from his wide shoulders and strong chest, and when she did she found that he lay watching her with half closed eyes. "Are you my nurse?" He sounded amused.

She licked her dry lips. "Would you mind very much if I were?"

Casey shut his eyes again and shook his head, turning on his side and pulling the pillow over his head. "Whatever you want," he said in a muffled voice. "Only...could you turn out that light, please?"

Regan was so relieved at his reaction that she would have done anything he asked. She switched on the bedside lamp and turned off the bright light overhead, and Casey's head emerged from hiding. He was smiling. "How about that! She's not yelling at me," he said in a low voice, as if talking to himself.

She ignored his reference to her temper. "Turn over

and let me prop you up," she suggested. "I've got some chicken soup for you."

"I'm not hungry."

"But Katy said you have to eat."

"I'm not hungry," he said again.

"Are you thirsty?"

He seemed to think about it. After a moment, he nodded.

"Okay, I'll get you something to drink."

He caught her arm. "Something cool, please."

Regan was shocked at the warmth of his hand. She bent to touch his forehead and the heat burned her skin. His face was flushed, his eyes feverish. In spite of her firm resolve and the traces of bitterness she still harbored over his disinterest, she suddenly wanted to put her arms around Casey and soothe away his sickness. She brought him a glass of ice water and helped him lift his head to drink. Casey gulped it greedily and then lay back looking satisfied. His eyelids dropped shut immediately.

Regan looked at the soup and sighed. Well, perhaps he'd feel more like eating later. She took the tray back to the kitchen and cleaned things up; went upstairs and showered and dressed for bed; and then began worrying about Casey. After an hour of cogitation, she realized she wouldn't rest easy until she checked on him again.

This time she found him shivering with the covers pulled up around his chin. At first she thought he was asleep, but when she approached the bed, his eyes opened and fastened on her face. "Angel," he mumbled drowsily. "You came back. Good. I thought you were gone."

Before she could remind herself that the fever must have confused Casey beyond all reason, Regan's heart began pounding with ridiculous pleasure. She stared down at the dark head on the pillow, aching to have the right to touch him, to cross the barrier he kept up between them, to get close to him, if only because he was sick and alone and needed caring for.

She thought she had only wished it, then, when his brown hand snaked out from under the sheet and the strong fingers closed around her wrist. "Come here," he said, his voice thick.

Wide-eyed, she let him pull her right against the bed. When he tugged at her arm, it was his weakness rather than his strength that prompted her to sit down on the edge beside him.

It was odd, seeing Casey like this with all his defenses down. Bemused, she could only gaze at him while he in turn stared back, the gray eyes a little glassy. Still watching her face, he released her wrist and ran his hand lightly up and down the smooth Qiana sleeve of her peignoir.

"Mmm," he sighed, sounding tired. "That's nice." His eyes began to close again, although she thought he was trying to keep them open, and her hand stole up to his forehead to rest on his rumpled brown hair. Her fingers buried themselves in the soft thickness, combing it back with gentle movements, and he let his eyes shut all the way and sighed again. "*You're* nice. I guess any minute now you'll be doing a disappearing act?" There was a wistful note in his voice.

She had been thinking. Suppose he woke up in the middle of the night and needed something? "I could stay here," she offered tentatively, "just in case."

He didn't open his eyes. "My own private-duty angel?"

"If you like."

Smiling, he turned his face into the pillow and settled down more comfortably. "I'd like that." Somehow he managed to regain possession of her right hand, locking their fingers together and drawing it under the cover to tuck it against his hot chest as if it were a cherished security blanket. The action bewildered her even more than she was already bewildered, and compounded her difficulty breathing by shortening the distance between them. She now sat snugly against his hip, leaning over him a little because of the way he gripped her hand.

In the lamplight she studied his firm jawline and sunbrowned throat and the one well-developed shoulder that had come uncovered, and she dropped all pretense of scorn for Casey. She loved him, dear God! The speeding *ka-thump, ka-thump, ka-thump* beneath her ribs grew louder in her ears, and she wondered that it didn't wake him up.

But instead, he seemed to fall more deeply into sleep, the lines of weariness around his mouth easing. After perhaps twenty minutes his fingers had relaxed so she could slip her hand out of his and pull it from beneath the cover. She could have moved at once and curled up in the overstuffed chair across the room, but she sat where she was, her hand resting cautiously on the sheet that stretched across his flat stomach. Her hungry eyes feasted on his face in repose, admiring the slightly parted lips that had lost their grimness, the thick brown lashes that lay on his cheeks, the straight aristocratic nose.

"I love you, Casey," she mouthed without sound into the quiet bedroom. He didn't stir, and she repeated it in a faint whisper this time. "I love you." Lifting her hand with absolute care not to disturb him, she touched one fingertip to her lips and then transferred the kiss to his, only a feather touch, light as air. She rose to her feet reluctantly and moved over to the chair to try and get some rest.

Although she dozed off with no trouble, every couple of hours Regan aroused herself enough to feel Casey's forehead experimentally and hold a glass of cold water to his lips so he could drink. Each time, he drifted right back to sleep without speaking.

As dawn approached she bent over him once more,

pressing her hand to his temple, and Casey moved restlessly under her touch.

"It's okay," she whispered, thinking that he felt a little cooler than before.

At the sound of her voice Casey's eyes opened in the dim light. He looked at her with a puzzled frown. "Regan?" he demanded in an uncharacteristically weak voice. Lifting one hand, he touched her cheek and then jerked the hand back as if startled to discover that she was flesh and blood. His eyes slid down to her peach-colored peignoir, and the confusion deepened. "What are you doing?"

"Just checking," she answered vaguely.

"Checking what?"

"To see if you still have a fever. And to see if you need anything. Are you thirsty or hungry now?"

"No." He suddenly seemed more alert. "What are you doing here?" he repeated curtly.

"I told you, Casey—"

He shook his head impatiently. "I mean, why *you*? Where's Katy?"

When she told him, his brows drew together in a mutinous scowl. "She left!" he exclaimed almost in disbelief.

"She had to," Regan tried to soothe him. "Her niece was sick, and Katy was needed there. We'll get by all right for two or three days without her."

"With you playing Florence Nightingale?"

"You didn't seem to mind last night."

Casey moved his head and looked at her without speaking.

"Casey?" Regan said doubtfully. "You didn't mind last night, did you?"

He gave a short, bitter laugh. "Last night I thought I was dreaming." He ground the words out.

She was puzzled by his attitude. "Was the dream so awful?"

"Not at all." Still the acid tone. "You make a beautiful nurse, with your cool, gentle hands. And that outfit." He looked at her now out of the corner of his eyes, as if he didn't trust himself to face her. "None of my real nurses ever dressed so obligingly."

"Obligingly!"

"And in my bedroom, with me half dressed and too groggy to know what you were up to."

"Just what do you think I was up to?"

"Seduction—"

"Seduction!" she gasped. Hadn't he really been asleep last night? Could he possibly have been fully aware of her sitting there with her hand on his chest, admitting her love into the silence of the bedroom?

"Or was it just curiosity to see how I handle myself in bed? No sex, just a sideshow?" Looking up at her from the pillows, he saw her pained horror and turned his face away.

Her right hand drew back to slap him, and she grasped it with the other hand to stop herself. *He's ill,* she told herself grimly. No matter how much she might want to kill him right now, she couldn't fight back.

"Go on to bed, Regan." Once more she heard the lack of strength in his voice.

Swallowing, she remembered her promise to Katy. "Don't you want something to eat?" she forced herself to ask.

"No! For Pete's sake"—it was a weary growl—"do I have to spell it out for you? I don't want your motherly concern! Just get out of here!"

Regan got out—quickly, silently, totally devastated by the rejection. Upstairs, she collapsed in a trembling heap on her bed and cried until her eyes were swollen.

Casey spent most of the day in bed. Distressed as she was at being unable to keep her promise to Katy, Regan nevertheless refrained from so much as glancing in his room. He had made his wishes perfectly clear, and her feelings were too raw to risk another scalding rebuff. Besides, she consoled herself, she had left a glass of water on the bedside table where he could reach it.

It was afternoon and she was in the kitchen, waiting for a pan of homemade bread to finish baking in the oven, when he pushed open the swinging door and came in from the hall. She looked up at him. Her quick appraisal told her it must have cost him dearly to dress as neatly as he had. His clothes were perfect, his hair combed. He headed straight for the table and sat down, dropping his crutches with more than the usual clatter to the floor. Regan watched as he clasped his hands in front of him and tried to stop their trembling. He saw her look and glared, daring her to mention his weakness.

Her heart felt as if it were being squeezed in two. *Don't shut me out,* she cried silently, but all she said was, "Hungry?"

Evidently he was ready to admit it, and even to let her cook for him. Using every scrap of cooking sense Katy had passed on to her, Regan concocted palate-pleasing dishes for Casey over the next few days, seeming to do it casually, without regard to whether or not he ate. She was rewarded by seeing his appetite improve to the point that he actually asked for another serving at dinner one evening. His temper also improved as he got over the virus, and by the time Katy returned, both were pretending the incident in his bedroom had never occurred. The trouble was, Regan knew it *had* occurred.

Though Katy was obviously dying to know how they got along without her, neither enlightened her. Casey was rapidly regaining his strength. Before long he was back to his old habit of rising at the crack of dawn and spending hours shut up in the library, working on the family business.

This time, though, there was a significant difference.

Early every morning Neva Jonsson arrived in her green Trans-Am and went into the library with Casey to work. He teasingly called her his assistant; and Regan saw that day by day it was later and later when they emerged.

She thought they were carrying it a bit far when she saw the girl's sports car on the circle driveway on Saturday morning. "Working today?" Regan exclaimed to Katy, who was scrambling her a couple of eggs.

"Mr. Casey would work seven days a week if he could find a willing helper. I was hoping Miss Geneva wouldn't be that willing, but I'm afraid she is. He'll work himself into an early grave if he's not careful."

Over breakfast Regan asked, "Exactly what does Neva do for him?"

"Oh, typing and some of the simpler research," Katy replied. "She gets the legal volumes down from the shelf for him whenever he needs one. With his crutches, he has trouble carrying things, you know."

Feeling more than a little miffed Regan said, "I can type! I could have done all that! Darn it, Katy, why didn't he ask me? It would have given me a way to help pay him back for my room and board."

"I pointed that out to him, Miss Regan, right after he hired Miss Geneva. He said there was no reason for you to feel you had to pay him back at all. He said you help him enough just by being here."

Seeing Casey's actions as merely another refusal to be thrown into her company, Regan resolved to try that much harder to hide how she felt about him. On Sunday morning when he asked her in an offhand manner if she needed a ride to church, she assured him that she did not, and then promptly drove off to church in her own VW. When he entered the sanctuary a few minutes after she did, he gave her an amused look and ended up sitting across the aisle beside Neva Jonsson, who seemed glad to see him.

Regan felt Casey's eyes on her more than once during the service. Bob and Mary Cox, who sang in the choir, had left their three young ones in her keeping, and it was all she could do to stop the little boys, ages three and two, from clambering onto her lap on top of their tiny baby sister. They bounced boisterously, sang lustily, and kept her busy murmuring apologies to the elderly lady in the pew in front of them whose feather hat they persisted in examining.

"Where's the bird, Regan?" Cory called out once after lifting the bright plumage in a vain search. Baby Jennifer began to howl, and Chad fidgeted in boredom.

While other members of the congregation smothered their chuckles Regan glanced nervously at Casey and found him watching her to see how she handled the situation. *Wondering if you made a mistake in hiring me?* she challenged him with her snapping green eyes, but his gaze didn't flicker.

She put a gentle hand on Cory's shoulder and sat him down, bending to whisper a firm order in his ear. Chad settled down with a mere stern look from her. The baby she raised up, nestling the small bald head in the hollow of her neck and patting her until she slept. When she looked back at Casey, there was an unfocused, faraway expression in his eyes, and she decided he wasn't really looking at her at all.

In the days that followed, Neva's car was in front of the McKeever house more often than not. The sandy-haired girl and Casey were usually closeted in the library, the closed door as good as a DO NOT DISTURB sign to shut Regan out. Regan often watched forlornly from her bedroom window as Neva swam with Casey before lunch or stretched out to sunbathe as he made his laps around the pool.

Any hopes that she too would be welcome to join him in the pool were shattered the day Regan came upon him unexpectedly. She had been swimming in the lake and was rushing back to the house to change clothes before lunch, and she was upon Casey before she realized he was there. He sat in one of the wicker chairs beside the pool, dressed only in his bathing suit, reading something in a legal folder. For once, Neva was absent.

Casey had been swimming, too. His hair was wet, his arms and shoulders sun-dried. Regan's swift glance told her that his legs were as brown as the rest of him and that they were too thin, with faint scars barely discernible beneath the tan. And then her eyes rushed upward and met his steady gray gaze and she wished fervently he hadn't caught her looking at his legs.

"Do you want something?" he asked, the chill in his voice travelling down Regan's spine like icy fingers.

Her already shaky pride took a nose dive. Casey swam with Peggy Dunivan and Neva Jonsson willingly enough. Yet he was showing Regan that once again she was overstepping her boundaries, trespassing where she had no business.

She bit her lip and shook her head in answer to his question, before hurrying past him through the open door to the dining room. As she showered and dressed, she reflected bitterly on his paradoxical insistence that she stay here and yet remain apart, isolated from him. The inconsistencies of her life in Casey's house disturbed her. Emotionally, she felt like a yo-yo—up and down, high and low, over and over and over.

She began to sneak out of the house for long walks during which she was positive no one even knew she was gone. She swam while Neva and Casey worked, and lunched while they swam, in order not to have to make conversation with them at the table. Soon they began having their lunch sent in to the library, so even if she had wanted to she couldn't have eaten with thcm. She felt effectively excluded from Casey's comfortable orbit.

But the maddening inconsistencies were to continue. One day near the middle of July she found him sitting at the table when she went down for breakfast. He didn't seem in any hurry to leave.

"'Morning," he said, looking up from the newspaper.

Regan involuntarily checked her watch. "Am I up early?"

Taking a sip of his coffee Casey shook his head. "Neva had some things to do, so I persuaded her to take the day off. Katy says I work the poor girl too hard."

"She docsn't complain, does she?"

"No. She's never said a word."

"Well, I wouldn't worry about her," Regan muttered, callously shrugging off concern for the other girl. She filled a bowl with corn flakes. When she sat down at the table opposite him and poured milk from the little white pitcher over the cereal, Casey eyed her with mild disapproval.

"Is that all you're having for breakfast?"

"It's all I want."

"No wonder you're so skinny."

"Thanks!"

"Sorry. I meant to say 'slender.'"

"I think you said what you meant."

Casey raised his eyebrows at her sharp tone of voice. "Did I offend you, Regan? I didn't realize you were sensitive about that. As I understand it, most women spend half their lives dieting to get the sort of figure you havc naturally."

She put down her spoon with a loud clink. "Do tell, Mr. McKeever, just what sort of figure do I have?"

His lips quirked. Morning light streamed in the windows behind him and streaked his brown hair with gold. "Do I hear a trace of vanity in that question? Never mind, it's a legitimate question." He assessed her with an odd gleam in his smoky eyes. "Your figure is nice," he murmured. "Very nice. You look healthy and straight, like a young willow tree." Strange words to be coming from the pragmatic lawyer who usually had little time and few compliments to spare for his houseguest. "Now am I forgiven for calling you skinny?"

She was in no mood to be pacified so easily. "Healthy and straight?" she repeated, sounding grumpy.

"You look as if you wouldn't break if someone were to hug you." He grinned at her and his charm twisted itself around her heart again. "As a matter of fact, you look as if it might be fun to hug you. And as I recall, it is."

Regan stared at Casey, mesmerized by his words. Somewhere inside her, a voice was protesting, *Don't turn your charm off and on with me, Casey McKeever! It's not fair! I won't be used like that!*

His eyes were laughing now and she saw that he was teasing her. Bristling, she finished her cereal in silence. He finished reading the paper at the same time and they rose from the table together. Regan dawdled, gathering up her dishes as he reached for his aluminum crutches.

"If you don't have one of your solitary walks planned for today," Casey said, making Regan wonder how he knew about those walks, "why don't you come along with me to Houston? I'd enjoy the company."

Regan groaned inwardly at the invitation. *Please, please, don't do this to me,* she wanted to beg.

Instead she asked reluctantly, "You're just going for the day?"

"That's right. I need to pick up some work from the office. It's not really a business trip, though. I promise I won't let you get bored if you go."

"Oh, I'm not worried about getting bored." She forced herself to speak slowly, wretchedly ashamed of the eager acceptance that wanted to trip off her tongue. It was a mistake to go with him, she reminded herself in desperation. Spending a whole day with him would only fan the flame of her hopelessly one-sided love. What she really ought to do was continue to avoid him at all costs. Against her will she asked him, "What time are you leaving?"

Casey gave her thirty minutes to get ready, but she was back downstairs in fifteen. The expression in his gray eyes warmed her, told her he was pleased with the way she looked in her sleeveless ivory linen dress with its orange accent scarf, her dark hair clean and silken as it lay smoothly on her shoulders. Climbing into the silver Mercedes beside him, Regan felt a twinge of excitement. She knew she would have to pay the price later, but for now all that mattered was that she was with Casey.

Chapter Twelve

Thirty-five miles downriver from Bowie's Landing, Casey pulled onto Interstate 10 and turned east toward Houston. He reached over and inserted a tape of Van Cliburn into the eight-track tape player that was built into the dashboard, and Regan recognized the opening strains of Tchaikovsky's First Piano Concerto. At the same time her eye was caught by a telephone receiver on the instrument panel. *Big business,* she thought, smiling to herself.

"What's so funny?" he asked.

"Nothing, really. Just that I've never known anyone with a telephone in his car. It's impressive."

"It's not there to impress people."

"Do you use it much?"

"For business, occasionally." Casey looked across the seat at Regan thoughtfully, as if debating something mentally. After a moment he added, "Mostly it's there as insurance, so that in case my car breaks down or I have a flat, I can call for help. Changing a tire is a bit beyond my skill." From the taut line of his mouth she recognized that it was a difficult confession for him to make.

Good for you, Casey, she applauded him silently, unable to recall another time when he had volunteered any such comment about his disability. Feeling brave, she wanted suddenly to jump all the other hurdles that existed between them.

"Tell me something." She tried to sound nonchalant. "How do your hand controls work, anyway?"

Prepared for a blast of his hot anger or icy scorn, she was astonished when she received a smile instead. Casey seemed to relax. "I'm glad you asked. Some day you may need to drive this car, or one of my other cars, and it will help if you're familiar with the controls."

Regan let out her breath in quiet relief. "You mean this isn't the only car you have with hand controls?"

"The other cars at the lake house are equipped with them, too," he said, referring to the late model brown station wagon that Katy drove and another nearly brand-new Mercedes that Charley sometimes used. "Unless I want to be chauffeured around," Casey went on, "it's essential that I have several cars I can drive. One of Dad's cars in Houston has hand controls. Charley's Porsche doesn't, though. Hand controls require an automatic transmission, you see, and the Porsche has a standard floor shift." He grinned. "Charley felt the four-speed was necessary to uphold his swinging bachelor image."

"Do they—Charley and Katy and your father—drive with hand controls?"

Casey shrugged. "They've learned, over the years. It's not difficult—just takes a little getting used to, I understand. Of course I can't speak from experience about that, as I've never driven any other way."

He demonstrated the shiny chrome bar extending from the left side of the steering column, pressing the bar straight down toward his thigh to accelerate and toward the dashboard to brake. "There's nothing terribly complicated about that, is there?" he asked.

"You make it look easy," she acknowledged, edging closer to him on the front seat and pointing to a small button and toggle switch on the control lever. "What are those for?"

Without moving his left hand from the control bar,

he pressed the button with his thumb and the horn honked. Nothing happened as far as Regan could see when he flipped the toggle switch on and off. "That dims the headlights," he explained. "Well? Do you think you could drive it?"

"I could honk the horn and dim the lights, all right, but as for actually driving, I'd be scared to try. What if I wrecked your beautiful car by accelerating when I should be braking?"

Casey looked amused at the horror in her voice. "With a bit of practice, I'm sure you'd do fine. But you can drive it with your feet, just as you would another car. My controls don't interfere with that." His eyes crinkled at the corners when he smiled at her. "One of these days we'll take a car out for a practice run. Not this car, I think." His smile deepened. "We'll work up to that later, when you're not such a novice."

Regan laughed with him, feeling amazed at their shared humor. Only this morning she would have thought the scene impossible. Yet here she sat, near enough to Casey that she could smell his clean masculine scent, her orange shoes kicked off and one smooth leg tucked beneath her as she watched him drive.

As they neared the coast the rolling hills flattened. Casey reached out once and touched Regan's shoulder, pointing out to her the huge round silver storage tanks in an oil field that he said belonged to one of his father's companies. Oil wells, cattle, and grain elevators were the only things to be seen on the vast green horizon. Before long, however, housing subdivisions, shopping centers and service stations marked the western edge of Houston's development. Traffic on the interstate thickened at the outskirts of town. Casey steered the Mercedes expertly through lanes filled with swiftly moving cars that hurried toward the distant smog-capped skyscrapers of downtown Houston.

"I thought I'd go by the office first, to get that out of

the way," Casey said. He left Interstate 10 at a down-town thoroughfare where the circling entrance and exit ramps and the merging freeways at various levels were shaped like a tangle of spaghetti. In almost the blink of an eye, they were edging along in bumper-to-bumper traffic on one of Houston's main streets, shadowed by tall buildings on all sides.

"This must be like New York," Regan breathed in excitement. "I've always wanted to go there."

Casey smiled at her as if she must be a glutton for punishment. "Houston traffic is bad—hundreds of cars are being added to it every day as people move here—but it still hasn't quite reached the proportions of New York's infamous snarls."

Another block farther he nosed the Mercedes into the parking garage of one of the city's taller buildings, a modern structure whose exterior consisted of solid bronze-colored windows reflecting the images of its shorter neighbors. He pulled into a numbered spot on the first parking level, just a few feet from an elegant lobby visible through smoked-glass doors. Bronze let-ters spelled out the name McKeever Plaza over the doors. "Coming in?" Casey asked, and she climbed out eagerly, not wanting to miss the chance to see another building named for Casey's family.

A doorman in a gray uniform with red epaulets hur-ried across the lobby to open the door for them. "Good morning, Mr. McKeever," he said. "Good to see you, sir." He nodded politely to Regan.

"Hello, George," Casey responded. "How's your family?"

He listened then with evident interest, and again when the stout cleaning woman approached him to tell him in detail about her arthritic hip joint and her rheu-matism. "It was getting so bad, I went to see that brother of yours last week, and you know what he told me? He said I ought to lose a hundred pounds!"

Biting her lip to suppress a smile Regan turned her head away from the woman's indignant face and felt Casey's conspiratorial nudge in the ribs.

"He said that!" Casey showed just the right amount of sympathy.

"Now I ask you, Mr. McKeever, would I need a doctor if I could lose a hundred pounds?" She cackled. "If I could lose that much, it would be a sure-enough miracle! Besides, I thought Dr. McKeever was supposed to concern himself with bones and things like that, not with how much a person eats. But he said if I lost some weight, half my problems would be taken care of, so I guess I'll give his diet a try...."

Still amused, Regan stepped off the elevator with Casey at the top floor and found a world of quiet, efficient big business, fronted by a gracious antique-decorated reception area that shielded obviously top-level offices beyond. An attractive middle-aged woman rose from an eighteenth-century English desk to greet them.

"Mr. McKeever! This *is* a surprise! We weren't expecting you today—"

"Hello, Scotty. I know you weren't, and I don't plan to stay. Dad has some papers ready for me to begin working on. By the way"—he indicated Regan with a nod—"I'd like you to meet Regan Allison, a friend of mine. Regan, this is Mary Scott, Dad's girl Friday. We call her Scotty, but we ought to show her the proper respect and call her Miss Scott. She really runs the place."

The woman eyed Regan with frank interest and acknowledged the introduction warmly before turning her attention back to her employer's son. "Your father is in conference with the board of directors right now. Would you like for me to call him out, or would you prefer to join them?"

"Neither. Dad told me about that meeting last night

on the telephone. They're voting on something like the color scheme for the executive washroom at the new clubhouse. If I went in there now, I'd be stuck all day. I'm on vacation, remember?''

"From what I hear, it's some vacation! You've been working as hard as you do when you're in town," Scotty chided him.

"Well, I really am on vacation today, so be a good sport and run get the papers from my office for me, will you please? And, Scotty—don't mention to anyone that I'm here."

She gave him an almost imperceptible wink. "No problem, sir. I'm covering the front, as you can see, because most of the ladies, *your* girl Friday included, are having a luncheon to celebrate someone's birthday. They won't be back until one thirty."

Regan was puzzled by the relief on Casey's face. Didn't he want to see Holly?

Scotty returned shortly with a bulky manila envelope and a stack of papers that she said needed Casey's approval and signature. He scanned them, then bent over the desk to flourish his pen with a bold hand. "There," he said, straightening up and pocketing his pen. His gray eyes came to rest on the large sealed envelope on the corner of the desk. In a rare nervous gesture, he raked a hand through his thick brown hair.

Regan found herself wondering how Casey could handle two crutches and the unwieldy packet too. Knowing his touchy pride she suspected he would ask Scotty to carry it to the car before he'd ask Regan. Casually, she picked up the envelope and slipped it under her arm without a word. From the corner of her eye she saw that Casey was watching her with an odd mixture of emotions on his darkly handsome face. She turned to Mary Scott and extended her hand. "I'm so glad I met you, Scotty," she said. The older woman smiled, nodded and squeezed her hand in approval.

After a silent ride down in the elevator Casey paused at the trunk of the Mercedes-Benz and unlocked the lid. "You can drop that in here, please," he said, and when she had done so, asked coolly, "Are you hungry?"

Regan didn't know what his mood signified, or how to react to it. She hesitated for a moment and then decided to be honest. "Ravenous."

"You should be, after that breakfast." He slammed the trunk shut, looking annoyed. "All the good places will be crowded, but let's go see what we can find for you to eat."

She was stung to flippancy by his displeasure. "A hot dog will do just fine."

He evidently did not agree, because he chose to take her to the plush Hyatt Regency, just a few blocks from McKeever Plaza. Wide-eyed, Regan stood next to him in the glass elevator that climbed the outer wall of the hotel. As they rose higher and higher into the Houston sky, she clutched his arm without thinking. "Fantastic!" she breathed, hardly noticing that everyone else around them looked bored. The expression in his eyes softened.

She was genuinely delighted with the Spindletop. The gracious circular restaurant and cocktail lounge atop the Hyatt Regency rotated slowly as they ate, so they had a panoramic view of the city along with their beef Bourguignon and strawberries Romanoff. Casey pointed out various landmarks as they came into sight.

"Can you see Hermann Park off in the distance?" he asked, indicating a large green area to the south. At her nod he said, "The park covers over five hundred acres and includes the planetarium and natural-science museum, as well as an outdoor theater and the city zoo. The complex of buildings just south of the park is the Texas Medical Center. I thought we'd run by there

after we eat. There's something I need to talk to
Charley about.''

"Is that where he works?"

Casey nodded. "We can probably catch him at the
hospital. He spends his mornings in surgery and after-
noons in his office, seeing patients.''

When they left the Hyatt parking garage, Casey
drove out South Main Street, turning onto Fannin near
the equestrian statue of the city's namesake, Sam
Houston. A mile or so farther he turned into the
sprawling grounds of what he described as the most
comprehensive medical center in the world.

There were, he told her, four general hospitals, one
of which was county-operated for indigent patients; a
world-famous cancer hospital; one hospital specializing
in treatment of children's diseases and another for
crippled children; a rehabilitation hospital; a mental-
health center; a speech-and-hearing center; two medical schools; a dental college and a nursing school.

Casey appeared to be completely recovered from his
earlier annoyance with her. In the lobby of a tall,
modern-looking brick hospital, he asked the switch-
board operator to page Dr. McKeever. While he waited
for Charley to answer his page, Regan browsed through
the gift shop and bought several small toys for the Cox
children. She saw a colorful educational book about the
United States and, thinking suddenly of Michael Cypert, bought it too. Perhaps it would interest him in
school.

Regan came out of the gift shop to find Charley and
Casey talking in the hall, Charley still garbed in his
baggy surgical greens. The blond doctor gave her a bear
hug that caught the attention of two young nurses
walking past who continued on, heads together, gig-
gling and whispering.

"There goes your chaste reputation," Casey observed in a dry voice and turned to Regan. "Charley wondered if we could have a cup of coffee with him in the cafeteria while he grabs a sandwich. Think we can work it into our schedule?"

They spent a pleasant half hour at a small table in the section of the big dining room that was reserved for physicians. Conversation was easy and relaxed between the three of them, and Charley seemed unhurried; but after a while Casey looked pointedly at his watch. "Your office nurse is probably wondering where you are about now."

"She's probably ready to kill me," Charley agreed, sounding cheerful. "I guess I ought to be going." Pushing back his chair to rise, he looked over at Casey and Regan. "I'm glad you guys came by today! What are the chances of your doing this more often?"

Casey looked startled, but he managed to smile as he stood up. "Don't worry, you'll be seeing us, Charley," he assured his brother, deftly avoiding the question.

As they left the Medical Center, they wound around one of the streets that wandered through Hermann Park and drove slowly past the zoo. "I wish we could stop here." Regan spoke wistfully. "When I was little, Daddy used to take me to the zoo in every city we visited. It's one of the nicest things I remember about my childhood."

"You really want to stop?" He gave an indulgent shrug. "Sure, why not?"

"You mean we have time?" she asked hopefully.

"It's your day from now on. Is there any reason for you to hurry back to the lake?"

"No."

"Good. Let's enjoy it."

They walked for what seemed like miles along shaded paths; through the cool dark reptile house; past seals sunning themselves beside a pool and bears hunting out a scrap of shade among their rocks; and lingered longest in Regan's favorite spot, the tropical aviary with its waterfalls, stone footbridges and jungle-like foliage. Regan thought Casey must be ready to drop, but when she suggested that they had done enough for one day, he raised a mocking eyebrow at her. They had returned to the car, parked near a placid blue pond on which ducks swam idly in the muggy afternoon.

"If you fizzle out that easily, Miss Allison, how do you plan to handle a classroom full of kids? We're only a couple of blocks from the Fine Arts Museum, and there's still an hour to go before it closes. Care for a look?"

Regan slipped her feet out of her shoes and bent to massage her aching arches. "It sounds interesting, but I think not. Even if you're not, I'm tired."

He studied her a moment as if he might not believe her. "This humidity can get to you if you're not used to it," he finally admitted. "Would you like to go somewhere quiet and cool to rest for a while?" At her nod, he reached for the key and switched on the ignition.

Having no idea what Casey planned, she looked about with curiosity as they drove through an area of formerly run-down older homes that had been restored and converted into art galleries, interior-design studios, and the like. Five minutes and numerous turns later, the silver Mercedes whooshed into the driveway of an enormous wooded estate in the exclusive River Oaks section, sliding to a stop on the brick paving before a Georgian colonial mansion that was even larger than Casey's lake house. He did not need to tell her that this was his father's home. A properly dignified butler with a faintly British accent and a bald pate met them at the door and at Casey's request ushered Regan into the large den. She sat stiffly alert on one of two white-yellow-and-coral printed chintz-covered sofas that faced each other in front of the fireplace. After what seemed like hours but was really only a few minutes, Casey joined her.

"What's the matter?" he asked her at once, seeing the tension in every line of her straight slim body. "I thought you wanted to relax. You certainly don't look relaxed."

"I don't feel relaxed, either, although I do feel better now that you're here."

Casey hesitated and then sat down on the couch beside her. For once she was too preoccupied to be disturbed by his proximity; in fact, she moved a little closer to him without thinking. "What's the matter?" he repeated, a frown drawing his eyebrows together.

Regan gazed all around the room with its Hepplewhite chairs, studying the eighteenth-century engravings on the cream-colored watered-silk walls and tilting her chin to inspect the high ceiling. She faced him again finally. "The house where you grew up is very impressive."

"Yes"—he spoke impatiently—"but would you please tell me—"

"I'm trying, Casey!"

"And I'm listening, Regan."

She sighed, sent another quick glance around the room, and pushed a wing of hair back from her temple. "I think I'm a little frightened that your father is going to walk in any minute."

He stared at her. "Is that all you're worried about, for heaven's sake?"

"Is that all? It's plenty! I've heard so much about him that he terrifies me. I've never met a millionaire before—"

"In other words, I don't count?" Leaning back, he eyed her with humor.

Regan stopped in consternation. "Well, I've—I've just never thought of you as a millionaire, exactly."

"Fine." He nodded his approval. "Don't change now."

Casey—a millionaire? She supposed he must be. There was nothing ostentatious about him; rather, he possessed a sort of quiet suavity that implied money was no object.

"Now I really am nervous!" She stood hastily, but Casey took her hand and pulled her back down beside him.

"Regan, don't run away. Listen to me. My father's really a pretty nice guy—"

"I'm sure he is." But Regan didn't sound very sure.

"What do you think he's going to do—eat you alive? Come on, be realistic. I'm not sure I understand why you're afraid to meet him."

Because he's your father. Because he might not like me. Because I'm afraid I won't measure up to those girls you've known who have always had everything.

She didn't answer him aloud. After a moment of watching the way she sat, head bent and lower lip caught between her teeth, Casey touched her delicately pointed chin and then her cheek. She looked up and met his eyes.

"I get the feeling," he said, his voice low, "that something more than just meeting my father is bothering you."

He was right. She felt a hysterical giggle rise in her throat and only just managed to stifle it. It wasn't until she saw his house and heard Casey admit to being a millionaire that she realized the extent of the difference in her world and his. It was a staggering difference. His life-style at the lake house, while elegant by most standards, was still informal enough for her to feel comfortable in his home. But here...

"Regan?" He pulled her closer to him on the couch with hands on her wrists and then put both arms around her, drawing her over against his chest. "Can you tell me about it?"

She could feel his heart beating, and she heard her

own heartbeat in her ears. "I—I don't know," she stammered, his very nearness playing havoc with the calm facade she usually maintained in front of him. A telltale flush crept up her cheeks and her stomach fluttered with hundreds of happy butterflies again. She ran the tip of her tongue slowly over her lips, moistening them.

"Try," he encouraged her when her silence continued.

"You won't understand."

"Maybe I will."

"You couldn't!"

Regan felt the sudden light pressure of Casey's lips on her hair and then her temple. She closed her eyes as he kissed her gently, sliding his mouth along her cheek to her ear, his breath warm on her skin. Every nerve in her body sprang to life at his kiss. A convulsive little shiver of pleasure went through her and she sighed.

"What couldn't I understand?" he asked.

She peeked at him through her thick lashes and what she could see of his face was solemn. "Mmm?" She tried to think. "Oh, what it's like to be poor."

"Who's poor?"

"I am."

"You!" His arm tightened around her and she thought he was smiling. "How can a beautiful young willow tree be poor?"

"Casey!" she reproached him, opening her eyes wide now. "I'm serious."

He was silent for a while. "So am I," he finally responded. He still held her, and her dark hair muffled his voice. "Don't think I'm putting down money. I'm not. It's a lot easier to live with it than without it. But it sounds as if you've gotten your priorities a little confused." He moved slightly and she realized for the first time how tight his muscles were. "You're a big girl— you're old enough to know money can't buy what really counts." His voice had an ironic note.

She remembered with sudden shame that all his father's wealth, all his grandfather's influence, hadn't prevented his becoming disabled, nor his being hurt by "that young witch," as Katy had said.

"Oh, Casey, I'm sorry!" Regan muttered contritely. "You're talking about love and good health and things like that...."

He pulled back a little, his mouth a stern line. "You're sorry?"

Blinking tears from her wide green eyes, she answered impulsively, without thinking, "I'm so sorry! If only I could do something—say something to make up for it—"

"To make up for what?" He gave a short hollow laugh, and she saw that his face had darkened. "For a pair of defective legs? Or for my having the misfortune to love the wrong person? Tell me, how could you possibly make it up to me for either of those things?" She cringed at the bitterness in the hard lines of his face, realizing too late that she had said the wrong thing. "And why should you feel you should make anything up to me, sweet, sympathetic Regan? You're not to blame for any of it."

Her misery was reflected in her eyes. "I know I'm not to blame, Casey, but—"

"But you're still sorry for me. So I gathered. Sorry enough to let me kiss you."

She had to tell him how wrong he was. "No, I'm not—"

"Just how far would your pity let me go, sweet Regan?" There was a dead quiet to his words that alarmed her. His arms closed around her again and one strong hand began stroking the base of her neck with rhythmic sensuous movements that made her tremble. "I felt you shudder when I kissed you a minute ago. It was difficult, wasn't it? Would your pity be great enough that I could get away with making love to you?"

I didn't shudder, she wanted to scream. *I wanted you to touch me!* She shut her eyes and shook her head to block out the intensity of his anger.

"The thought disgusts you. Admit it, Regan. It may even surprise you to learn that I'm not a monk. There are women around who don't feel repulsion when I touch them. Does that shock you?" His arms like bands of steel clasped her to him in a painful embrace. "Answer me, Regan!"

She could barely breathe. "No!" Gasping for air, she shook her head again in denial. "It doesn't shock me!"

"Don't lie to me!" Casey snarled in her ear, tightening his hold. "It really doesn't matter whether or not I repulse you. If I wanted you, I'd have you, and there wouldn't be a damn thing you could do about it."

Oh, dear heaven, how had this happened? It had to be a bad dream! Regan turned her head aside, searching for air, unable to struggle. She squeezed her eyes shut against hot tears. "Casey, please let me go! You're hurting me...." She dropped her head to his shoulder and sobbed into his collar.

Though his muscles were still rigid, his hands loosened their grasp and he cradled her limp form. She felt his heart pounding heavily beneath his shirt, but it was no more out of control than her own.

Too tired to move, she stared up at his frozen expression. In her relief at being released, her anger started. "You wanted to hurt me!" she accused him in a surprised whisper. "Is that how you make love? By brute force?" There was a flicker of something deep in Casey's eyes. "I've often wondered if you were afraid of being thought weak—if that's what drives you to be so hard and unkind." Having been wounded, she struck back at him with words she would never have dreamed of uttering if she hadn't been so distressed. "Does it make it easier to bear being handicapped—knowing you're a bully, as well?"

Casey's mouth tightened and he turned his face away from her, but not before she saw him flinch. She felt him thrust her away from him blindly. With great effort Regan rose from the sofa and moved over to stand by the window overlooking the estate. She stared out in blank confusion, not interested in the view, not focusing on anything but her chaotic thoughts, her arms clutched together across her chest, while Casey sat and gazed into the cold fireplace.

Meeting Charles McKeever, Sr., would have to be less of an ordeal than bearing the glacial silence in the room, Regan thought.

Casey's father, when he finally came in, was a young-looking sixty, an inch or two taller than Casey, sun-browned, lean and handsome. Gray hair added to his distinguished attractiveness. Not at all the pompous businessman Regan had feared to meet, he was warm and friendly and he asked interested questions about Regan and how she had come to be trained in special education. Something about him made her think of a college professor. Casey watched the two of them without expression, and if Mr. McKeever wondered at his son's constraint or Regan's forced gaiety, he didn't comment on it.

Elizabeth McKeever, Casey's stepmother, was probably not much older than forty. Her hair was a silvery blonde, pulled back into a severe but stylish chignon that revealed the perfect bone structure of her classic face. That Casey got along well with Elizabeth was evident from the moment she swept into the room and gave him her slender hand. Casey stood up, holding her hand, and kissed her cheek. He stood for a moment with his arm around her waist and introduced her rather brusquely to Regan.

Regan thought he only agreed to stay for dinner because there was no way he could get out of it gracefully. Elizabeth had been planning since noon, when she found out from Scotty that Casey was in town, to serve one of his favorite dishes—stuffed Cornish hens roasted in wine.

"Since the cook has a cold, Liz even gave up her Tuesday-afternoon tennis game to shop for groceries," Charles said significantly, so of course Casey had to stay. Except for a brief technical exchange with his father about the board-of-directors meeting, he let the others carry the conversation in the dining room.

"Have you made a decision about that other matter you've been considering?" Charles asked Casey at one point, sounding deliberately vague, Regan thought.

Casey didn't look up. "No, I haven't." His voice left no doubt that he didn't want to discuss the subject now, in the present company.

"Casey, dear, you must bring this lovely girl back to visit us!" Elizabeth insisted as they were leaving.

"Charley's quite an admirer of yours, Regan, and I can see why," her husband added. "Casey"—he leaned down to address his son, who was already behind the wheel—"bring her back soon. And Regan—please see what you can do to keep Casey from working till he drops, will you?"

It was a long uncomfortable drive back to Bowie's Landing, and Casey made no effort to stay within the speed limit. His anger was so thick in the air it was almost tangible, seeming to grow by the mile. Shutting her eyes Regan went over and over the bitter words they had exchanged. If only she could have foreseen the impact her simple expression of sympathy would have on him; if only she could erase those words *I'm sorry.* He had misinterpreted her meaning completely, and she had been inept at explaining. What had ever deluded her into thinking she could spend a day with Casey McKeever without there arising between them a misunderstanding of unbelievable proportions?

It was after ten o'clock when Casey pulled into the driveway and stopped in front of the big white house, letting the engine idle as he waited for her to get out of the car. Neither had spoken since they left Houston. Regan glanced over at him reluctantly. "Aren't you coming in?"

"No," he snapped. "Tell Katy to lock up. It may be late when I get back."

She got out slowly, remembering Neva Jonsson for the first time all day. Was he going to see her? He was no monk—he'd said so himself. Still, wherever he was going, he ought not to tear off in the car in a mood like this.

"Casey—" she began, but he cut her off.

"Drop it, Regan. I'm not interested. Just go into the house like the good little girl you are." He sounded cool and bored.

Her face went hot, and she slammed the car door quickly. She turned to run up the shallow steps and across the veranda and let herself into the entry hall. The Mercedes, she saw through stinging tears, didn't circle the driveway and leave until she was safely inside.

Chapter Thirteen

Every time she thought she heard a car in the driveway, Regan glanced at her wristwatch. David wasn't due to pick her up for the community picnic for another quarter of an hour, but Regan was all dressed and ready to leave and this waiting was driving her up the wall. She stood before the full-length mirror in her dressing room and nodded approval at the tall slender girl in white T-shirt and khaki slacks who looked back at her. *Nice tan,* she thought. *Hair's thick and long; needs trimming a bit. Face is too thin. Eyes too sad. She looks sad. She is sad,* Regan confirmed.

Grabbing up her house key from the top of the chest of drawers, she ran out of her room and shut the door. She'd spent far too many hours in there these last few days, hiding.

"What's the matter with you two?" Katy had come up to her room to ask bluntly yesterday.

"What do you mean?"

"You know what I mean, Miss Regan. You moping around up here. Him snapping my head off down there and staying out till all hours of the night. You two aren't yourselves at all." There was a suspicious gleam in Katy's eye. "Did something happen on your trip to Houston?"

Fingers crossed Regan had said, "No, of course not. He's working too hard as usual, I imagine. I've been reading." She held up a novel she kept conveniently close for just such an excuse. Katy wasn't fooled, but at least she asked no more questions.

Regan had ventured out once, when she thought she couldn't stand the silence of the lovely room another minute. She'd asked for directions from Ronald Barnes and had driven out the highway toward Springer to find the beaten-down little house where the Cyperts lived.

She almost wished now she hadn't gone. Perhaps she was more sensitive to poverty these days after living in luxury in Casey's house, but the place had seemed miserably depressing with its brown yard and shabby furniture and its air of drabness. Tammy Cypert welcomed Regan into the still, hot living room where Michael sat in his wheelchair watching television.

"Look who's here, Mike!" the girl exclaimed, her enthusiasm a little too forced.

The boy raised serious blue eyes to Regan. "Hello," he said in a voice so low Regan wondered if she had only imagined that he spoke. He turned immediately back to the cartoon show and ignored her attempts to draw him into the conversation. Even the book she had brought him from Houston elicited only a brief wistful glance before he shoved it aside.

Regan wanted to know what Michael liked to do and where his interests lay, but he refused to answer her. In desperation, she finally clutched the boy's thin arm and shook it gently to get his attention. "Don't you like to do anything in particular, Michael?" she demanded. "Isn't there *something* you enjoy doing just for fun? Maybe I could arrange for you to do it."

He had a look of bewilderment in his eyes when he stared back at her. He shook his head slowly, and Regan couldn't tell if he comprehended her question. She was convinced he was not at all retarded.

"Where's your mother?" she asked the boy's sister

when the girl accompanied her outside to the little white Volkswagen.

"At work. Why?"

"I'd like to talk to her about Michael."

"I'm sorry, Miss Allison, but we can't bother her there. She might lose her job, and then we'd really have problems." Tammy was old for sixteen, wise beyond her years.

Regan glanced over at the front porch and frowned at the two rough boards that slanted over the steps. "Is that your ramp? Is that how Michael gets in and out?" Her voice revealed her stark dismay.

"It's the best we can do, Miss Allison," Tammy had replied with dignity. "Michael—Michael doesn't go in and out by himself anyway. We have to help him. He stays right where he is most of the time."

It was an awful situation, she told herself now as she waited for David. What would happen if the house caught fire and Michael couldn't get out in time? Would he refuse to go to school in September? And what about his future? At the moment it looked about as dim as the house he lived in.

She shook her head to clear out the depressing thoughts. This evening was supposed to be fun. No good could come from dwelling on an unpleasant situation that couldn't be changed.

Regan crept cautiously down the stairs, tiptoed across the cool foyer and froze with her hand on the doorknob when the telephone shrilled and echoed through the huge silent house. Before she could decide whether to run, or answer it just to shut it up, the phone rang again.

"I'll get it, Katy!"

At the sound of Casey's voice Regan jerked her head around and watched him emerge from the living room, moving quickly across the polished floor toward the white telephone on the table near the door. When he saw Regan, he didn't slow down or speak. He gave her a short nod, his gray eyes only a few degrees warmer than when they had parted the other night. *Anyway,* Regan thought with relief, *I don't have to speak either.* She turned her back on him and opened the door to slip out, just as Casey's hand reached for the receiver.

"Hold it!" he ordered her curtly, and she looked back at him, panic-stricken. "This might be for you," he added, grimly amused by her fear.

Regan's face clouded with resentment, but she closed the door and stayed where she was. Her hand still gripped the doorknob, proof that she was poised for flight. Casey watched her with a sardonic expression as he spoke into the phone.

The call was for him, as she had known it would be. From Casey's easy familiarity, she thought it must be his brother on the line. Remembering another long-distance call Casey had accused her of eavesdropping on, she made up her mind not to be guilty a second time. Once again she turned the doorknob quietly and started to escape, and once again Casey stopped her, this time by raising a crutch and forcing the door shut. She spun to face him, indignant.

"Can you wait a minute, Charley?" From his three-inch advantage of height, he glared at her arrogantly. "Would you please stop trying to run away? You're acting like a two-year-old!" His voice was scornful, his words distinct, and Regan flinched because Charley was hearing it all. Casey gestured toward the ladder-back chair beside the table. "Sit down," he said roughly. "I want to talk to you when I'm finished."

Tongue-tied with fury Regan stomped over to the chair and sat.

"Now, Charley," Casey said apologetically, "what were you saying about a party?"

Regan didn't want to listen. She stared down at her lap, trying to shut out Casey's incredibly handsome image in his light blue Lacoste sport shirt with the alligator insignia and his navy blue slacks. His thick hair was smooth, his gray eyes dangerously alert, and cords of muscles stood out on his strong tanned arms from his savage grip on the crutches.

"Yes, I'm aware of what day next Saturday is," he was saying, his tone dry. "I appreciate your thinking of it. Tell Dad and Elizabeth that, will you? But I don't know if I can make it for what you have in mind.... What do you mean, it's all set? Shouldn't you have discussed it with me first?... How many?... Well, it looks as if I don't have much choice.... I don't know.... I doubt it.... I really don't know, Charley!" His voice was growing impatient. "Look, she's right here. You can ask her yourself."

Casey thrust the receiver at Regan and she took it warily, as if it might bite.

"Regan?" Charley sounded as if he could have been calling from Bowie's Landing rather than Houston. "What's going on, anyway? Are you two fighting again?"

"Umm," she mumbled, avoiding Casey's watchful eyes. "About as usual."

"That bad, huh?" Charley was grinning—Regan could tell that even on the telephone. "Listen, you made a huge hit with Dad and Elizabeth the other day. They were a little concerned about Casey's behavior— said he acted like a bear—but they loved you. I'm extending an invitation on their behalf to a birthday party for Casey. You probably didn't know he will be thirty-three next Saturday, did you?"

"No, I didn't know that."

"Dad likes to make a big deal out of birthdays. He's gotten tickets for the Houston Ballet and Symphony performance Saturday night, and we'll come back to the house afterward for a late dinner. Just a few close friends. How about joining us?"

Her fingers closed convulsively around the phone as

she tried to think of an excuse that wouldn't be terribly rude. A darting glance at Casey told her he was enjoying every minute of her discomfort.

"Regan? Still there? Listen, I know he can be a devil to get along with. When we were kids, we used to yell at each other until Katy was ready to kill us both. But I'm concerned about what's likely to happen at the party. I'm afraid Casey's going to be in for a real blow unless—by the way, he can't hear me, can he?"

"No, I don't think so." She was clutching the receiver with both hands by now, and she flicked her eyes nervously at Casey. His face no longer registered enjoyment but rather shrewd interest.

"As I was saying, I'm worried about Casey's reaction to an out-of-town guest who has wangled an invitation to the dinner. Without going into detail, let me just tell you it's an old friend he may not be happy to see."

"Uh-huh."

"You do know the kind of friend I mean?"

"Female?"

At that, Casey leaned forward, his eyes narrowed, his expression puzzled.

"Right," Charley said, "but don't say anything else. I don't want Casey to know Tiffany's coming until he gets here. If he has any advance warning, I have a feeling he won't show up."

Tiffany. The name rang a bell and Regan remembered Katy's description: "the young witch." Charley must be talking about Tiffany St. James.

Charley spoke into Regan's silence. "I hate to seem overprotective, but I think he's going to need the right person there for moral support."

She looked away from Casey. "Not me, Charley."

"Yes, you, Regan!" he insisted. "You won't be committing yourself to anything permanent, for heaven's sake! You don't have to be afraid of getting involved with Casey—"

"You don't understand!" she cried in distress. Charley was dead wrong if he thought she didn't want to get involved with Casey. Her main point in objecting was that if Casey needed someone to help him get over the shock of seeing Tiffany, it should be someone he was genuinely attracted to, someone like Holly Bridges or Geneva Jonsson. "You don't understand," she repeated helplessly, near tears but unable to explain with Casey listening to her end of the conversation.

Looming suddenly over her Casey took the phone from her hand without preamble, his face an emotionless mask. "The lady said no, Charley. For God's sake, you don't have to *beg* people to come to my party, do you? Maybe you're inviting the wrong people. If you're worrying that I won't have a date, you can stop. I'll bring one.... Right.... Okay, see you."

His hand reached out and placed the receiver in its cradle slowly. Regan watched as his slim brown fingers closed over the crutch grips and he turned to look down at her where she sat. Self-consciously she lowered her eyelashes and twisted her hands together on her lap, dreading the awful scene that was sure to follow.

"I apologize," he said, to her complete surprise.

She raised her head, not quite trusting her ears. "You...apologize? What for?"

"For Charley. I'm sorry he tried to pressure you about coming to Houston. He had no right to do that."

"Charley didn't try to pressure me."

"Look, don't be nitpicky. I apologize for whatever method of persuasion he used. Playing on your pity for the handicapped or for the poor little rich kid or whatever. What line was it, by the way?"

Unwilling to break Charley's confidence about Tiffany St. James, Regan flushed and kept silent. From Casey's expression, she knew exactly what he was thinking: that Charley had tried to stir her pity. Her heart beat painfully against her ribs. Regan wanted to deny Casey's unspoken accusation, but she fought down the urge. Much as it galled her, perhaps it was best to let him think that. It would save further explanations, and right now she didn't think she could come up with a believable one. She bit her lip and clenched her nervous fingers until they hurt.

"Anyway," he went on, grimly determined to finish with the distasteful subject, "I'm glad you refused to be coerced into what could only be a boring weekend for you."

Regan nearly laughed aloud at the absurd notion that spending a weekend with him would be boring, but she choked back the sound. "I thought there must be plenty of other girls you'd rather take. After all"—she swallowed—"it will be special... your birthday."

He moved over restlessly to push back the draperies and look out the window onto the veranda. "Yes," he said, "it will be special." She was wondering why his voice sounded so flat when he turned to face her again. "It's just as well you don't want to go. God knows what David would do to me if I tried to take you to Houston again. He might want to fight me for your fair hand, and I wouldn't be much of a challenge for him." Before she could do more than gasp at that, he hurriedly added, "Look, I'm sorry. Forget I said that, would you? I don't usually indulge in such blatant self-pity." Shaking his head in evident disgust, he continued resolutely, "As long as I'm apologizing, I may as well confess I'm not very proud of the way I acted the other day. You were absolutely right to resent it. In case you haven't noticed, I don't deal with kindness very well; however, that's no excuse for my display of bad manners."

She stared at him, her mind searching for words to tell him that kindness had nothing to do with her feelings for him. It hadn't been kindness that had weakened her and made her melt in his embrace. She had honestly wanted him to make love to her.

But it was unthinkable for her to tell him that. Once again, he would have to go on thinking the worst—that she felt only pity for him. "I suppose you have quite a problem with tenderhearted females," she said in a quiet voice.

"Being the recipient of constant kindness does get to be a problem, yes."

"Isn't it possible that you misinterpret what other people are feeling for you? That it's not kindness or pity at all?"

"It's possible," he conceded wryly. "But after dealing with it all these years, I've become pretty adept at recognizing the symptoms. If I act like a brute at times, it's self-protection against the maternal instinct that inevitably seems to surface in the women I know."

"David told me once you always have more feminine admirers hanging around than you know what to do with."

Casey acknowledged that with a shrug. "I've never lacked for female companionship. It just gets a little tiresome having to screen out the ones who want to mother me, and those who are attracted to me because my name is McKeever."

"Oh, really Casey! You're starting to sound paranoid!"

His mouth hardened. "So I'm a paranoid, crippled bully. You've diagnosed me pretty thoroughly." His voice had an edge to it. "Tell me, can you cure any of my problems or do you just criticize?"

Regan was saved from having to answer by the sound of a car on the driveway outside. She jumped up and moved past him to look out the window. "It's David," she announced needlessly and came back to stand beside him. In spite of his truculence, she longed to reach out and touch his hand, to make some physical contact with him, but of course she couldn't. Knowing any gesture of love would be misunderstood, she just looked at him, her green eyes miserable.

"Poor Regan," he muttered, and it was he who touched her. One hand released a crutch and spanned the short distance between them to caress her cheek with gentle fingers. "I didn't mean to make you look like that—all wide-eyed and sad. David will wonder what I've been doing to you." His eyes darkening at some private thought, he drew back his hand. "Go on and have a good time at the picnic. That's where you're going, isn't it?"

She nodded, strangely reluctant to leave him. "And you, Casey? Are you going to the picnic?"

He shifted his weight restlessly, reaching up to rub one hand down the back of his neck as if the muscles there were uncomfortably tight. "I'm not sure, but I probably will." With a forced smile, he moved over to open the door for David.

Regan and David were settled with plates of barbecue beef and potato salad at one of the many long tables which had been set up in the park for the community-wide picnic. Nearby, noisy children participated in organized sack races and games; and groups of adults sat under the pecan trees, the ladies busily sewing quilts or crocheting while the men smoked. David was still in uniform but was officially off duty. His curly dark head was bare, the wide-brimmed hat lying beside him as he ate.

"Did Peggy go to Houston for the weekend?" Regan asked him.

He looked around at the chattering throng of summer people and year-round residents. "No, she's here somewhere. She brought a group of therapy patients from the nursing home. Charley was scheduled to work all weekend anyway, so his partner will cover for him next weekend. Saturday is Casey's birthday, you know."

She nodded, her eyes on her plate. "So I heard. Are you going to his party?"

"Unfortunately, no. I had already agreed to work that weekend so one of the other deputies can go on vacation. Of all the rotten luck, Peg can't make it, either. She promised to help with the fund-raising bazaar for her PT clinic."

"That's a shame," Regan sympathized. "I guess Charley's disappointed that she won't be there."

"That's putting it mildly. He really hit the ceiling. I've never seen him so angry." David winced, no doubt recalling the scene that had taken place.

It was hard for Regan to imagine Charley McKeever blowing up. "He's probably already gotten over it, don't you think?" she suggested hopefully, but David looked doubtful.

"If this had been an isolated incident, he wouldn't have lost his temper in the first place. Charley's one of a kind; *nothing* seems to upset him. But this is just one more time he's had to put up with playing second fiddle to Peggy's job. It's starting to get to him. I'm afraid she's going to lose him if she doesn't watch out."

That shocked Regan. "Oh, no, David! Those two are perfect for each other!"

"They're also both used to being looked up to in their work. Peggy's not really egotistical, but she's not ready to give that up just yet."

Charley had said something to that effect once.

"Well, it doesn't necessarily have to be Peggy who gives up her job, does it?"

David stared at her. "You're surely not suggesting that Charley ought to stop practicing surgery? Do you have any idea how good he is at it?"

"But Peggy's good at her work, too! Anyway, couldn't

Charley open a practice in Bowie's Landing or Springer?''.

"Not bloody likely! How well do you think an orthopedic surgeon would do in a dinky little twenty-bed
hospital in a town with two traffic lights?''

"You mean there's not much demand here for his
particular skills?''

"Exactly. He couldn't even pay his overhead ex-
penses. But that's not the only drawback. Imagine having his healing expertise denied the thousands of
people who go to Houston each year for medical con-
sultations and eventually have surgery there. Think of
all the people he helps in the Medical Center. People
from all over the world, literally!''

"Okay,'' she conceded reasonably. "So why couldn't
Peggy quit her job and get another in Houston? Surely
she wouldn't have any trouble getting a job there?''

"As a matter of fact,'' her brother said, "she's had a
couple of fantastic job offers over the last few years.
She turned them all down.'' Before Regan could speak,
he explained, "She says she feels responsible for the
programs she started here: the pediatric clinic, the therapy department at the nursing home, all the rest of
it...''

"She *would* be difficult to replace, I guess.''

"Difficult, but not impossible, Charley knows a
therapist at his hospital who wants to apply for the job,
if Peggy ever gives any indication that she'll quit—''
He stopped and shook his head. "Regan, how did we
get off on this subject?''

"Talking about Casey's birthday.''

"Oh, yes.'' He turned his direct blue gaze on her.
"Well, then, tell me. Are *you* going to his party?''

"I don't think so.''

A puzzled frown drew his eyebrows together.
"Weren't you invited? Charley said he was going to
call you—''

"Yes, I was invited, but ... well, I didn't think Casey would consider me essential company at his birthday celebration. Not the way we get along."

"Oh, come on!" he protested. "Casey said you were getting along fine now."

"When did he say that?" she asked with faint irony. "Before or after he took me to Houston?"

"Did things fall apart then?"

She sighed. "David, things just keep falling apart where Casey and I are concerned. I think we're chemically incompatible or something. Sometimes I think I should pack up and leave his house." She stared off into the crowd thoughtfully. "I could stay at my cabin the rest of the summer at least and decide what to do."

"Listen, Regan." David put his hand on hers. "Don't do anything unless you talk it over with Casey first, okay? He's got a good head on his shoulders, and he'll help you work it out."

She knew beyond a doubt she would never attempt to talk it over with Casey McKeever, because he could talk her into or out of anything. She simply wasn't strong enough to win an argument with him. That had been proved several times.

"Anyway," David continued, buttering a roll as he talked, "I think you ought to go to Casey's party. You're hung up on the idea that he dislikes you, which is a lot of bunk. Casey wouldn't be so determined to keep you around if he disliked you."

"What are you implying?"

"Just that the two of you seem to spend an awful lot of time in a stew about each other, which makes me highly suspicious of your emotions. I think you've fallen in love with the guy." His face was gloomy. "I don't know how Casey feels. He's pretty good about hiding that. But you don't hide it so well."

Flushing, she was silent for a while. All her attempts to force a spark between her and David, to respond to his romantic overtures, had failed. She hadn't fooled him, and she probably hadn't fooled anyone else either.

So... David knew how she felt about Casey. Had anyone else also figured it out?

David finished his barbecue before he spoke again. "I wish I thought there was a possibility something would work out between you and me," he muttered, and it dawned on her that she wasn't the only one who was hurting. "If there had ever been a chance, I wouldn't have minded competing, even against Casey."

"I wish we could make it too," she responded, her voice husky with feeling. "Why is it that we always seem to fall for the wrong person? You're much too nice to be hurt, David, and I'm sorry if I led you on."

He gave her a rueful grin. "Apology accepted. It wasn't your fault, anyway. I just kept hoping."

No longer hungry, she pushed a bit of food around on her plate. It seemed amazing to think that couples ever progressed to the point of actually getting married. Look at Peggy and Charley. For that matter, look at Casey and Tiffany. Once upon a time, things hadn't worked out for them.

She took a deep breath and asked the question she had known all evening she would have to ask. "He's still in love with Tiffany St. James, isn't he?"

"Who on earth told you about her?" David asked in astonishment. "Not Casey—"

"Oh, no! Not Casey," Regan reassured him. "I've just heard bits and pieces about her. He does still love her, doesn't he?"

"Heaven only knows! As I said, he keeps his feelings pretty much to himself. I don't have the guts to ask him that question, and I don't know anyone else who does, either. Not even Charley. The subject is off limits and has been for years."

"It seems to me," she said with painful honesty,

"that he must have declared the subject off limits because it's so important to him."

David leaned toward her and touched her hand again. "Regan, I wouldn't even begin to speculate about Casey's feeling for Tiffany. He loved her when he was young, and she nearly shattered him when she broke off with him. Charley blames her for the fact that Casey has never let himself get serious about any of his girl friends. Maybe so, but that's no reason to consider Tiffany competition. She's not a part of his life anymore. He hasn't seen her in fourteen or fifteen years."

The table was starting to fill up, and Regan didn't want anyone to overhear their talk. Strolling away from the picnickers, she and David sat down side by side on a smooth flat rock overlooking the lake.

"And if he saw her again?" Regan persisted.

"Why worry about such an if?" David burst out in exasperation. "Tiffany lives in London, I believe. Charley told me once that she married a Polish count. She's safely out of the way."

No, she's not, Regan wanted to tell him, but instead she swallowed with difficulty. "Did you know Tiffany, David? I suppose she was very beautiful."

He nodded, twirling his hat thoughtfully as he stared at the lake. "She was small and blonde with huge blue eyes the color of cornflowers. Her beauty was the fragile kind, sort of like Dresden china, but with a strength that wasn't apparent. She loved to swim and ride horseback. It's crazy, as beautiful as she turned out to be, but I still remember her best as a selfish, spoiled little rich kid, a ten-year-old snob lording it over Peggy and me because we were year-round residents and not in the same class as the summer people."

"That must have been pleasant for you!"

"It was good training for life." David shrugged his broad shoulders. "Casey and Charley ignored her when she acted that way, and she grew more bearable as she got a little older." He squinted down at Regan as if debating how much more to tell her. "Thinking back on the kind of person she was, it really surprises me that she stuck with Casey as long as she did after he got sick. Her family lived on the estate next to the Mc-Keevers in Houston, and she came up here to spend part of every summer with Casey and Charley. She was really fond of Casey, I think. His having polio must have been difficult for her too, but at the time all anyone thought about was how Casey felt, how *his* life had changed. She was good company for him during the first year, when he was confined to a wheelchair. When he was old enough to drive, they dated quite a bit. By that time he was walking with crutches and braces, and no one knew he'd improve to the point that he wouldn't have to use braces at all. I guess it got to be a drag on her, young as she was. She split when they were eighteen. For years they had been planning to go to the University of Texas together, but at the last minute Tiffany enrolled in a school in the East. Casey almost refused to go to college at all. It took every argument his father and grandfather could come up with to convince him he should go on with his plans."

David's voice became apologetic. "That's all I know. I was several years younger than Peggy and Casey, so I wasn't aware of all that went on."

"Hey, thanks for telling me what you know about it," Regan said soberly. "It helps me to understand him better." She leaned against David's sleeve, putting her arm around his neck and drawing his head down to kiss his cheek gratefully. She hoped the kiss conveyed her deep affection or him. They exchanged a long look that comforted her, because it told her they were still friends.

"Good. If I can't have you, I'd rather see you with Casey than anyone else I know. He's the best friend I have in the world. Maybe you can help him get over

Tiffany, if as you suspect he really is still hung up on
her." David rose to his feet and reached down a large
hand to pull Regan up.

Brushing off the seat of her pants, she turned around
and her green eyes widened when they met Casey's
opaque ones. He sat not far away at a table with a crowd
of other well-to-do summer people, an unsmiling witness to the kiss Regan had given David.

Chapter Fourteen

The house was dark and silent when Regan stole down the stairs and into the long hallway behind them. Although it was past midnight, a sliver of light under the farthest door in the hall told her Casey was still awake. Perhaps he was reading in bed. As she shut herself furtively in the library, she sent up an urgent prayer that he wasn't prone to nocturnal wandering.

She eyed the wall-to-wall books with doubt, nearly overwhelmed by the task of finding a single volume among so many. The most perplexing aspect of her search was that she wasn't even certain the book she looked for existed.

"If you want to know what Tiffany looked like," David had said earlier, "surely you can find a snapshot of her at Casey's house. She lived next door to him in Houston for ten years. There's bound to be a picture of her somewhere."

What he said made sense. The more Regan considered it, the more convinced she became that she wouldn't sleep a wink tonight until she found out what sort of girl was walking back into Casey's life on his birthday. Taking the books a shelf at a time, she ran her fingers along the bindings, looking for a photo album. It was tiring work, standing on the step ladder with arms raised to inspect books on the higher shelves. By the time she had covered half of the room, Regan had come to the reluctant conclusion that if Casey had any pictures, he kept them somewhere else. More likely, he'd destroyed any pictures he ever owned of Tiffany. But she refused to give up, and as luck would have it, she had nearly completed her survey when she found the book on the very top shelf in the corner behind the door.

It was bound in fine red leather and engraved in gold with Casey's name, his birthdate and a year that Regan calculated must have been his seventeenth. Feeling like a snoop—albeit a triumphant one—she climbed down from the ladder to spread the album on Casey's desk.

The pictures on the pages of the book were a charming record of a relationship between a boy and girl. Regan knew without a doubt that the small brown-haired boy and his towheaded playmate on an elaborate set of playground equipment were Casey and Tiffany as eight-year-olds. They were together in each photograph: at ten, dressed up for someone's birthday party; at twelve, in formal riding habits astride horses; at what must have been fourteen, a stunningly beautiful blond girl standing beside a thin pale boy who smiled wanly from a hospital bed. In a later picture, it appeared that someone had forced the rather impatient Casey to stand still for the camera. Looking sturdy and tanned again, he stood straight, not leaning at all on his crutches, while the girl smiled enchantingly at the photographer. In another snapshot, he leaned against a gate and patted the nose of a small black mare on whose back sat the lovely girl. The unseen photographer had captured them in a backyard swimming pool; on the veranda of the lake house; and elbow to elbow, Casey in tuxedo and the girl ethereal in a filmy long dress, looking as if they were on their way to a school prom, which wasn't very likely in view of Casey's handicap.

The final picture in the album showed them again in tux and evening dress, standing close together on a patio lit by Japanese lanterns, with other young couples dancing nearby. Casey held the girl in his arms as if he were dancing with her, smiling with adoration down into her face. The crutches propped against a nearby chair were a poignant reminder that they were only pretending to dance.

Regan picked up a birthday card that was tucked away in the back of the book. Inside, a note in a neat young script read:

Dear Casey,
    These pictures symbolize all we have shared. You will always be part of me—my finer part by far, as you are finer than I can ever hope to be. All my love forever,

Tiffany

Beneath the card lay a yellowed sheet of good-quality stationery that appeared to have been crumpled at one time and then smoothed out flat. The upper left-hand corner held the engraved initials T.S.J. In the same schoolgirl handwriting, someone had penned:

I know you hate me now. Perhaps you'll understand one day that I had to do it. I'm sorry, Casey, but there is my whole future to think of. I hope someday you'll meet a girl who doesn't care for dancing and skiing and riding and all the things I love, and the two of you will be very happy together.

There was no date or signature.

Nearly blinded by tears of anger and pain for Casey, Regan slammed shut the book and returned it to the almost inaccessible niche where he must have ordered it banished. Although Tiffany hadn't said it in so many words, the implication was clear that she didn't want to spend her life with a man who was handicapped—that if Casey had been able to dance and ride, Tiffany would have chosen to stay with him.

Regan dropped into the brown leather chair across from Casey's desk and hugged her elbows to her, hating Tiffany St. James with an awful passion. She put herself in eighteen-year-old Casey's place, still not fully recovered from a crippling attack of polio, rather unsteady on his feet and perhaps not yet very sure of his ability to create his own place in a family of super-achievers. She tried to imagine how he must have felt on reading such a good-bye note from the girl he had loved for ten years. No wonder he'd never married! The experience must have convinced him he was unacceptable. Even evidence to the contrary when he was older failed to reestablish his feelings of self-worth in that one area that Tiffany had shattered in his youth. His callous arrogance was a shield against both the hated pity and the feared involvement that might lead to more hurt.

Casey, Regan told herself with sudden certainty, was still vulnerable where Tiffany St. James was concerned. Charley was right: Casey needed help to get through his encounter with her, if only to keep him from falling under Tiffany's spell again. Regan didn't know if she could help, but she did know she wasn't going to let him go off to Houston alone.

Casey looked up from the book he was reading and raised an eyebrow at Regan. "You *what?*"

Nervously, she cleared her throat. "I said I've changed my mind about going to Houston with you."

"That's what I thought you said." He closed the thick volume and set it aside on the redwood patio table at his elbow. Leaning back in his chair to scrutinize Regan, who stood across the sun-dappled terrace from him, he asked bluntly, "Why?"

She was prepared for the question. "Charley said your father has tickets to the Houston Ballet. I've been thinking—I'd really like to see them perform again."

The sun overhead beat down with a dazzling brilliance that Regan thought must be unique to Texas. When it hit the surface of the lake, it sent silver arrows up the hill. Casey narrowed his eyes against the shimmering brightness. "You like the ballet?"

His low-key attitude didn't fool Regan. She knew he was tuned in to catch the slightest intonation in her voice that didn't ring true, so she spoke carefully. "That's right. I saw the Houston company a couple of times while I was at the university . . . in *Swan Lake* and *The Nutcracker,* I think."

Casey reached for his frosted glass of iced tea, took a long swallow and set the glass back down with a clink. His gray eyes met and held hers with a challenge. "Did you stop to think I may have asked someone else by now?"

Regan bit her lip until she tasted blood. "Yes," she said meekly, "I thought you might have."

"And if I have?"

She swallowed her pride. "If you have, I would still like to come, too. I assure you, I won't be any trouble."

Eyes veiled, he stared off at the lake in silence for a while, his fingers drumming on the arm of the chair. "In other words, you don't really care whether I have a date or not?" he drawled with dry amusement.

"No." But the lie didn't come easy to her.

More silence. Then, "What about David?"

"David?"

Casey gestured impatiently with one hand. "Your good friend David." His poorly disguised sarcasm surprised her. "Does he want you to go?"

"Oh!" Regan remembered suddenly the kiss Casey

had observed at the picnic. Was that little scene responsible for Casey's apparent hostility toward David? She puzzled over it a moment before deciding that she must be imagining things. If Casey was hostile to anyone, it was Regan, and that had nothing to do with her relationship with another man. "David thinks I should go, yes," she answered honestly. "He can't go, you know, but he thinks I should."

"I see." Casey's eyes met hers squarely once again, but they didn't tell her what he was thinking behind that calm mask. After a moment, an ironic half smile eased the sober mouth. "All right, Regan. If you want to come along, you'll be welcome." He picked up his book and opened it as if to dismiss her.

"Casey?"

He looked up again and waited.

She braced herself. "*Have* you asked anyone?"

"You said it doesn't matter," he pointed out.

Shrugging, she lied in a soft voice. "I'm just curious."

With his charcoal eyes examining her face, she felt as if he could see beneath her skin. Finally he turned his attention back to his book, muttering in a terse, let's-drop-the-subject manner, "No, I haven't asked anyone."

Casey and Neva Jonsson worked long hours in the library during the week that followed. More than once Regan was tempted to put her ear to the door to find out if they were really concentrating on McKeever business inside. She couldn't help wondering why Casey hadn't invited Neva to be his date for the weekend in Houston.

She got up her nerve to ask Peggy's opinion on the matter when the two girls had lunch together on Monday. They had chosen a corner booth at the pizza parlor, and the place was dark and nearly deserted, so Regan had no fear that anyone would overhear.

"I know it's none of my business," she admitted
after they had finished their pepperoni pizza and salad,
"but he does see a lot of her. It would have seemed
logical for Casey to want Neva to be his date, don't you
think?"

Peggy shrugged. "Oh, I don't know. He's always
telling me they're just friends. Neva has a pretty bad
crush on him, but that part of it may be all one-sided.
Casey's been helping her prepare for her entrance ex-
ams to law school."

"I had no idea she was going to law school!"

"Well, now you know. She's just one of many young
people around here who've been influenced by Casey
in that direction. In fact, David's seriously considering
it. Casey makes it hard to resist, with his offer to foot
the bill for tuition and his guarantee of a job with his
father's company when David graduates."

Sipping her iced tea as she thought that over, Regan
was startled when Peggy asked softly, "You haven't by
any chance been jealous of Neva, have you?"

She looked up quickly, then back down at the table,
hoping her blush wasn't visible in the dim interior of
the restaurant.

"Hey, Regan, pretend I didn't ask you that, okay?"
The older girl sounded sympathetic. "That wasn't very
tactful of me."

Lifting her eyes again, she saw that Peggy's smile
was contrite.

"You can hardly be blamed if I wear my heart on my
sleeve," Regan murmured. "I suppose I've been pretty obvious?"

"Not at all," Peggy denied. "You're almost as hard
to read as Casey. But I think I've gotten to know you
fairly well, and I have a rather unique relationship with
David and Casey, so that's given me the chance to observe all three of you. I have to admit, I've spent a lot
of time trying to figure out what's going on with you

guys this summer. I've known for a while how David feels, so I took a guess just now, and I'm sorry if I embarrassed you.''

"That's okay. I'd appreciate it, though, if you wouldn't say anything. I mean, David knows, but I really don't want anyone else to find out. I'd hate to be the laughingstock—"

"Your secret is safe with me, Regan," Peggy cut in gravely. "Charley told you who's coming to the party on Saturday, didn't he?"

"Tiffany St. James? Yes." Leaning forward, Regan spoke urgently. "Peggy, I'd feel so much better about everything if you'd come too. You used to know Tiffany. You know how much in love with her Casey was when he was young. Maybe together we can figure out some way to stop her—"

But Peggy was shaking her head slowly, her lovely blue eyes filling with tears. "I can't, Regan!" she whispered, her voice trembling. "You have no idea how badly I want to go to Casey's birthday party, but I can't break my word to the volunteers at the clinic. They do so much to support my program, I can't let them down at the bazaar." She smiled through her tears. "You'll just have to outfox Tiffany on your own. I'm betting on you."

Although she thought Peggy's confidence was misplaced, Regan lifted her chin. "I'll do my best." She paused, then asked anxiously, "Is Charley still mad?"

"Furious!" Peggy sighed. "He says I'm so wrapped up in my work these days that I don't care whether or not he's around. That's not true, of course, but I just seem to have gotten myself in over my head. One obligation has led to another, and I'm afraid if I withdraw from a single thing, the whole structure will collapse. I know it sounds as if I'm full of my own importance, but I'm not, really. I just want to be sure the people who need therapy are getting it. I grew up with the adage that if you want something done right, you should do it yourself, and I still operate on that principle."

"At the risk of destroying the most important relationship you'll ever have?" Regan asked quietly.

Peggy stared at her. "Do you think I'm wrong?"

"I don't know." Regan lifted one shoulder and dropped it. "I can't say what's right or wrong for you. I only know what I'd do if I had that decision to make."

"What would you do?"

"If Casey wanted me—if he asked me to give up my job in Bowie's Landing and live with him in Houston or Alaska or—or Tibet, I'd go in a flash. Oh, I'd hate to give up this place, because I've never really had a hometown before, and it's something I've always wanted, but I'd do it in a minute if Casey loved me. I think you're lucky to have that choice, Peggy."

"Maybe," Peggy muttered, looking pensive.

The rest of the week, Regan saw so little of Casey she might have thought he was avoiding her, but she was aware that he was tied up with evening school-board meetings and church administrative-board meetings and meetings of the Chamber of Commerce. On Thursday night she attended a meeting of a citizens' group concerned with building an airport near Bowie's Landing. She went on impulse, because she suspected Casey would be there, but it was a complete surprise to her to find out that he had been elected to chair the group.

He led the meeting with such cool authority that Regan felt a ridiculous possessive pride, watching him. *I live with that man,* she found herself wanting to announce irrelevantly to the well-dressed woman in the next chair. His crutches, propped where everyone could see them, had never seemed less significant as he listened to subcommittee reports on construction costs, possible funding sources, and established and projected need for air facilities.

The meeting was held in the cafeteria of the elementary school. Regan thought perhaps Casey didn't see her in the large assembly. As soon as he adjourned the meeting, however, he edged his way toward her through the milling crowd of both summer and year-round residents until he was within earshot. "Wait for me," he ordered her curtly as three or four determined gentlemen vied for his attention to further discuss the project.

When the rest of the throng had finally drifted off, Casey—by this time sitting on the edge of one of the conference tables—looked across the empty room at Regan. "Why didn't you tell me you were coming tonight?"

She spread her hands. "When would I tell you? When have I seen you?"

"Let's see," he mused. "I saw you for a minute at breakfast on Tuesday, and before that I think we passed in the foyer on Sunday evening. You seemed to be in a big hurry."

That was because you had Neva with you, Regan thought. *I wasn't about to linger.*

Changing the subject, she murmured, "I was impressed tonight with your charisma. You seem to have quite a flock of admirers here in Bowie's Landing."

Casey shrugged off her words. "I've known most of these people so long, they're like distant cousins." He grinned suddenly. "You thought it was charisma? I'm flattered."

"But it *is* charisma!" she insisted. "I know how they treat you, and it's very unusual for the townies to give that kind of devotion to a summer person. I notice you get appointed to every civic committee Bowie's Landing comes up with. Somebody's trying to tell you something."

"Oh?" Casey looked interested. "What might that be?"

"It's pretty obvious to me. They'd like you to live

here year round like your grandfather. You see, they treat you like a native—which you're not, technically— because they want you to be one. I'll bet someone has even approached you about running for district attorney or some other major office."

"Very astute of you, Miss Allison," he acknowledged, crossing his arms across his chest. "Or was it just a lucky guess?"

Smiling, Regan tilted her head at him. "I was being astute, of course. What was your answer? When they asked you to run for office, I mean."

"Simply that I'm a corporation lawyer, not a criminal lawyer, and that I prefer to practice corporate law. My legal advice on community affairs is probably worth almost as much to the town as would be my service as district attorney, anyway, and I give that gladly."

Green eyes solemn, she accepted what he said with a small nod. "I guess there isn't much hope Bowie's Landing could entice you away from Houston permanently. After all, what can such a tiny place offer you, other than a quiet place to relax every once in a while?"

He bent his head to study his feet in their polished oxfords, so that Regan couldn't see his eyes when he answered. "Bowie's Landing has its own unique attractions." He spoke quietly. "It's the kind of place in which I'd like to live and raise my children." There was a brief pause before he added, "If I had any."

Regan's stomach knotted. "It is that sort of place," she mumbled, hoping she didn't sound as unhappy as she felt.

"I almost forgot." Casey looked up abruptly and reached for his crutches. "I asked you to stay for a reason." He stood and moved toward the hallway that led to the classrooms. "I want to show you around."

He took her on a tour of the building and pointed out the changes that had been made since school had been dismissed in May: gently inclining ramps where steps had been, widened doors, water fountains lowered to accommodate wheelchairs, remodeled restrooms. The tour ended in a large classroom with enormous windows, white walls trimmed with green, and a profusion of plants in colorful ceramic pots and hanging baskets.

"What a beautiful room!" Regan breathed when she saw it. "It must be a pleasure to teach children in a room like this."

"I'll ask you in a few months if it is." Casey motioned toward the nameplate on the desk that spelled out MISS ALLISON.

"You mean this is my room?" Regan gasped. "Oh, Casey, I love it!"

She examined at length the books and educational toys on the shelves around the room. Casey watched her with a smile as she sat down behind her brand new desk and then rose to print on the clean chalkboard: "My name is Miss Allison."

When she had inspected everything to her heart's content, Regan turned to him shyly and murmured, "Thank you."

"It's a pleasure, I assure you," he answered. "Speaking for the other board members, we hope you'll be happy enough to stay here."

"I'm sure I will, Casey, only...." Regan stopped, thinking of Michael Cypert. Her sudden frown drew attention to her delicately arched brows.

"Only what?"

"I was just wondering—what's the use of having this marvelous classroom if the kids who need it can't even get out of their own homes?"

Casey looked at her blankly. "You sound as if you have someone in mind when you say that."

Nodding, she asked, "Do you know the Cyperts out on the Springer highway?"

When he shook his head, she rushed on, spilling the words out in her haste to share a problem that had been bothering her for some time now. She told him all she knew about the little boy and his pretty sister, describing the dingy little house down to its paintless exterior and the makeshift ramp leading up to the front door. "And I think—no, I'm positive Michael won't even try to come to school!" she concluded with passion. "Why should he, knowing somehow he'll fail? That little boy has never known anything but the same dreary existence he's living now. He has no motivation to make the effort."

Casey, a thoughtful audience to her story, asked a couple of questions about the situation and then turned to leave abruptly, giving Regan the impression that he had lost interest in Michael Cypert.

"Casey?" she asked. "What should I do?"

"Do?" Rather absently he ran a hand through his hair. "You've done enough by bringing it to my attention. I'll see that it gets taken care of. The school district just bought a van that's equipped to carry wheelchairs, you know. That solves at least part of the problem." His eyes were on her face, but she got the feeling that his thoughts were elsewhere. "Don't worry about it, Regan."

Theirs were the only two cars left on the dark parking lot when they emerged from the building. Casey walked down the newly built ramp and, still somewhat preoccupied, accompanied Regan to her small VW.

"By the way," he said, "I've received an offer from a man who wants to buy your cabin."

He dropped the bombshell so casually that he might have been telling her that rain was expected tomorrow. "It's a very good offer, and I think you should accept it," he added.

Regan stared at him. "What?" she stammered, and then corrected herself. "No, I heard you. How in the world did you get an offer on my cabin? I mean, it's not listed with a real-estate agent. How did it happen?"

"Come on, Regan, surely you understand how the grapevine works in Bowie's Landing. Everyone knows by now about our arrangement—that you're living with me." A grin split his dark face in the moonlight and his white teeth flashed. He reached out and tugged gently at a strand of her hair. "Now don't get upset. I'm only teasing you. Seriously, I believe this prospect is somebody's brother-in-law's third cousin, or an equally close relation. The point is he's offering you twice the market value. It would be quite a good deal for you financially." When Regan didn't say anything, he went on honestly, "Of course, if you sell the property at a substantial profit so soon after inheriting it, you may have to pay a larger inheritance tax, but you'll come out ahead anyway. We can invest your money in some blue-chip stocks if you like."

The idea of selling the cabin her parents had owned overwhelmed Regan. She stood in shocked silence for a moment, staring at Casey. The frantic thought occurred to her that if she sold it, she would be giving up her real ties to Bowie's Landing. Even having a job was somehow not quite the same as being a property owner.

"This prospective buyer happens to like the site of your property," Casey went on, "and he can afford to pay a good price, so naturally I'm concerned that he doesn't lose interest and look elsewhere. He might find other property he prefers. I'd feel a lot better if you went ahead and sold the cabin—got your money and invested it wisely for the future. I'll be glad to handle the legal end of it."

"Thank you, Casey. You can't imagine how much I appreciate your help." She took a deep breath and added hopefully, "If I get a really good price for my cabin, maybe...maybe I could buy another place of my own—something that's already in good shape."

In the darkness she couldn't read Casey's expression. He didn't speak for a moment, and when he did, his voice was strained. "Look, Regan, let's not get into that tonight. This may not have been an ideal time to bring up the subject, but it's the only chance I've had." For the first time she noticed the way he leaned back against her car, as if he was tired. "Frankly, owning property can bring with it a whole slew of problems that I'd rather you didn't have to bother with. I worry about you," he admitted reluctantly, as if the confession was being forced from him.

Feeling a sudden shame at causing more work and problems for Casey, who certainly didn't need the added burden of responsibility for her, she put her hand on his arm in an impulsive gesture. "I'll try not to make you worry," she promised him. "You've been a good friend."

Casey's hand closed over hers. "Will you sell your place, then?" His voice was taut.

The warm pressure of his hand electrified her. Her skin tingled and her heart pounded alarmingly as she nodded, knowing she would do anything he asked.

"And will you hold off awhile on buying another place?" he persisted. "After all, you assured me you'd share my house for at least six months."

She sighed. "Whatever you think is best."

"Then it's my turn to say thanks." Casey's voice was low and husky. Before she knew what he was going to do, he had straightened up and pulled her against him, pressing his lips on hers in a kiss that was like a bolt of lightning coursing through her body. There was nothing casual or friendlike about this kiss. One strong hand flattened against the small of her back; the other twisted its fingers in the thick dark hair at the base of her neck, holding her close to him while his warm lips sent trails of delicious fire across her face and temple.

Regan was only remotely conscious that she was returning his kisses with a passion she had never felt before in her life. The movement of Casey's hand along her spine, the pressure of his body against hers and the warmth of his breath in her ear awoke in her a desperate need that begged for fulfillment. All she could do was cling to him, her hands reaching hungrily beneath his sport jacket to explore the hard-muscled surface of his back, pulling him ever closer to her. Their bodies seemed charged and fused together with a vital current.

When her slender form had molded itself pliantly against him, he untangled his hand from her hair and slid it slowly across her shoulder and then down her side. His searching fingers were firm but gentle, tracing the shape of her breast and drawing her to a painful awareness of how little she knew of her body's capacity to respond to a man. Casey's touch was an education, the nerves he stroked became sharply sensitized, so that she seemed to feel everything more intensely than ever before. Light-headed, almost dizzy with the intoxicating experience, she drank in his clean and spicy scent and felt her need explode deep within her. Her thighs, her stomach, her breasts burned from their contact with his taut length, and at the same time her whole being ached for more intimate contact.

Love me, Casey! She thought the words, but her throat was closed, her lips incapable of voicing aloud her desire for him to make them one.

It couldn't possibly happen here, anyway. She acknowledged that vaguely, even as her blossoming senses cried out with pleasure at the lovely things Casey's hands were doing to her. Brushing feather-light promises of rapture over the slight swell of her stomach, the curve of her hips, they lulled her into a waiting trance. She was his prisoner, immobile, bewitched.

Love me!

Sweetly caressing at first, his hands became more urgent by the minute. His lips seared her throat with kisses that flamed, white-hot and dangerous. Finding her mouth again, he demanded entry, and she gave it eagerly, welcoming the invasion.

From the evidence, it was apparent that Casey was rapidly losing the usual calm self-control that was so characteristic of him. His breathing ragged, he groaned against her ear, "Dear God, Regan, don't—don't torture me!"

Forgetting their previous disagreements, forgetting what had happened the last time he kissed her, forgetting that Casey loved Tiffany St. James, Regan could think of nothing but how badly she wanted him to make love to her. Her fingers dug into his back as her excitement rose to a fever pitch. With her breath coming in shallow gasps, she buried her face in the hollow of his neck and whispered, "Please...please, Casey...." Her mind finished the thought: *Please love me. Please don't leave me dangling like this, too agonizingly aware of what can be ours. Please, Casey, finish what you've started....*

Suddenly he shuddered and was very still. After a moment, Regan felt him withdraw from her physically, pushing her carefully but firmly away from him. While she stared at him, unable to believe this was happening, he leaned back against the car, his face haggard in the pale moonlight.

"Sorry," he said shortly when his breathing had finally evened out. "I'm sorry. I didn't mean to get carried away. We'd better go home."

Just like that, the passion was clicked off.

Regan felt strung out, tense almost to the snapping point, but she somehow managed to drive her VW home and park it safely in the garage. Casey, who followed in his car, slid the silver Mercedes into the space next to hers and together they walked into the house, his footsteps now slow, apparently tired. As she watched him slide the bolt lock on the door and turn to face her with remote charcoal eyes, it occurred to her that he was keeping his distance. He had no desire to set off another spark as he had done in the parking lot.

I have to show him he needn't worry about my getting too involved, she thought desperately.

Nerves screaming, she walked over to him and kissed his cheek. She felt his rigidity, saw him relax visibly when she drew back. "Good night, Casey," she said with a nonchalance that was entirely faked but utterly convincing. She even managed to smile at him before she climbed the stairs with the graceful walk of a dancer. Casey, watching her, didn't respond.

Chapter Fifteen

There was rain in the forecast for Friday. Standing on her little balcony that morning and studying the low-hanging black clouds, Regan hoped the storm wouldn't break until she and Casey left Bowie's Landing.

She had slept later than she intended, having had some difficulty getting to sleep the night before. It was with trepidation that she went down to the breakfast room. She didn't know what sort of mood Casey would be in, after their unnerving interlude in the parking lot; but he had finished eating earlier, Katy said, and had driven over to the courthouse in Springer to take care of some business.

"He'd like to get started as soon as possible," the housekeeper informed Regan tactfully, "so if you could be ready by the time he gets back, I know he'd appreciate it."

Since her overnight case was already packed and waiting, Regan had no trouble complying with the request. As soon as she heard Casey drive up, she called a quick good-bye to Katy and carried the bag out to his car.

Before she could tell him not to bother—she'd just stash her suitcase in the back seat—Casey had gotten out of the car, reached back inside for his crutches and started to the rear, keys in hand. Regan bit back her automatic objection, meekly watching as he opened the trunk, took her bag from her and stowed it next to his in the roomy gray-carpeted receptacle. Once again she guessed from his dark expression that he was out of sorts at being unable to carry her things for her.

A couple of large splashes of water on the silver fender of the Mercedes drew Casey's eyes heavenward and set both of them in motion. They barely made it into the front seat before the bottom dropped out of the clouds.

Altogether, not a very prepossessing start to their trip, she decided as Casey turned the car downriver, all his attention on the rain-drenched road ahead.

Sneaking a peek at him, she noted his brooding eyes and the determined set to his mouth. Was he still regretting what had happened last night? In the light of day—lowering as this particular day might be—he certainly appeared grim and forbidding...not someone she could imagine pulling her into a healthily passionate embrace just a few hours ago. He looked as if his mind could be a thousand miles away.

"This is awful weather for driving," she offered on a tentative note. Focused studiously on the limited view through the windshield, he gave a noncommittal grunt. "Casey," she said after a few more intent and silent miles, "there's no sense in your fighting the elements like this. Why don't you pull over and wait until the rain slacks off?"

He shook his head. "I've driven through worse than this."

"But you can hardly see ten feet ahead!" She gestured at the frantic windshield wipers that were making little headway against the torrents of water. "Surely we can take our time getting to Houston. We're a whole day early. Your party isn't until tomorrow night—"

"I have some work to do at the office this afternoon," he interrupted her, sounding impatient, "so I need to get there as quickly as possible."

"Important business?"

"I think so, yes."

"Couldn't you declare a holiday for once?" she asked lightly, intending to take his mind off whatever it was that occupied it so completely. "Katy said you were over at the courthouse bright and early this morning, hard at work on some project. Good grief, Casey, what can be so all-fired crucial to you?"

At that, his head turned swiftly and he spared her a close look. A moment later, he shifted his gaze back to the road, his hands tightening perceptibly on the steering wheel. "We should be coming to a roadside park soon," he said without answering her question. "I'll stop there for a while and give the rain a chance to ease up. I didn't realize my driving would make you so nervous."

His driving hadn't made her nervous at all; as Katy had once observed, Casey handled a car with exceptional capability. "I just thought how tiresome it must be for you," she murmured.

He ignored the faint protest and concentrated on delivering them safely off the ramp to the right of the highway, onto the paved rest area with its covered picnic tables and fully enclosed bathrooms.

There—along with five other cars, two semitrailer trucks, and a recreational vehicle—they sat out the worst of the deluge, neither of them talking. Casey slumped in his corner, watching the clouds dump their wet burden over the rolling countryside, his fingers tapping restlessly on the seat between them.

Chafing at the bit he might be, but he gave his usual fine display of will power. He forced himself to wait until the rain was a mere patter on the roof of the car before he shot an inquiring, somewhat mocking glance at Regan. "Okay if we go now?"

"Of course!" She was bewildered by his purposeful resolve to get to Houston just as soon as he could. As he steered the car back out onto the highway, looking relieved to be on his way again, Regan affirmed what she had long suspected about Casey McKeever: He was a powerful opponent who liked to come out the victor in every endeavor.

Of course, she reminded herself, he hadn't invited Regan on this trip in the first place. That had been Charley's doing, and Casey's moodiness might well be resentment at having her company foisted off on him. That thought, more than the weather, had the effect of dampening her already uncertain spirits.

The rain drizzled steadily on them all the way to the coast. Once in Houston, Casey dropped Regan off at his parents' estate, not even bothering to come inside himself, and he spent most of the afternoon downtown.

Elizabeth McKeever shared a scrumptious light luncheon of fresh fruit salad with Regan and saw her settled into a comfortably elegant guest room upstairs before setting off to visit her own hairstylist. Regan's bedroom was a virtual flower garden with its soft pastel hues and the vases of fresh-cut pink and yellow roses scattered about the room. Best of all, the sunken tub in the bathroom sported a whirlpool that went a long way toward soothing her tight muscles as she soaked in it for an hour.

That evening before dinner when Casey called her into his father's study and presented her with the papers for the sale of her Bowie's Landing property, she developed a sudden strong hunch that this was the urgent project he had been involved in all afternoon. Indeed, it could even explain his business at the Springer courthouse that morning. He showed her a cashier's check made out to her for an incredibly large amount, and suggested that he have his bank transfer the money to hers, to avoid carrying such a sum with them back to the lake.

"Fine," she mumbled, in virtual shock at the enormity of the cash payment and the speed with which Casey had arranged the whole thing. He showed her where to sign, and she affixed her signature on duplicate and triplicate forms until her hand developed writer's cramp.

"Casey?" She looked up suddenly. "Who is this man who's buying my cabin?" She searched the contract again. "This A.W. Fisher. You said he was a relative of someone in Bowie's Landing. I've never heard of any Fishers—"

"Actually," Casey explained, "he's acting as agent for the party who is buying your place. Fisher's a real estate broker. The new owner has some tentative plans to build an executive lodge for a large corporation to use as a weekend retreat for the staff."

Casey whipped the papers away from her and it wasn't until much later that she realized she still didn't know who had bought the cabin.

The rain continued intermittently all evening, a hot steamy mist that dripped off the eaves of the McKeever mansion onto the flagstone terrace and formed a screen to blur Regan's view of the beautifully landscaped grounds. Charles and Elizabeth had gone out for the night to an engagement they couldn't avoid. Regan stood at the windows in the den and gazed out at the wet dusk, while behind her Charley mixed a pitcher of drinks at the bar.

"I still think we should have gone to the Astros game." Casey sat back comfortably on one of the coral-and-yellow couches. "It's a shame that Regan's never been to the domed stadium. She may not be a baseball fan, but visiting the Astrodome is quite an experience in itself."

"You're right," Charley responded amiably. "Bring her back next weekend and take her to the 'Dome. I'll have Dad reserve the company box for you. But tonight I want to talk to you."

"Seriously?" At Charley's nod, Casey laughed. It seemed to Regan that his mood had lifted radically just since she had signed away her property, and she wondered if she had only imagined that he wanted so badly for her to sell it. "I hate to disillusion you, big brother," he joked now, "but I know all about sex."

Charley didn't smile. He met Regan's eyes when she turned from the window and glanced his way nervously. Casey intercepted the sober look that passed between them and his smile faded, replaced by a slight frown. The frown deepened when Regan asked, "Do you want me to leave, Charley?"

While Charley hesitated, Casey demanded, "Why should she leave? What do you want to talk to me about?"

For once Charley was at a loss for words, his usually glib tongue tied. He delayed a moment by crossing the large splendidly furnished room to deliver a slender-stemmed glass to Regan and another to Casey. Resuming his protected stance behind the bar, he took a swallow of his own daiquiri. "I need to talk to you about"—he visibly steeled himself to say the name—"Tiffany."

"Tiffany?" Casey repeated.

"Tiffany St. James."

"I presumed that was the Tiffany you meant," Casey said wryly. He held the glass up and stared through it intently for a moment as if fascinated by the frosty liquid. In one swift move, he brought the rim to his lips, downed its entire contents without pausing, and reached over to set it on the walnut tea table beside the sofa. "Well? What's the latest news about Tiffany?" His voice was low and perfectly calm.

Clearly dreading the discussion to come, Charley came around the bar and sat down opposite Casey. "I got a letter from Tiffany a month or so ago in which she asked about everyone—you in particular. She mentioned that she was planning to make a trip to the United States soon and would like to come for a visit."

Scarcely breathing, Regan watched from the window as Charley talked and Casey listened, his lean dark face impassive. "Go on," Casey ordered his brother.

"Tiffany knew your birthday was coming up. She said she would like to be here to help celebrate it, to surprise you." Charley leaned forward, elbows on his knees, to assure Casey, "I didn't answer the letter. Quite frankly, I was shocked to hear from her after all this time. I had no intention of inviting her to come here at all, much less for your birthday. But she called from New York last week. She talked to Dad one evening and invited herself. You know how he is—super-polite and kindhearted. And realistically I'm not sure I could have withstood her charm when Tiffany started pouring it on thick. So she's coming tomorrow night. Hell, she may arrive before then! I don't know when to expect her. Anyway, I'm sorry, and so is Dad. It won't help much, but he feels rotten."

Casey had been watching the floor between his and Charley's feet, but he suddenly raised opaque eyes to meet Charley's apologetic ones. "That's it? Just that Tiffany's coming?"

"*Just* that she's coming?" Charley asked ironically. "You don't sound upset at all."

Shrugging, Casey said, "I certainly am curious. Why were you so secretive about the whole thing?" His eyes slid over to Regan, who had come to lean on her elbows over the back of the sofa next to Charley. "And you, Regan. Just exactly what do you know about Tiffany?"

"M-me?" she stammered in surprise.

Charley came to Regan's rescue. "She doesn't know anything except what I've told her. I said an old friend was coming that you might not be too pleased to see." He cleared his throat. "I told her it would help if she came, too—just to let Tiffany know you haven't exactly been pining away since she's been gone."

"Ahh!" Casey breathed. "I see. And Regan agreed to pretend to be my date so my pride would be spared." He gave her a long look. "You're very kind to be so concerned about me."

She straightened, alarmed at the direction his thoughts were taking. "That's not exactly why I came. I told you, I enjoy the Houston Ballet tremendously."

"Yes, you told me." Casey's voice registered cold skepticism. He speared Regan with hard gray eyes. "Tell me the truth," he commanded. "Did you honestly come here just to see the ballet, or was there another reason?"

Drawing in her breath, she knew she had no choice but to tell him the truth. "There was another reason," she admitted in a small voice.

"Did that other reason have anything to do with Tiffany St. James?"

She bit her lip and nodded.

Sheer fury darkened Casey's face, flaring his nostrils and turning his mouth into a thin line. A muscle jerked convulsively in his cheek and his hands clenched and unclenched. When at last he spoke, he bit out the words with a rage that made Regan flinch. "I would have thought you'd understand by now that I don't need any favors from you, Regan!"

In a rush Regan remembered other times Casey had made it clear he didn't want her help—small hints like his disapproval when she carried the parcel of papers to his car from his office, and unmistakable messages such as his edict when he was sick: "Do I have to spell it out for you? I don't want your motherly concern!"

A heavy weight settled on her chest, squeezing out the air and causing pain so intense that tears came to her eyes. "I understand now," she managed between shallow breaths. "I'm sorry it took me so long." Casey didn't want to be in her debt; he didn't want the intimacy that went along with accepting help from her.

"Well, I don't understand!" Charley exploded. "You're angry with Regan all out of proportion to the offense, yet you're not upset in the least that you're going to see Tiffany again. I'd like to know what's going on. I expected—" He stopped abruptly.

"You expected what?" Casey asked. "That I'd fall apart when I heard about Tiffany? Why the hell should I? Did you think I've been nursing a broken heart all these years?"

"Haven't you?" Charley's tone was kind. "Hasn't the subject of Tiffany St. James been taboo since you two split?"

Casey sat back and eyed his brother with cool amusement. "If she has been taboo, it's because you kept her that way. At first, I'll admit, I was reluctant to talk about what had happened, but later I discovered no one would mention her name, even when it would have been the obvious thing to do. Everyone went to great lengths to avoid referring to her."

"Wait a minute!" Charley protested. "Are you telling me that you haven't been supersensitive about the way she treated you?"

"This may surprise you, Charley, but Tiffany and I are on the best of terms. We've been in touch for some time."

Casey's calm announcement shocked Charley into momentary silence. Regan was glad that she was still holding on to the back of the sofa. Otherwise she might have collapsed in a heap on the Persian carpet when her knees turned to water and buckled beneath her.

"What do you mean, you've been in touch?" Charley's voice sounded strangled when he finally spoke.

"We've been corresponding for a year at least—ever since her divorce."

"Divorce?"

Charley uttered the word aloud, but Regan echoed it silently. Tiffany was no longer married? No longer safely out of circulation?

"That's right. Didn't you know she had divorced her husband?"

"No. No, I didn't!" Charley stood up and crossed over to the bar to refill his glass. He didn't look pleased. "She's been divorced a year?"

Casey nodded.

"And the two of you have been in touch all this time? Mind if I ask who renewed the relationship?"

Casey answered smoothly, "I don't mind at all. Tiffany wrote me a letter and I answered it."

"What was her purpose in starting up with you again?"

"What the hell kind of question is that?" Casey snapped.

"I'm sorry. I only meant—wasn't it a little late for her to be pursuing you, so many years after she dumped you unceremoniously?"

For the second time in five minutes Regan watched Casey flush with anger. One hand, resting on his thigh, doubled into a fist that was white with restraint. She sensed that he would have reacted swiftly and aggressively, had he not been forced because of his physical handicap to sit and wait out his frustration. "Tiffany isn't pursuing me," he managed after a moment, and his voice shook with fury. "She just thought we should resume our friendship. It was a nice gesture."

"Very nice, indeed," Charley muttered with acid sarcasm. "Come off it, Casey. Don't be naive. If friendship is what Tiffany wants, why did she wait until she got rid of her husband to write you?"

Casey held his tongue, although Regan recognized the cost to his iron self-control. "You've never liked Tiffany, have you, Charley?" he asked quietly after a moment. "Even when we were kids, you ignored her. I used to wonder why."

"I can answer that for you. Because even as a kid she was the biggest snob I've ever known. You used to agree with me about that, even if you did love her."

"She was shy."

Charley raised a hand in protest. "Spare me, Casey. You go ahead and remember her however you want to. Heaven forbid that I should shatter your beautiful memories. If you honestly think she's after your friendship, then you've dreamed up a totally different Tiffany St. James from the one I knew."

"Okay, drop it," Casey said in a deadly soft voice. "I don't want to hear any more."

Looking back and forth from brother to brother Regan longed to cover her ears with her hands to shut out the tense bickering. Casey had cut her deeply by rejecting once and for all any help from her. Now, on top of that, she had to struggle with the knowledge that Tiffany had been very much a part of his life the past year. In fact, Casey was defending his former girl friend as if perhaps there was still a special relationship between them. It was a frightening possibility that Regan wanted to escape. She pushed a lock of dark hair back from her temple and edged toward the door as Casey and Charley glared at each other.

She would have made it, she thought later, if the doorway hadn't suddenly been blocked by the petite figure of a fair-skinned young woman whose chic blonde hair and cream-colored silk evening pants and tunic made her look as if she had just stepped off the pages of *Vogue*. Enormous cornflower-blue eyes raked over Regan and dismissed her before sweeping the room almost possessively. They inspected Charley with speculation and focused with unconcealed pleasure on Casey's handsome profile. It didn't take the woman's

British-accented greeting to tell Regan that the much-discussed Tiffany had arrived.

"Casey, *darling!*" she said theatrically.

Casey turned his head and stared at Tiffany for a long moment. Even though she tried desperately to interpret the expression on his face, Regan knew she was seeing a mask—that Casey wouldn't allow anyone to know what he was thinking. Tiffany was trying to read him, too, Regan thought. The lovely fragile-looking blonde seemed to be devouring him with her eyes, as if she couldn't get enough of him.

"Casey?" Tiffany begged. "Can't you speak? Aren't you even a little bit happy to see me?"

The smile he finally gave her was lazy. His eyes flicked to Regan, who watched the reunion with sinking heart; then returned to travel slowly over Tiffany's sophisticated form. "Of course I'm glad to see you. You're more beautiful than ever, Tiffany. Not that I would have expected any less," he murmured, and Tiffany beamed at him.

Turning her charm on the orthopedic surgeon, she drawled, "Hello, Charley. It's been a long time."

Charley rose and busied himself mixing another pitcher of daiquiris. "Yes, it has. Let's see, what was it—fifteen years ago that you shafted Casey?" He raised his eyes just in time to see Tiffany color faintly.

"Charley!" Casey's voice was sharp.

"Sorry," Charley said as he poured out fresh drinks in crystal goblets. "I could have sworn you just implied you weren't sensitive about how Tiffany treated you."

Casey's narrowed eyes studied Charley icily before he turned his attention back to Tiffany and gave her a lopsided grin. "You'll have to pardon Charley. He gets in one of these foul moods every time his surgery schedule gets a little overloaded." Waving a hand at the other couch, he said, "Sit down and tell me how you are."

"Do I have to sit way over there?" Tiffany asked with an appealing wistfulness.

"By all means, sit here." He patted the empty sofa beside him.

"I can't quite believe I'm really here in this house with you again after all these years," Tiffany sighed, sitting next to him and gazing up at him with delight.

"Casey, shouldn't you introduce the ladies?" Charley interrupted their intimacy brusquely. "Never mind, let me. Regan, I'd like you to meet an old family friend, Tiffany St. James. No, wait—St. James wouldn't be your last name anymore, would it? You're married."

"Divorced," she corrected him tightly.

"Indeed?" Charley raised an eyebrow in pretended surprise. "What's your name?"

"St. James." With so many eyes focused questioningly on her, Tiffany must have felt obliged to explain. "I've resumed use of my maiden name." She shrugged. "We had no children." Her expression added the heartfelt comment, "Thank heaven!"

Charley let the silence stretch a moment before he continued. "Well, Regan, as you've just heard, this is Tiffany St. James. Tiffany, our beautiful young friend is Regan Allison. Regan is Casey's date for the weekend."

Both Casey and Tiffany looked startled by the announcement. Even though she knew Charley meant well, Regan nearly groaned aloud.

"Casey, darling, I was hoping to have you all to myself. Do you mean I have to share you with this . . . this *child*?"

Child! Regan drew her breath in quickly and straightened under Casey's sudden curious gaze. He gave her a long thoughtful stare, as if he were really seeing her for the first time. Enjoying her rancor, he let his eyes slide from the top of her head, with its mane of thick dark hair, down her simple mint-green blouse and skirt, along her suntanned legs to her sandaled feet. Regan suffered under his look, chewing the inside of her lip when she realized he must be comparing her with the exquisite Tiffany, but she stood with rigid dignity and her eyes didn't falter.

Charley abandoned the drinks to come around to Regan and encircle her with his arm. "This child, as you call her, is a special-education teacher. She's a fantastic asset to Bowie's Landing, and Casey was smart enough to hire her."

"A teacher?" Tiffany echoed lightly. "How sweet." She was clearly not impressed. "But seriously, Casey, can't we have some time for just us? There's so much to talk about!"

Casey looked down into her face. Lovely blue eyes blinked up at him beseechingly. He glanced over at Charley and Regan. "It looks as if our talk is finished for tonight, Charley." His lips twisted cynically. "Maybe you'd like to reconsider and take Regan to the 'Dome after all?"

"I'd be delighted," Charley said, "but frankly, I'm tired. As you said, my schedule's been murder the past couple of weeks. I think I'll just stay right here and relax. How about you, Regan? Care to spend the evening here with me?"

She nodded at him, unable to answer aloud for the ache in her throat. Charley gripped her hand in a warm tight squeeze that conveyed his support before he turned back to Casey. "Sorry," he said, not sounding sorry in the least. "Looks like you and Tiffany will have to find someplace else for your rendezvous, unless you choose to share it with us." Still holding Regan's hand, he steered her over to the opposite couch and pulled her down beside him, as if they were settled in for the evening.

Charley had such an easygoing manner, it would be safe to assume he possessed none of Casey's iron will.

In reality, Regan realized, the agreeable warmhearted orthopedic surgeon could be just as steel-hard and unbending as his lawyer brother when he felt strongly about something.

Tiffany put her hand on Casey's cheek. "Let's go to my hotel where we can talk—just the two of us."

Not a one of them believed Tiffany was interested in talking to Casey. Regan's stomach gave a sickening lurch at the knowledge of what would happen if Casey went with the divorcée.

Light from the bronze Dutch chandelier overhead struck highlights in Casey's brown hair when he tilted his head a little in thought. After a moment, he reached for his crutches where they leaned against the sofa beside him. He got to his feet and fitted the crutch cuffs over the sleeves of his expensive brown sports jacket without speaking.

Tiffany, who had risen too, stood back to inspect him. "I've heard rumors—I keep up to date on gossip about you, darling—rumors that you get around so much better these days than you used to. I've been dying to see for myself."

It seemed a cruelly tactless thing to say to him, in Regan's opinion, and Charley must have agreed because she thought he was going to come up off the couch in fury. Unconsciously she placed her hand on his arm and pressed him down in the seat, watching the other two.

Casey gave Tiffany a hooded glance. "Did you just come here for a demonstration? To see if you made a mistake when you left?"

"Oh, Casey, no!" Tiffany sounded hurt. She put out her arms and hugged him, the top of her silky hair just brushing his chin. "I already know the answer to *that!*" When Casey said nothing, she tipped her head back to look at him. "Don't you want to know?"

He shrugged. "If you want to tell me." Casey wasn't

going to make a fool of himself over Tiffany twice.
That didn't mean, however, that he wasn't still in love
with her.

Nodding, Tiffany pressed her cheek against the front
of his white shirt and murmured, her voice muffled,
"I've known for years that I shouldn't have left you.
You've haunted me ever since. It's been my one hope
that I could persuade you to forgive me for the hurt I
caused you. How terrified I've been that you'd fall in
love before I could see you again! You can't imagine
my relief in knowing you haven't—that you're still
free!"

Casey's gray eyes, hosting an odd expression, flicked
toward the pair seated on the couch and then back
down at the crown of Tiffany's head. "What about
your husband?"

"Stan—Stanislaus never stood a chance against you,
darling. I used to tell you you were a finer person than
any I knew, remember? Well, the same is true now.
You're a finer man than my husband ever dreamed of
being. It always infuriated him to realize I compared
him to you and found him sadly deficient."

Casey's lips twisted as he looked down at his crutches.
"I can see how it would upset him, losing out to me."

"It did upset him." Missing the irony in Casey's
voice, Tiffany nodded emphatically. "But I don't want
to spend the night talking about my ex-husband. I can't
wait to get you alone, darling, so we can *really* talk!
There's so much I have to say to you."

Casey glanced at Regan and Charley one last time. "I
hope you'll excuse me, Regan. I'm sorry to break our
date." He smiled meaningfully, his eyes hard.

At the door, he paused and glanced down at Tiffany,
who had watched his steps keenly. "Well?" Regan
heard him ask in a low voice. "Do I pass?"

She didn't hear Tiffany's soft reply. The slender-
framed young woman with the breathtakingly delicate

beauty embraced Casey in another dramatic hug, reaching up to pull his dark head down and kiss him long and fervently on the mouth.

A moment later, Regan and Charley sat staring at the empty doorway where Casey and Tiffany had disappeared. As the front door slammed off in the distance, tears built up behind Regan's eyelids, threatening to spill and run down her cheeks. Charley let his breath out in a long sigh, as if he'd been holding it in for some time.

"Well," he said, his voice flat with disappointment. "She won the first round."

"I didn't help much." Regan hated the way her voice quivered, betraying the depth of her feeling. She swallowed hard. "I'm sorry, Charley."

Wrapping an arm around her shoulder, the surgeon pulled her against him and squeezed gently. "Hey, Regan, don't look like that. It's not your fault, for heaven's sake! You tried."

"Not hard enough!" she cried in anguish, and the tears began to fall. "N-Neva would have done more. She might have been able to persuade Casey not to go off with that—that witch!"

Blotting the tears from Regan's eyes with his clean white handkerchief, Charley wore a bemused expression. "Neva? Why would Casey choose to stay for her and not for you?"

"B-because he cares about Neva," Regan sobbed. "For that matter, he cares about Peggy! Oh, I wish she were here! She would have stopped him!"

"Regan," Charley addressed her quizzically, tilting her face back with his knuckles so he could study her, "don't you think Casey cares about you at least as much as he does about Neva or Peggy?"

Her laugh had a slightly hysterical quality. "You've got to be kidding! I'm not a person to Casey—I'm a special-education teacher, someone he hired to do a job. Oh, it's an important job, and he cares very much that it's done right, and that I don't get—get murdered or become so downright miserable that I quit—but care about *me?* Sometimes I think he cares about everyone in Bowie's Landing except me!'' The bitterness in her own voice frightened Regan. She clamped shut her mouth and wiped the tears from her eyes with one hand, wishing she hadn't revealed to Charley how much it hurt that Casey didn't care at all.

But Charley, looking thoughtful and sympathetic, didn't ask any more questions of Regan. He held her hand for a few minutes, and then he got up to bring her one of the drinks they had forgotten earlier. Charley and Regan spent the eve of Casey's birthday getting blessedly and quietly drunk.

Chapter Sixteen

From the sidelines Regan surveyed the noisy crowd drifting back and forth between living room and den and told herself sternly that if she wasn't having a good time, it certainly wasn't the fault of Charles and Elizabeth or Charley McKeever. The perfect hosts, the three had gone to great lengths to treat her as an honored guest all evening at Casey's party, despite the fact that Casey himself was blatantly ignoring her.

He had ignored her, in fact, from the time he'd returned home at noon that day. He gave no excuse for having been out all night. His mood had been flippantly casual when he greeted his family and the friends who had arrived from Dallas by private jet that morning, but not once had he so much as looked at Regan, much less spoken to her.

Regan was somewhat amused at the McKeevers' version of "a few close friends." By the time they departed for the music hall at seven, an entourage of limousines lined the long private drive, and most of them pulled in behind Charles McKeever's chauffeur-driven Rolls-Royce for the ten-minute trek downtown. Regan went with Charley in his Porsche, which followed Casey's gleaming silver automobile until it swooped out of the caravan and up to the entrance of the stately white Warwick Hotel, where Tiffany was staying. When Regan saw Casey next, in the enormous glittering foyer of Jesse Jones Hall, Tiffany's hand rested possessively on the dark sleeve of his tuxedo.

Because it was opening night of the ballet, the crowd was huge, with press and photographers very much in evidence. Flashbulbs blinked around the McKeever party as reporters recognized the elite members of Houston society.

Sensing Regan's unhappiness, Charley stuck close to her, his arm as often as not draped over her shoulder in what she knew to be a brotherly gesture. But although several others in the group eyed Regan and Charley with speculation, Casey kept his gray eyes averted. During the performance, Charley and Regan had the misfortune to sit directly behind Casey. From that vantage point, Regan was painfully aware every time Tiffany looked at him, every time she touched his arm. Regan would have preferred not to see his dark head bent near Tiffany's blond one as he listened to her whispered comments in the darkened theater. Regan had begun wishing on Friday night that she had not come to Houston. Saturday evening, watching the beautiful dancers acting out Prokofiev's haunting tale of Romeo and Juliet, she wondered with a lump of tears lodged firmly in her throat how she could manage to make it through the rest of the performance, much less the party to come.

The dinner afterward was scarcely more pleasant, although Regan was mercifully placed at the other end of the long oak table from Casey. It wasn't until later that Charley left her unattended when he talked shop with several of his doctor friends. Regan thought she might not have minded so much the awful time she was having if Casey hadn't appeared to be having such a good time. Of course, it was *his* party, and these were *his* friends, but still it hurt to feel so alone when she could see him surrounded by congenial guests, laughing more than she had ever seen him laugh before.

What hurt perhaps most of all was the way in which, when he was opening his birthday presents, he hesitated when he came to the small flat gift from Regan and then shoved it aside without opening it. Regan had pondered for days before giving in to a sentimental whim and buying him an eight-track tape recording of the singer whose concert they had attended together. It had been a foolish purchase, one that revealed more than she would have liked how she cherished that memory, and now he was rejecting it sight unseen. Probably no one but Regan noticed the gesture that told her plainly he didn't want anything from her.

"I understand you teach school in Bowie's Landing, Miss Allison."

The expensively tailored banker, who had been introduced to Regan as a close friend of Casey's from his college days, interrupted her reverie when he joined her near the windows that led to the terrace. There were two wine glasses in his hands, and he held one out to her.

"Thanks," she said as she accepted it. "Yes, I teach."

"Umm...." he said, sipping his wine. "Was it my imagination or did I actually hear someone say you live with Casey?" The man—his name was Bill Westmoreland—wasn't especially handsome, but he carried himself like a person who knew his own worth. Since he was president of one of Houston's biggest banks, she supposed his self-confidence was justified, but she hoped this wasn't going to be a come-on. He had arrived at the party with a beautiful woman Regan presumed to be his wife.

"I live at his lake house," she acknowledged reluctantly. "With Katy. You know Katy?"

"I know Katy." He grinned boyishly, revealing slightly uneven front teeth. His blondish brown hair was starting to thin in front, and to his credit he made no attempt to hide the fact. "Katy can be a great ally."

"You sound as if she might also be stout opposition."

"I suspect she can be if she wants to. Luckily, I've never had to find out. In all the years I've known Katy, she's never so much as spanked my hand. She seems to approve of everything I do." His quick brown eyes locked with Regan's. "Can you guess why?"

Regan shook her head. If he was fishing for a compliment from her, he would be disappointed.

"Because I'm Casey's friend." Bill's answer surprised Regan. "You might call it innocence by association. It has nothing whatsoever to do with my own good character, although Katy has a way of ferreting out those acquaintances of Casey's who like him for himself, and the ones who just want to hang out with money. I suppose you and Katy get along all right?"

Regan bent her head and studied her wine. So he was curious about her relationship with Casey! "We get along fine," she murmured, her lips curving in spite of herself. "I have no interest in Casey's money, and Casey has no interest in me."

Bill turned to glance across the room at Casey, who sat talking to a regal-looking white-haired lady. Tiffany St. James was perched on the arm of the sofa next to Casey, her hand on his shoulder, leaving little doubt that she had assumed her former position in his life.

"Uh-huh." Bill's face was mildly puzzled. "It would certainly appear that his interest is engaged elsewhere, but one thing I've learned is that with Casey appearances are deceiving. He's damned good at hiding his feelings."

Regan had heard all this before. "If you want to know where his true interest lies," she suggested dryly, "why don't you ask him? Or do you just like to play amateur detective?"

"How'd you guess?" Bill grinned again, and Regan

thought she liked this shrewd, nosy, honest man. "Playing detective makes me feel macho, like Casey. He has a reputation among the women—so my wife tells me—as a Byronic type: moody, tragic but strong, and totally out of reach. You should have heard all the rumors that circulated in college about why he didn't date. I knew him four years at the University of Texas, and he didn't date at all. He studied like a man obsessed and graduated summa cum laude with Phi Beta Kappa and every other honor you can name. Everyone was consumed with curiosity. We all suspected there was a Tiffany St. James lurking somewhere in his past, but we never knew for sure, because Casey kept us all at arm's length." Bill looked at Regan and shook his head. "And you wonder why I don't ask him where his interest lies! We're good friends, but Casey would no more tell me now than he would have told me fifteen years ago about Tiffany. He never parades his weaknesses in front of others."

Nodding absently, Regan thought she knew only too well how proud Casey was, and how independent.

"So," Bill said, "Charley's not so aloof. Maybe I'll ask him who *he's* interested in." A twinkle in his eyes told Regan he was teasing her now.

"Do that." She smiled back at him. "I can save you the time, though. Her name's Peggy Dunivan, and she'd be here tonight if she could."

"Ah, yes, Peggy!"

"Ah, yes!"

When Bill's wife beckoned him away a moment later, Regan slipped out unnoticed through the French window onto the dark terrace. An afternoon shower had left the air fresh and clean. She could smell the heavy-boughed magnolia trees that grew up against the house, and crickets chirped a loud symphony that drowned out the party sounds inside. Regan felt her way to the balustrade edging the flagstone patio and, making sure it was clean and dry, sat down on the cool top of the low wall. It would be a shame to ruin her slinky white silk dress by sitting in a puddle of rainwater. She remembered the excitement she had felt when she packed the lovely gown. Never having had an opportunity to wear it for Casey, she had hoped to inspire his admiration tonight. Instead, she doubted if he had even noticed what she was wearing, so engrossed had he been in Tiffany and his old friends.

Through the thick trees she could see lights from the neighboring estates, and the sound of Ciao barking drifted up to her from the kennels behind the garage. *Ciao, you devil,* she thought, *I wish I'd never seen you or Casey!*

The seclusion of the darkness was a relief to her; she was weary with the effort of hiding her pain. Her mouth hurt from smiling when she wanted to cry. Here in the warm night she could let go and stop pretending for a while until Charley, acting like her protective big brother, sought her out and made her come back to the party.

Lost in thought Regan jumped when the windows opened to fan light onto the stones at her feet. She was shocked to see Casey and Tiffany framed in the opening, shadowed silhouettes recognizable only by Casey's crutches.

Although the light didn't quite reach her, Regan shrank back, terrified of being discovered, hardly breathing. The other two stood in silence until Tiffany turned and implored in dulcet tones, "Please, Casey!"

Casey's response was low and reasonable. "I'm sorry, Tiffany, but I can't."

"Why not? You're free, aren't you? Do you have to answer to someone for your nights? To your young school teacher, for instance?"

"No," he said. "I answer to myself. And she's not *my* young school teacher, so I wish you'd stop referring to her that way. I can't go with you because I have some business to go over with Dad in the morning."

"Then tell me," she asked restlessly, "do you have any regrets about last night?"

Casey didn't answer at once, and Regan held her breath, more than half afraid to learn what had gone on between them. "I suppose my only regret," he said at last, "is that I didn't see you again a long time ago. I've wasted too many years."

In her sorrow Regan released her breath on a tiny hiccuping sob that caused Casey and Tiffany to whirl and peer into the darkness beyond their sphere of light. "Who's there?" Casey asked sharply.

For a brief hysterical moment Regan considered running away, but she knew she couldn't make it. The unfamiliar turf held too many unseen obstacles on a dark night like this. She gritted her teeth until her jaws ached and rose from her seat on the balustrade to step forward.

"Regan!" Casey's displeasure was evident in his surprised exclamation, but she couldn't see his face because of the light at his back. "What are you doing out here?"

"Can't you guess, darling?" Tiffany drawled. "She's been eavesdropping. I'll bet she's just dying to know all about our night together."

"You forget." Regan's words were quiet. "I was here first. You intruded on me."

"That's right," Casey agreed. "Regan has no interest in what you and I do, Tiffany. Why should she eavesdrop?"

"You think not? Casey, my innocent, you're deceiving yourself if you think Regan's not interested in you. I knew the first time I saw her that the poor child was in love with you." Regan heard the words with a numb kind of horror, praying silently that the earth would open up and swallow her. "Naturally, it's a shame to hurt her, but she has to find out about last night—that you stayed at my hotel—that we made such beautiful love." The small delicate shadow turned and put her arm around Casey's taller, sturdier form. "After missing you so dreadfully all these years, Casey, I'll never let you get away from me again!"

Regan listened stonily, hearing what she had been so afraid to hear. Casey had made love to Tiffany. She had won him back as surely as if the past fifteen years had been erased and they were eighteen years old again. Tiffany, who had once discarded Casey because he was handicapped, had finally learned what Regan knew— that his handicap didn't matter, that he was a man, strong and masculine, capable of arousing a passionate response in her by his very touch. He had chosen Tiffany; and Regan, who needed his love so badly, would never feel the pleasure and sweet pain of his body joined with hers.

"Tiffany." Casey raised his head and held off the elegant divorcée. "You've made a mistake about Regan. What she feels for me is pity, not love. She doesn't even like me. I'm old—eleven years older than Regan— and my handicap isn't one that can be easily overlooked. It's not very likely that a girl as young and beautiful as Regan would imagine herself in love with me, now is it? Have you forgotten how *you* felt at that age? You didn't want to be tied down to a man who couldn't dance or ride."

"Shh, Casey, shh!" Tiffany put her finger to his lips. "Don't remind me! I was young and foolish. I didn't realize how little those things matter—how small a portion of one's life one spends dancing."

"I want you to see how wrong you are about Regan. She's not in love with me now, and she never has been. Nor has she fancied herself in love with me. Have you, Regan?"

Regan's chest ached, but she managed to keep her face composed. "What difference does it make?"

"Deny it," Tiffany challenged her brutally. "I'd like to hear you deny that you love him. I've seen the way you look at him, like a lovesick schoolgirl. You'd fall all over him if he gave you the slightest encouragement, which he hasn't."

All I have left, Regan told herself as she stared at the silhouettes against the lighted doorway, *all I have left is my pride. I will not let her take that away from me!*

"I don't love him," she said in a deliberately cold voice. "He's right. I don't love him. Why on earth should I? He's too old for me and he's bossy and cranky and—and—"

"Crippled," Casey put in calmly.

Regan wanted to deny violently that his handicap had anything to do with her feelings, but she wondered suddenly, why? Why bother? Let him think what he wanted, as long as he didn't guess how much she loved him. With tears sliding down her cheeks, she added huskily, "And crippled. Now please, please, just leave me alone."

"Come along, darling," Tiffany urged. "The girl's rather unbalanced, I think. Let's go back inside and leave her to herself as she wants." She sounded smugly satisfied with Regan's answer.

Casey half turned to go so that the light struck one side of his face, revealing the remote expression Regan knew so well and the hard mouth with a tightly clenched look to it. He glanced back at her once, searching her face as if to be sure of something, and then he bent his head and went inside.

Chapter Seventeen

Candles on the altar and in recessed sconces along the walls provided dim light in the church when Regan stole in through the half-open door. She entered the last pew and dropped to her knees, bowing her head as the rest of the Sunday-evening congregation meditated silently. She pushed at a wing of dark hair on her temple and waited for the organ music to soothe her pounding heart. The youth choir sang in soft sopranos of hope and dawn.

Sighing, Regan sank back onto the seat for the rest of the service. There had been many times recently when she had doubted if there was anything worth seeing beyond the darkness of the present. The dawning of a new day no longer seemed full of promise, and she asked herself sometimes if she was destined to spend her life looking to the past.

In the last month she had learned to discipline herself, so that tonight she was able to concentrate on the words the minister spoke without letting her mind dwell on things it was best to forget. When the Reverend Mr. Tillman talked about the sanctity of marriage, Regan told herself that she would not covet someone else's husband, no matter how much she had loved him before he was married. *And I will not cry for myself,* she vowed. Feeling a glimmer of hope, she remembered that it had been weeks since she had shed a tear.

That first awful night when she had known Casey was lost to her, she had cried all the tears inside her, and her eyes had been dry ever since.

Regan allowed herself only one concession to what she considered her weakness, and that was to leave church before the benediction, so none of her neighbors had a chance to ask her about Casey. The idea of having to talk casually and objectively about him filled her with constant dread. She doubted if she would ever reach the point where she could think of him without pain, especially while she lived in his house. It was impossible for her to continue living there, when he would probably want to bring his bride home for a visit before long. But Casey, even from a distance, was adamant in insisting that she keep her end of the bargain and stay with Katy at the lake house.

She hadn't seen him since his birthday. To avoid having to make the return trip with him to Bowie's Landing, she had persuaded Charley to drive her back after the party. Several days after she left Houston, she had received a letter from Casey.

Dear Regan,

At the risk of seeming not to trust you, I'd like to remind you of our agreement that you will stay in my home for at least six months. Whether or not I benefit from keeping the lake house open, Katy will enjoy living there, so I'll hold you to your word. Remember, we shook hands on it. It seems to me that it will be best for all concerned if I stay away. Please tell Katy I'll be in touch with her.

The signature was a bold black slash on the heavy stationery.

He had been in contact with Katy by telephone on several occasions during the ensuing month. Once Regan had answered the phone, only to be told by an operator with a decided New York accent that there was a person-to-person long-distance call for Katy Danetz. Katy had confirmed later that it was Casey who had called, but she showed an unusual reluctance to volunteer any of his news. The idea occurred to Regan that Casey and Tiffany might already be honeymooning in Manhattan, and that Katy was hesitant to tell Regan.

She knew Casey had made at least one quick trip to Bowie's Landing before leaving for New York, although he hadn't come near his lake house. She had found out about it the previous week when she had driven out to the Cyperts', determined once and for all to persuade Michael that he should attend school in September.

When she reached the small frame house, Regan could only stare in astonishment at the changes in progress there. A crew of workmen were busy painting the outside walls a fresh white, and from the looks of it, a new roof had already been added. The porch had been repaired and a safe, sturdy ramp built with a slope gentle enough for a ten-year-old child to manage by himself. But the greatest transformation Regan saw was in Michael, who sat in his wheelchair out under a tree, eagerly chattering with the workmen.

"Miss Allison!" he exclaimed when he saw her drive up. "Look at our house! Isn't it beautiful?" His arms struggled with the wheels of his chair and maneuvered it closer to her.

"Absolutely beautiful, Michael!" she agreed as she got out of the car. The little boy's face had a healthy flush that made her think he had spent some time out in the sun lately. His arms seemed somewhat stronger than they had been the last time she saw him. "What's been going on around here, anyway?"

"Lots of things," he said expansively. "You should see what Tammy and my mom have been doing inside! It's gonna be the prettiest house in the whole world."

"I'm sure it is. You're looking good too, Mike. It's nice to see you outside."

"Oh, I come out all the time now. I can get up and down the ramp all by myself."

Could this grinning little imp with shining eyes be the same withdrawn child she'd tried to talk to before?

"You know something else, Miss Allison? I'm going to come to school in just—let's see, I forget, but I think it's only about thirteen or seventeen days. I'll be in your class, just like Tammy said. A bus will take me. It has a hytro—hydro—"

"Hydraulic?"

"Yeah! A hydraulic lift that will just pick me up—whoosh"—he motioned upward with his hands—"and put me inside."

"Is that right?" Regan's throat was full of tears. "How wonderful for you, Mike! I'll be glad to have you in my class. We'll have so much fun!"

"I know." He nodded, full of confidence. "I can't wait."

It wasn't until Tammy heard them talking and joined them outside that Regan learned the house repairs had resulted from an unexpected visit from Casey McKeever.

"It had been a really rotten day, Miss Allison," Tammy said. "Mike was just so—so down in the dumps, and Mom had been cross and tired that morning, and I was crying when he came. Feeling sorry for myself, I guess. He knocked on the door and came in and sat down to talk. I mean, we really talked! He asked me all about everything, and he was so nice, I just poured it all out. Spilled my guts. Maybe I shouldn't have." She bit her lip, worrying about it. "I don't think anyone's ever listened to me the way he did that day. He's just fantastic!" She smiled then, as if she couldn't suppress it. "Mike thinks so, too. He was in bed, acting stubborn as a mule, refusing to get up and do anything that day. Casey—" She blushed and corrected her mistake. "Mr. McKeever went into his bedroom and talked to Michael a long time, while I stood in the hall and listened." In spite of her blush, she looked rather defiant. "I'm glad I did! The things he told Mike— well, there's just no way Mom or I could have helped Mikey that way! Mr. McKeever knows exactly what kind of problems Mike has, and after seeing *him* get around so well, Mike's beginning to think the future might not be so bad. Mr. McKeever showed us his car and the hand controls, and promised Mike that he'll teach him to drive when he gets old enough. He invited us to come and swim in his pool. If he's there, he'll swim with us, he said. You can see Mike's happiness." She turned to look at her younger brother where he sat nearby, supervising the painters with gusty enthusiasm. "He's decided he can become anything he wants to be. Isn't it sort of like a miracle!"

Tammy showed Regan through the renovated interior of the house. Walls had been plastered and painted, and Tammy and Mrs. Cypert had sewn curtains and slipcovers for the furniture. "After he left here, Mr. McKeever went by and talked with my mother where she works, and told her how she could get a low-interest loan from some government agency to put the house in good shape. Mom was a little hard to convince, but he won her over when he pointed out that the electrical wiring was old and dangerous and Mike might be stuck inside in case of a fire. Anyhow," she concluded, "it wasn't long before things started happening. We've been working as hard as we can to make the place look nicer, and it's really lifted our spirits—all of ours. I can't thank you enough for sending Mr. McKeever. I think he's"—Tammy took a deep breath—"I think he's super." Her sky-blue eyes were full of hero worship.

Regan felt her chest constrict. *I know, I know,* she

echoed silently, but aloud she merely demurred, disclaiming any credit for Casey's intervention.

She herself had been helpless to remedy the Cyperts' dilemma. It had been Casey who had the knowledge and who had acted on behalf of the struggling family. What a shame for all the other residents of Bowie's Landing that they were to be deprived of Casey's able assistance, merely because he felt compelled to avoid Regan.

Now, absently chewing her lip, Regan didn't notice the sheriff's car parked next to her white VW in the church parking lot.

"Quarter for your thoughts."

She looked up quickly. "David! Hi!" She smiled across at him where he sat behind the steering wheel of the official vehicle, a streetlight overhead clarifying his features in the soft evening shadows. "I thought the going rate was a penny."

"Haven't you heard about inflation?" he joked.

"Seems like I have heard something or other about it."

"You should keep up with current events!"

"I should, shouldn't I?" She tried to be flippant, but her underlying sadness was too great, and she merely sounded wistful.

David studied her with a look of concern until Regan squirmed uncomfortably. "You know you've lost weight," he observed. "Your eyes are enormous." He shook his head. "You look like hell." And while she was still recovering from that: "I'd like to take you to a movie tonight."

"Your technique for asking is lousy, David."

Nodding, he tried again. "May I have the pleasure of your company this evening, Miss Allison? There's a good movie playing in Springer."

"What movie?"

"*King Kong Bites the Dust,* I believe."

Regan winced. "No, thanks."

"Come on, love. You look like you could use some recreation."

"That's recreation? It sounds more like punishment."

"Are you referring to the movie itself or to going out with me?"

"Dope! The movie, of course." She smiled at him, genuine fondness in her eyes. "Some other time, maybe. Sometime when I'm not so tired."

"You look tired, Regan, as if you're not getting enough sleep. Is anything in particular bothering you?"

"Whatever could be bothering me?" Her smile became as bright and as artificial as a clown's mask.

David gave her a long look and was quiet for a moment before he said, "Come with me tonight. It'll do you good. Help you forget."

"Forget what, David?" Her voice dared him to say it.

He sighed. "You know very well, Regan. I haven't forgotten why you were never really free to get involved with me. I'm aware that Casey's been in New York since a couple of days after his birthday, and that Tiffany's also in New York. Putting two and two together—"

"Are you sure that's where she is?"

"I've heard rumors."

"Can the sources be trusted?" she demanded, wanting to doubt the dreaded fact that she had suspected all along.

"I'd say so. Charley told Peg, and she told me."

Charley and Peg? It would be hard to question the reliability of that particular source.

She swallowed. "Did they say—has there been a wedding yet?"

He shook his head. "Not that I know of. Not between Casey and Tiffany, at any rate. But Charley and Peggy have finally set the date for theirs."

"They have!" The news took Regan by surprise. The last time she had talked to Peggy, the older girl had been despondent over what seemed to her to be an insoluble problem. The weekend of Casey's birthday, Charley had managed to avoid discussing the situation, and he hadn't been back to the lake for a visit since then.

"After all these years," David observed, "my big sister finally came to her senses and realized just what she would lose if Charley got tired of waiting. It must have scared her to death when she thought about it. She got up at midnight the other night and went tearing off to Houston without telling any of us where she was going. She tracked Charley down at the hospital—he'd been doing emergency surgery half the night—and proposed to him." He chuckled. "I'd give anything to have seen Charley's face. He probably would have married her on the spot if he hadn't been so exhausted. As it is, they decided to get married next weekend. Peggy wanted me to tell you you're invited to be her maid of honor, and to say thank you for everything."

"Thank you?" Regan echoed.

"She said you'd know what she means. Something about your advice being just what she needed to hear at just the right moment."

"Oh." Her eyes stung a little. "Oh, yes."

Peggy and Charley...getting married! Slowly a warm glow of happiness for them suffused Regan, intermingled with a regret that brought a haunted look to her wide green eyes.

"Look, Regan," David murmured. "Maybe this is an omen that there's hope for you yet. After all, a month ago I wouldn't have given two cents for the chances that those two would work out their differences, and now here they are, ready to live happily ever after. Don't *you* give up, okay?"

Chattering voices drew Regan's attention to the fact

that the service had been dismissed and the crowd was spilling out the door.

"Don't be an idiot, David!" she snapped, unable to soften her sharp tone. "Their marriage has absolutely no significance for my future. I'm thrilled for them, of course, but then I've always liked happy endings." She turned away. "I have to go now. Give Peg my best and tell her I wouldn't miss her wedding for the world." Jerking open her car door, she climbed inside and started the engine before David could answer. Driving away down the street, she felt strangely torn between joy for and envy of Charley McKeever and Peggy Dunivan.

Regan found it almost impossible to sleep that night, and sleep when it came to her was restless and dream-filled. In one of her dreams, she was confined to a wheelchair for some obscure reason and Casey, who walked without so much as a limp, was her constant companion. She knew she loved him, but she bickered with him constantly because he insisted on waiting on her and doing things she felt perfectly capable of doing for herself, taking away her cherished independence. When he got down on his knees and begged her to marry him, she laughed shrilly and slapped his face.

At that point she woke up and lay for a while, wide awake and staring through the dark at the ceiling, confused and sad. After an hour, when she still wasn't sleepy, she slid out of bed, drew the floor-length blue silk robe over her nightgown and stepped out onto her balcony.

A quarter moon hung, pale and delicate, over the lake. The wide expanse of Texas sky spattered with stars looked just as it had when she was a little girl. She was overcome with the same choked sensation that she'd had at the age of seven when she went outside at night and looked up to say her evening prayers. There was a pain in her chest that had no physical cause. A childish prayer slipped out through her sudden tears: "Dear God, please make the hurt go away!"

Bending her head and reaching up a hand to wipe her eyes, she saw it—a light in one of the downstairs rooms casting a straight yellow beam across the bricks on the patio. Sniffling, Regan studied the shaft of light with faint prickles of alarm before she decided that she must have forgotten to turn it off earlier tonight when she returned a book to the library.

It won't hurt to leave it on, she thought as she padded back through her bedroom to go downstairs, *but I'll never get to sleep at this rate, so I may as well get something to read in bed.* Not wanting to disturb Katy, Regan tiptoed in her bare feet through the foyer to the hall and turned the brass doorknob carefully, pushing open the heavy library door without a whisper of a sound in the big sleeping house.

She halted abruptly in the doorway. Casey McKeever sat slumped in the swivel chair behind the desk, his head resting against the chair back and his eyes closed.

Chapter Eighteen

Regan's heart beat in erratic jerks while she struggled with the shock of seeing Casey. As if in a trance, she stood still and watched him silently and hungrily, devouring his features, aching to touch the brown hair that lay for once in disarray on his forehead. His cheeks had a leaner, sharper look than she remembered, as if he hadn't thought much of eating lately, and everything about him spoke of exhaustion. There were lines etched near his mouth, lines that she was sure hadn't been there the last time she saw him.

Regan knew she probably ought to leave, to shut the door quietly and go back to her room as if she hadn't seen him, but his appearance troubled her. She was concerned at the fact that he was here in the library in the middle of the night when David, and perhaps Katy, thought he was in New York. If he planned to stay, why didn't he go on to bed?

As she watched, Casey opened his eyes to stare up at the antique brass chandelier in the middle of the ceiling, his mouth grim, his throat tightening and relaxing as if he was swallowing with difficulty. With a sudden impatient gesture, his fist pounded on the chair arm and he lowered his eyes. It was then that he saw Regan in the doorway, still holding on to the doorknob. For just a second there was a look that might have been stunned pain in his eyes, and then it was gone. "What are you doing here, Regan?" he asked without moving.

She searched but could not find a trace of welcome in his face. Instead she saw extreme weariness and heard it in his voice, and it startled her. "I saw the light and came down to turn it off," she said. "Casey, what's the matter? You look ill."

He ran one hand through his hair and straightened in the chair, his wide square shoulders straining against the cream shirt with its brown-and-cream-striped silk tie. "Nothing's the matter." He sounded annoyed. "I'm just fine, thank you. What the hell are you doing, staring at me like that?"

"I didn't mean to stare. You look so... tired, you worried me. I thought you were in New York."

"I was. I just flew in to Houston tonight and drove straight here."

"Do you plan to stay long?" In attempting to sound casual, her words were downright stiff.

"No! You don't have to worry about that, Regan. I have no intention of making your life miserable around here. As a matter of fact, I'll be driving back to Houston as soon as I finish up some work I had to do." He motioned to an open folder in front of him on the desk.

"You just can't get away from me fast enough, can you?"

Casey opened his mouth, then shut it. He looked away from Regan and didn't answer.

"Don't you think I know," she went on, "that I'm the reason you don't want to come back here—that you don't want to be around me?" Casey turned brooding gray eyes on her again at that. "Do you honestly think that I'm going to let you sacrifice your beautiful lake house just so the poor special-education teacher will have a place to live? I know how much you love Bowie's Landing, Casey—not just the town but the people too—and I'm aware of how everyone here feels about you. I know what you did for the Cyperts—what you'd do for others if you lived here. If you imagine for one minute that I'm going to remain in your house and banish you to Houston or New York or anywhere else, then you're hallucinating. I'll move out tonight first!"

"Don't start that up again, Regan," he warned her. "I don't want to hear it."

"Well, that's just too bad, because you're going to hear it!" She shut the door and advanced into the room until she stood across the desk from him, green eyes snapping. "This time I mean it—I'll find the strength to make myself leave this house of yours. There are such things as apartments, if not in Bowie's Landing, then in Springer or some other town nearby. I'll find one."

"No!" His voice was quiet but firm. "I won't hear of it. You don't need to be out on your own. You need someone like Katy to take care of you."

Regan laughed without humor. "If anyone needs Katy, it's you. Look at you. You don't have the sense to see that you're killing yourself, working too hard, not eating properly, driving yourself to the breaking point!"

He raised his proud head and she saw bitterness in his eyes and in the straight line of his mouth. "I don't want to be mothered, Regan. I've managed to get by for thirty-three years and I can do very well now without your concern."

"Oh, yes, I forgot! You're the original Mr. Independence! 'No, thanks, Regan,'" she mimicked. "'I don't *want* your help. I don't *need* your help. Never mind what *you* need, Regan. *I* don't need *you!*'" She broke off, ashamed of her outburst. Casey was looking at her oddly, as if he saw but didn't quite understand the deep hurt beneath her scorn. She ran a shaky hand across her forehead.

"I wonder about Tiffany," she said after a minute. "What was she thinking of to let you make a trip like this—all this flying and driving back and forth. Don't you allow *her* to be concerned for you? I would have thought she'd have some objections to the trip, as your fiancée."

"As my what?"

"Your fiancée. I would have thought she'd at least come along to help with the driving, since you insist on breaking all kinds of speed records for cross-country travel. It surprises me, too, that you haven't considered how she feels about having me live here. Doesn't she have anything to say about it?"

"Oh, Tiffany had plenty to say about *that*," he agreed dryly. "Most of it was unprintable." Shaking his head, he murmured, "I must be hallucinating, as you suggested earlier. I could have sworn you just called her my fiancée."

"I did. Isn't that what she is?"

"No." His voice was cool. "She's not my lover, either, despite what you heard at the party."

The news stopped Regan. "If she's not your fiancée and not your lover, what is she exactly?"

Casey shrugged. "Just a friend."

"But— but Charley— Katy— David— everyone thinks—"

"I know what everyone thinks," he said curtly. "They're wrong. I haven't loved Tiffany in years. I stopped loving her at the same time I outgrew a lot of other teenage habits. Oh, I wasted a lot of time holding on to the pain, but I got over it long ago. I always knew she did the right thing by leaving. It would have been an awful mistake for both of us if she'd stayed. Seeing her again only made me realize how glad I was it ended when it did.''

Regan swallowed. ''But why did she tell me you had—had spent the night together? You could have set me straight! Why does Charley think the two of you have been in New York together all this time?''

He suddenly leaned back in the chair with a hint of a mocking smile. ''Shame on you, Miss Allison, for listening to gossip. It didn't occur to me that you were susceptible to unfounded rumors. The truth is Tiffany's been in New York and I've been in New York, but we haven't been together. She happened to come by my hotel one afternoon while I was talking to Charley on the telephone. I suppose he drew his own conclusions from that. As for why she tried to make you think we were lovers, I think she just wanted to upset you. I didn't bother to contradict her because I didn't think you cared whether or not we had slept together. Did you care?''

Regan dropped her gaze under Casey's scrutiny and stood with her head bent, her face shaded by a fall of dark hair over each cheek. When she didn't answer, he reached for his crutches and stood up to walk around the desk. He stopped beside her and, half sitting on the desk edge, put aside the crutches to touch her chin and tilt her head up. ''Regan?'' He was puzzled. ''Did Tiffany upset you?''

''Don't make me say it, please, Casey,'' she begged in a whisper.

''I have to know,'' he insisted. ''Tell me.''

Closing her eyes, she sighed and felt a tear trickle down her cheek. ''Yes, she upset me. What did you think the news would do? It convinced me she had won you back. I knew then I would never have a chance to make you love me.''

What a fool he must think her! What presumption—to think she'd ever had a chance! She had sworn she'd never let him see her love, yet here she was, blurting it out and crying at the same time, like the lovesick schoolgirl Tiffany had called her. She tried to turn her head away in shame, but Casey's hand cupped her face, holding it gently but firmly still.

"Casey," she babbled, her voice hoarse, "please don't hurt me anymore. You have to let me go. I can't stand it!"

When he didn't say anything, she opened her eyes and found him staring at her, his face just inches from hers, his brow knit with frown lines. "Am I hallucinating, Regan?" Disbelief clearly marked his features. "Did I misunderstand you, or did you really say you wanted to make me love you?"

A sob tore from her throat as she drew back from Casey. "Please! I've begged you not to make me say it! I can't bear it if you laugh at me for loving you."

"Laugh at you!" he repeated incredulously, and placed both hands on her upper arms to pull her closer. Holding her against his hard warm shoulder, he stroked her dark hair back from her temple, then traced the trail of a tear down her cheek with a brown finger. "I assure you, the last thing I'd do is laugh at you, my love. Have I really hurt you? I wanted to fix things so no one could ever hurt you! I've changed my will so that if anything happens to me, this house is yours."

"You have?" she gasped and felt him nod. "Casey!" She pulled back to look at him in astonishment. "You can't give me your grandfather's home!"

There was a totally out-of-character tenderness in Casey's gray eyes that softened the steel. For once his mouth didn't look hard. "Why can't I?" he demanded. "I've wanted to give you so much and I've been afraid to. I was terrified that you'd walk out of here before I could convince you to stay permanently. The greatest pleasure of being rich, you know, is sharing what you have with the one you love."

"The one you love?" She felt weak. "I thought you loved Tiffany or Neva or—or Holly Bridges at the very least."

He shook his head. "For a smart teacher you sometimes neglect to use your brain," he chided, but there was no sting to his words. "I was certain any half-witted observer could see the way I felt about you, although God knows I tried not to show it."

Unable to tear her eyes away from Casey's sunbrowned face, Regan let her breath out on a trembling sigh, finding it hard to believe this was really happening. "Well, you had *me* convinced you didn't care a thing about me!" Her voice was shaky and mildly reproachful. A shadow darkened her face as she remembered the bittersweet summer that was almost over. "Every time I tried to get close to you, you pushed me away. Every time I thought you needed my help, you cut me to shreds for so much as offering."

"Ah, Regan." Casey bent his head and pressed his forehead against hers for a minute, staring down at his feet. "I've had a long time to adjust to my handicap, and most of the time I think I cope pretty well with the frustrations. When I met you, though, I started resenting all over again the things I can't do. Every time you offered to help, it reminded me that I need more help than David or Charley...."

"Casey, everyone needs help sometime."

"I know, I know. But I didn't want your help. That time I was sick, when I woke up and realized you were really there in my bedroom with me—that you weren't just a product of my wishful thinking—I said anything that came to mind. In my fever-inspired logic, it seemed that it would almost be better to have you hate me than feel sorry for me. I felt so damned helpless, sick in bed like that with you nursing me. I hated myself because I *wanted* you to go on holding my hand, stroking my forehead. Yet I didn't want your pity, and it looked as if that was all you were giving me."

"No, Casey," she denied it. "Never pity."

He looked at her, obviously still doubtful. "Oh, God, can I really believe you don't pity me? You can be so tenderhearted, Regan, and so compassionate, but I don't want your help or your pity. All I ever wanted from you was your love. I wanted to hold you in my arms and dance with you as David did. More than anything, I wanted to sweep you up and carry you to my bed." He raked his eyes over her tall slender figure in the blue silk nightgown and grinned at her sheepishly. "I had wonderful, wicked dreams about us, Regan. Sometimes it was all I could do to keep my hands off you—to keep from giving myself away completely—and I got so frustrated I could only snap at you. Don't you think I despise the arrogant grouch I become whenever you're around? I tried so hard for so long to keep away from you for sheer self-protection. But, Regan, you've got to believe I never meant to hurt you!"

While she leaned comfortingly close against him, her body very much aware of the hard contact between them, wide green eyes gazed for a long time into smoky ones. "I do believe you, Casey," she said at last. "Now I want you to believe me when I say I haven't felt an ounce of pity for you since the week after I discovered your handicap. You have so much to offer the world, and you offer it so easily—your mind, your friendship, your ability to help people. You go everywhere you want and do just about anything you want. Besides"—she made a face—"it was pretty obvious that a man with as many women chasing him as you had certainly didn't need my pity."

She remembered suddenly the picture she had seen in the photo album. "There's something I want to do with you, Casey." Before he knew what she had in mind, she had taken one of his hands and was tugging at him, urging him to his feet.

Sitting tautly still, he eyed her with mild alarm. "What are you doing?"

She reached for his other hand and pulled again. "Stand up," she ordered him, not answering his question, and when he hesitated, she added, "Trust me, Casey."

A moment later he stood facing her, smiling slightly at the tender way she held his arm to steady him. "I'm not going to fall," he informed her. "I can stand without the crutches, you know."

"I know. I just like to touch you," she admitted. Still gripping one of his hands, she flipped a switch on the built-in stereo in one wall of the bookcase and quiet music soared around them.

Regan looked startled. "That song sounds like—"

Casey nodded. "The tape you gave me. It's been to New York and back." He looked embarrassed. "Does it sound well-worn?"

"It sounds beautiful." She turned back toward him. "Now we can dance."

Regan lost track of time within his arms. She slid her hands up his chest and clasped them behind his neck, while he locked his together at the small of her back. Standing in one spot, the two of them held on fiercely to each other, never wanting to let go, swaying slightly to the gentle music. Like a potent drug, his proximity had an immediate effect on her, alerting her senses to the soft curling hair on the nape of his neck that invited her fingers to lose themselves in the thickness there ... the expression glinting in his eyes that she would never tire of seeing ... the male scent that was soap and fresh air and unconscious desire and some elusive spicy cologne all mixed up together ... the warm hard strength of him pressing against her....

Applying sudden tension to his neck, she pulled his head down to kiss him on the mouth, a kiss that she felt like an electric charge all the way to her toes. Her stomach fluttered as something came alive inside her—something she thought had died a month ago. "I've been wanting to do that for a long time," she gasped with satisfaction when she finally had to break off the kiss in order to breathe. Laying her head on his shoulder she sighed, "Dear God, I feel as if I've loved you forever!"

"No longer than I've loved you," he murmured in her ear.

"Have you loved me awhile? Really?" She couldn't hide her delight.

"For a very long while. Why do you think I went back to Houston last year rather than spend the summer here?"

"I often wondered. That had something to do with me?"

"It had everything to do with you!"

"But I'd only met you once!"

He nodded. "And I knew from that one meeting that I was doomed if I saw you again."

"Doomed?"

"To fall in love. To spend my life loving you."

"And that frightened you?"

"It scared the hell out of me."

She worried over that a minute and then demanded, "Is it so awful, Casey? Be honest."

"Well..." he drawled thoughtfully. "It has been a pretty rough year. Remember, we met in rather misleading circumstances—me in the pool and you on dry ground. Just when I thought how foxy you were—a real spitfire who didn't mind yelling at me—it dawned on me that you didn't know about my handicap. It was like a dash of cold water in my face. I didn't know whether I wanted you to find out or not, even though we obviously could never develop any kind of relationship if you didn't know *that* about me."

"So you ran."

"I wanted you to keep thinking of me with spirit rather than the compassion I've come to fear. I knew you'd find out eventually, and I didn't want to be around when it happened. Imagine my surprise when you showed up at the school-board meeting, still not realizing I was one of those disabled whose rights you were championing."

"You let me blunder around in the dark those first few times we met—wondering why we couldn't seem to get along!" she rebuked him. "Your handicap doesn't matter to me now, and it wouldn't have mattered then—especially not after I got to know you. I could shake you for being so sensitive!"

Instead of shaking him she snuggled closer against him letting the warm friction of their contact do all sorts of chaotic things to her pulse and respiration. Running her hands over his back, kissing his earlobe, she felt his answering response in the strong tremor that passed through him. From his ragged breathing she knew his own vital signs were acting up. His arms tightened, and she felt safe and loved as the seductive music swirled around them.

After he had calmed down a little, he drew back to see her better. "Are you sure you won't mind that we can't really dance?"

She shook her head vigorously. "As Tiffany said, one spends so little of one's life dancing, Casey. It won't bother me at all."

"Will it bother you that I can't pick you up and carry you to bed with me?"

Her lips curved as she lowered her lashes demurely. "All that matters is what happens when we're in bed."

Casey laughed, a hearty sound of genuine delight.

"And I can hardly wait for that! I have a feeling it will be well worth waiting for." As he hugged her again, his expression turned quizzical. "But haven't you heard the rumor that those of us with physical disabilities are also sex cripples?"

Regan stiffened. "Let's get one thing straight, Casey McKeever," she said sternly. "You're not a cripple. I hate that word, and I don't want to hear it again!"

"Yes, ma'am," he answered, looking amused at her temper. "Tell me the truth," he insisted abruptly. "Aren't you the least bit worried about my performance in bed?"

"Should I be?" she countered.

Desire reflected in his suddenly clear gray eyes, he shook his head. "I don't think we'll have any problems there."

"I don't think so either. I have no use for outdated myths like that." Smiling playfully, she couldn't resist one last dig. "Anyway, I have it on the best authority—your own admission—that you're no monk!"

He grinned at the reminder. "I got my message across, did I?" His look intensified and he lowered his mouth to hers, warning her in a husky whisper, "I want you, Regan, more than I've ever wanted any woman." His kiss was hungry and demanding, his hands on her shoulders persuasive, and before very long Regan found herself clinging to Casey and shivering with her need.

When he finally managed to lift his head again, it was to take a deep shuddering breath, and then he pressed his face against her neck, nosing into her silky dark hair. "I want you in my bed," he said in a muffled voice. "I want you across the table from me every morning, and I want to come home to you at night. I want you to be the mother of my children—"

"Oh, Casey!" The very thought of it sent a tingle through her. "How many children will we have?"

"A girl, like you." His face was still buried in her hair, but he sounded more like himself, more nearly in control of his emotions than he had a moment earlier.

"And a boy, like you," she added. "That's two."

At that he straightened up, took another steadying breath and smiled at her. "Bless my soul, I believe the teacher can count!"

She ignored his affectionate teasing. "Is that right, Casey? Will we have two children?"

"If you want two, we'll have two. Between your teaching and my work and traveling back and forth to Houston, we may decide two is enough. But if you want a dozen, I'll do my best to oblige you."

Laughing softly, she assured him, "I think two sounds like a manageable number." She had surrendered herself to his firm embrace and was leaning against him, at long last daring to consider how heavenly it would be to bear Casey's children, when it dawned on her what he had said. "Casey!" she exclaimed and drew back with alarm. "How could we forget! Your work is in Houston, and mine is here! What will we do? I can't bear the thought of seeing you just on weekends!"

"Absolutely not," he agreed. "If I've learned anything from my brother, I've learned how hard it is to make a relationship like this work when the partners live a hundred miles apart. I don't even care to attempt anything like that."

"Then will I have to resign before I've started teaching? You worked so hard to hire a special-ed teacher—"

"And teach you shall."

Regan was comforted by Casey's calm tone, and the tangible reassurance of his hands on her waist. "For a long time I've wanted to make this my home all year long, as you must have guessed," he continued, "and I've been working toward that end. Dad and I believe the corporation would do well to develop a retreat on the lake for conferences—a place we can bring business associates and clients from Houston or out of state for meetings in a relaxed comfortable setting, and where I can get much of the legal paperwork done, the same as I'd be doing in my Houston office. For a while there it looked as if I'd have to scrap the idea"—he smiled wryly—"but now I think we can go ahead. The compound will include guest houses, and offices for me and a number of assistants and secretaries."

"This compound you're planning to build," Regan said suspiciously. "Just exactly where on the lake will it be?"

"Oh, down the road a little from here. Not very far."

"Have you bought the land for it yet?"

One corner of Casey's mouth lifted in a half grin. "Part of it. We're in the process of obtaining the rest of the land we'll need."

"I don't suppose the land you've already bought was mine at one time?"

"In a manner of speaking, it still is. You'll be part of the McKeever family as soon as I can arrange it." As she watched, uncertainty crept into his smoky eyes and he added, "If you'll have me, that is. I—I haven't really asked you to marry me. Maybe I'm presuming too much—"

She silenced his words with the soft pressure of her mouth, and when the kiss finally ended he could have had no remaining doubts as to her answer. Smiling at her, he traced the outline of her lips with his thumb. "Thank you," he said, his voice almost too low to hear.

"You're thanking *me?* After all you've done for me? You bought my place just so I couldn't leave your house and run home to my cabin, didn't you?"

"That was my primary reason," he admitted gruffly, "although it should turn out well for the business too. And the local economy will get a boost as we move more of the workload from Houston to Bowie's Land-

ing. I intend to hire town people whenever possible and
only bring a skeletal staff from the Houston office."

"Will you bring Holly?"

Casey narrowed his eyes to study her for a moment.
"I love you, not Holly."

"I know," she said, and the knowledge was sweet. "I
trust you. It's Holly I'm worried about. I've heard she
has designs on you."

He shook his head in amazement. "I'm having a
hard time adjusting to the idea that you've been jealous
on my behalf. I want you to rest assured, dear one,
Holly won't be coming to Bowie's Landing. Last month
I helped her get a job with another oil company. She's
probably already falling in love with the owner's son."
A caressing sort of humor that Regan was starting to
recognize and adore entered his voice and brought a
gleam to his eyes. "You'll notice I haven't asked if
you're going to see our friend David anymore."

She was shocked. "Oh, we have to see David! Casey,
he's a dear, dear friend! He considers you the best
friend he has in the world. You have nothing to worry
about where David's concerned."

Casey nodded. "I know. That's what he told me. As
a matter of fact, he told me that every week for the past
month—each time I called him from New York hoping
he'd mention your name. He always obliged me too.
He said I was a fool for breaking your heart."

"David said that?"

"Uh-huh. I didn't believe I had done so, of course. I
suggested rather sarcastically that he could help your
wounds to heal."

"Casey, you beast!"

"That's more or less what he called me, only he
wasn't so polite."

"Whatever came over David?" Regan marveled.
"He thinks you can do no wrong."

"David's a great friend." Casey's voice was warm.

"I'm glad he'll be around to look out for you when business takes me out of town."

"You'll have to travel some, won't you?" She couldn't hide her disappointment about that.

"Yes. I can't do an adequate job as legal counsel for the McKeever interests unless I go where I'm needed, but I've been thinking of hiring a couple of capable lawyers to assist me. I'm sick of hearing how overworked I am. If I turn over some of the workload to others, maybe the complaints will stop. Besides that, it will give me a chance to take my wife on some of the more pleasurable trips."

"You want me to go with you?"

His groan told her he didn't quite believe she could ask such a question. "If I had my choice, I wouldn't let you out of my sight for even an hour."

Casey was still standing with his arms around her, and now he bent his head a fraction so he could nuzzle her neck. "Regan?" He sounded hesitant, his mouth close to her ear.

"Yes, Casey?"

"I... think I'd better tell you something."

The reluctance in his tone worried her. What could be so difficult for him to say? She tried to prepare herself for the worst. "All right. Tell me."

He waited another half a minute and then muttered apologetically, "I'm tired. I've enjoyed dancing with you—more than you'll ever know—but I'm damned tired. Would you mind if we sit down to continue this discussion?"

"Oh, Casey!" Relief swept through her when she realized he wasn't confessing to being a philanderer or a bigamist. That emotion was chased away swiftly by self-reproach when she remembered that it was the middle of the night and that she had kept him standing all this time when he had come halfway across the country in the last few hours.

Handing him his crutches, she scrutinized his darkly handsome face and found with relief that the exhaustion that had been evident an hour ago had vanished. He did indeed look tired, but only normally so, and his charcoal eyes held the same happiness that she thought must be glowing in her own.

He moved over to the brown leather couch and sat down with a sigh. When he had stretched out his legs and leaned back against the cushions, he met her eyes directly. "That's better. Now—" he patted his lap— "you come here."

She obeyed him and was enfolded immediately in his powerful arms. "Do you realize what you just did?" she demanded.

"Uh-uh. What?"

"You just told me you're tired!" Her smile expressed her pleasure. "You didn't shut me out! Oh, Casey, do you know how good I feel about that? And do you have any idea how much I love you?" Before he could answer, she put her hands behind his head, lacing her fingers in his soft brown hair, and gave him a kiss that left both of them breathless and shaking.

"Here," she murmured, placing his hand over her breast. "Feel my heart pound! You did that to me, Casey. Promise you'll be kind to me. You have the power to make my life heaven or hell, you know."

Casey opened his mouth to speak and then shut it again, tears welling in his gray eyes as he looked at her. He pulled her closer until her head nestled on his shoulder, her breath warm on his lean cheek and her arms entwined loosely around his neck. "I'll be kind," he whispered to the clean-smelling lock of silky hair that tickled his nose.

They remained on the sofa, half sitting, half lying in each other's arms against the deep, comfortable cushions, and it felt right to Regan. Her eyelids were growing heavy and she yawned once or twice.

"Promise?" she mumbled drowsily after a while, and when he didn't answer she realized he was asleep.

Her heart was filled to overflowing with love for Casey. Smiling to herself, she settled down against his chest and slept.

Harlequin reaches
into the hearts and minds
of women across America
to bring you

Harlequin American Romance ^{T.M.}

YOURS FREE!

Enter a uniquely exciting new world with

Harlequin American Romance T.M.

Harlequin American Romances are the first romances to explore today's love relationships. These compelling novels reach into the hearts and minds of women across America... probing the most intimate moments of romance, love and desire.

You'll follow romantic heroines and irresistible men as they boldly face confusing choices. Career first, love later? Love without marriage? Long-distance relationships? All the experiences that make love real are captured in the tender, loving pages of **Harlequin American Romances**.

What makes American women so different when it comes to love? Find out with **Harlequin American Romance!**

Send for your introductory FREE book now!

Get this book FREE!

Mail to:

Harlequin Reader Service

in the U.S.
2504 West Southern Avenue
Tempe, AZ 85282

In Canada
649 Ontario Street
Stratford, Ontario N5A 6W2

YES! I want to be one of the first to discover
Harlequin American Romance. Send me FREE and without
obligation *Twice in a Lifetime*. If you do not hear from me after I
have examined my FREE book, please send me the 4 new
Harlequin American Romances each month as soon as they
come off the presses. I understand that I will be billed only $2.25
for each book (total $9.00). There are no shipping or handling
charges. There is no minimum number of books that I have to
purchase. In fact, I may cancel this arrangement at any time.
Twice in a Lifetime is mine to keep as a FREE gift, even if I do not
buy any additional books.

Name	*(please print)*	
Address		Apt. no.
City	State/Prov.	Zip/Postal Code

Signature (If under 18, parent or guardian must sign.)

Begin a long love affair with

SUPERROMANCE.
Accept LOVE BEYOND DESIRE, **FREE.**

Complete and mail the coupon below, today!

- -